# THE HACHETTE BOOK OF INDIAN CRIME FICTION

Tarun K. Saint was born in Kenya, and has lived in India since 1972. His interests include the literature of the Partition, science fiction and detective fiction. He is the author of *Witnessing Partition: Memory, History, Fiction* (2nd edition, 2020), based on his doctoral dissertation. He edited *Bruised Memories: Communal Violence and the Writer* (2002) and co-edited (with Ravikant) *Translating Partition* (2001). He also co-edited *Looking Back: India's Partition, 70 Years On*, with Rakhshanda Jalil and Debjani Sengupta (2017). He has edited *The Gollancz Book of South Asian Science Fiction*, Volume 1 (2019) and Volume 2 (2021). The bilingual (Indian–Italian) science fiction anthology *Avatar: Indian Science Fiction*, co-edited with Francesco Verso, appeared in January 2020, and the bilingual SF collection *Kalicalypse: Subcontinental Science Fiction* (co-edited with Bodhisattva Chattopadhyay and Francesco Verso) in 2022. *Ecoceanic: Global South SF* (co-edited with Francesco Verso) was published in January 2024.

He has most recently edited the two volume books, *The Hachette Book of Indian Detective Fiction* (2024).

# THE HACHETTE BOOK OF INDIAN CRIME FICTION

## Twenty-first Century Crime Fiction in English

*Edited by*

TARUN K. SAINT

hachette
INDIA

First published in 2025 by Hachette India
(Registered name: Hachette Book Publishing India Pvt. Ltd)
An Hachette UK company
www.hachetteindia.com

1



Print ISBN 978-93-5731-906-5
eBook ISBN 978-93-5731-538-8

Hachette Book Publishing India Pvt. Ltd
4th & 5th Floors, Corporate Centre,
Plot No. 94, Sector 44, Gurugram 122003, India

Typeset in Bembo Std 11/14.5
by R. Ajith Kumar, New Delhi

Printed and bound in India
by Manipal Technologies Limited

MIX
Paper | Supporting responsible forestry
FSC™ C043100

# CONTENTS

INTRODUCTION 1

THE LIBRARIAN 18
*Vaseem Khan*

KING PHISHER 33
*RV Raman*

SOCIETY MURDER 57
*Madhulika Liddle*

THE BARAAT 76
*Meeti Shroff-Shah*

STRIDE 86
*Arnab Ray*

THE LEOPARDS' LEAP CRIME FICTION WORKSHOP 105
*Manjula Padmanabhan*

MURDER BY A RAISED EYEBROW 121
*Tabish Khair*

THE MERMAID'S SONG 136
*Ajay Chowdhury*

OUT OF MERCY 155
*Nev March*

CRIME AND CRIME 171
*Tanuj Solanki*

THE LAMPLIGHTER 186
*Anuradha Kumar*

A DIVINE MADNESS 209
*Anil Menon*

BURDEN 228
*Salil Desai*

IN THE POISONED ENTRAILS 257
*Sumit Bardhan*

ABOUT THE AUTHORS 289

ACKNOWLEDGEMENTS 296

# INTRODUCTION

*Tarun K. Saint*

The genre of crime fiction has seen a remarkable resurgence in recent times in India. The popularity of crime and detective series on OTT platforms, as well as films like *The Buckingham Murders* (dir. Hansal Mehta, with Kareena Kapoor Khan, 2023) indicate the continuing hold of dramatic stories with a crime-related theme on the popular imagination.[1] This has extended beyond the traditional bastions of Hindi *lugdi sahitya* (pulp fiction), Bengali *goyenda* (detective) tales and Tamil detective fiction to Indian writing in English, as a host of recent publications bear out, besides the often bilingual series and films aforementioned.[2] There has been a movement away from the at times confining models of classic British Golden Age fiction, with its characteristic clue–puzzle structure, to a set of stylistic innovations and a diverse set of subjects that are distinctively Indian, in recent times. We also find an invigorating dialogue with global modes of crime fiction afoot, beyond the Western sources that were influential to begin with. This move can also be seen in the domain of films and series, such as *Manorama Six Feet Under* (dir. Navdeep Singh, with Abhay Deol, 2007), which takes Roman Polanski's noir style treatment of the politics of water in California in *Chinatown* (with Jack Nicholson, 1974) and relocates this in a western Rajasthan setting, and the Punjab-based series *Kohrra* (dir. Randeep Jha, with Suvinder Vicky, 2023; a second season has been announced), inspired in part by Korean director Bong Joon Ho's *Memories of Murder* (2003).[3]

In the Introduction to *The Hachette Book of Indian Detective Fiction* (2024, 2 vols.), the history of the genre in the Western and Indian contexts was sketched out in greater detail, albeit in synoptic form, including inevitably, the history and evolution of crime fiction.[4] The category of crime fiction, the focus in this volume, is somewhat more capacious, incorporating works that deal with the subject of crime, which do not necessarily feature a detective as protagonist. Such works veer towards noir terrain, often marked by ambiguity in conclusion, rather than neat resolutions of plot. [5]

To revisit the origins of the genre in Britain, racy and moralizing stories about true crime and criminals were produced in the form of *The Newgate Calendar* in the eighteenth and nineteenth centuries, and sold in pulp form in large numbers, also at the gallows where executions of convicted felons took place.[6] While several novels based on Newgate material were published at this time, crime fiction arguably first came to the fore in a serious way in William Godwin's *Things as They Are; or, The Adventures of Caleb Williams* (1794, retitled 1831), a trenchant novelistic critique of an unequal and unjust legal system, susceptible to manipulation by the influential and powerful landed class, raising the question of who is the real criminal in this society.[7] After the setting up of the Metropolitan Police Department in 1829 (replacing the constabulary and the Bow Street Runners), policemen began to appear in novels for the first time in various guises. Charles

Dickens's *Bleak House* (serialized in 1852–53) is an important Victorian novel which centred on a seriously inadequate judicial system (embodied in the institution of the Court of Chancery), and a murder mystery eventually solved by the indefatigable Inspector Bucket, despite attempted misdirection and red herrings strewn by the embittered French perpetrator.[8]

However, as David Lehman puts it, the ground zero of the (noir) mystery is the Hobbesian view of the moral universe, that '...man is not a noble savage but a natural born killer'.[9] Perhaps the best-known early work dealing with existential questions arising from the struggle for survival in a Hobbesian world ('...nasty, brutish and short...') and the descent into criminality as a reasoned (if misguided) choice, is Russian author Fyodor Dostoyevsky's *Crime and Punishment* (1866).[10] Rodion Raskolnikov, as the tortured protagonist, embodied the ethical dilemmas of an impoverished student aspiring to Napoleonic heights, thwarted by the lack of money and straitened circumstances. His act of murdering an elderly pawnbroker, however, saddles him with an unbearable burden of guilt and remorse, as well as an existential dislocation of selfhood. His interrogation by Detective Porfiry Petrovich, who has read Raskolnikov's essay 'On Crime' (in which he apparently justifies crime by 'extraordinary' individuals in certain contexts) further unsettles Raskolnikov, leading to the confessional denouement.

This psychological perspective on violent action unmoored in sound ethical grounds and its consequences has resurfaced in crime novels written across the world. Ethical conundrums come to the fore prominently in the no holds barred exploration of ambivalent moral states during the era of American hard-boiled crime fiction (the 1920s onwards) by

Dashiell Hammett, Ross Macdonald and Raymond Chandler and their many successors, reinterpreted in turn by feminist crime writers like Sara Paretsky and African-American authors like Walter Mosley, as well as later by Nordic noir writers like Stieg Larsson (Sweden), Jo Nesbø (Norway) and Henning Mankell (Sweden).[11]

While the subject of crime and the unravelling of its consequences (often according to the logic of karma) has been reflected in the subcontinent, at least since the time of the Mahabharata (think of the Game of Dice episode),[12] this anthology restricts itself to contemporary crime fiction in English from India. The idea, as charted in the concept note circulated among the authors, was to redo and reinvent the inherited conventions and formulas of the genre, especially the clue–puzzle structure with its codified approach to finding a solution to criminal actions, the 'whodunit'. Exemplars of this style, which eventually took the shape of 'cosy' crime stories, so named for the reassurance provided that all will be well at the end of the day as a mature detective solves a crime in a tightly knit community setting (as in the novels by Richard Osman and many others)[13] had been incorporated in the previous two volumes in fair measure. Here, the aim has been to elicit instances of the representation of the darker side to crime and criminality, and to further the questioning of received wisdom, whether from colonial era models or established and clichéd ways of depicting breaches of law and order, as well as attempts to solve the crime in narrative form in the Indian context. Thus we can see a change in focus in many recent Indian crime novels and stories from 'who-dun-it' to 'why-dun-it', with an emphasis on the social and psychological basis for the descent of individuals into lawbreaking and violence.

The advent of the Industrial Revolution and capitalism, the new economic system, from the mid-eighteenth century onwards, led to the burgeoning of cities and the migration of multitudes to the centres of production, with consequent effects of anonymity and loneliness, not to mention the fear of faceless crime, in the imperial centers, and later in the colonial cities. In this context the detective/police inspector in fiction appeared as a figure that might provide some reassurance, as a mediator and interpreter of the maze of the metropolis. Subsequently, we can see the influence of Marxist analysis of the effects of capitalist structures, with the alienation of the worker from his/her labour, which may culminate in collective revolt against structural injustices (and a redefinition of crime from the point of view of the oppressed) on popular forms like crime fiction in the West (see the work of Dashiell Hammett, as well as Maj Sjöwall and Per Wahlöö in Sweden in particular).[14]

Later, Freudian psychoanalysis, and the concept of the unconscious as a driving force for action that may be rationally inexplicable, as well as his concept of the uncanny, further destabilized the binary oppositions that underpinned early crime narratives, as borne out in the work of Patricia Highsmith.[15] Even as cataclysmic events like the two world wars and the Partition in the subcontinent ruptured normative patterns of belief and behaviour, there was a search for new formal possibilities of critique and resistance to dominant and hegemonic modes of understanding. Furthermore, epistemological uncertainties and questions as regards received knowledge (including modes of religious belief) ushered in by the modernist movement in the arts made an impact on the consciousness of authors (not only of crime fiction) across geographical boundaries. No wonder that in

France, poet Charles Baudelaire translated Edgar Allan Poe's detective stories (set in Paris) into French extensively from 1852 to 1865.[16] Post-modern detective fiction took such epistemological incertitude further, with the form providing a vehicle for an exploration of philosophical quandaries generated by scepticism of grand narratives.[17]

Crime and detective fiction have generated fascinating new perspectives and alternative methods of coming to terms with such rifts and disturbances of the status quo, as we have seen in work from Latin America (Gabriel García Márquez, Jorge Luis Borges), Scandinavia (Peter Høeg, Sjöwall and Wahlöö), besides the aforementioned Anglo-American scene, and now Japan (Seishi Yokomizo, Keigo Higashino) and India.[18] The genre at its best has become a vehicle for sophisticated critique, whether of historical crimes perpetrated in the past or contemporary instances of injustice, often unsettling assumptions that have remained in place in the more conventional exemplars of the genre such as cosy crime.

This eventual transformation and redoing of formulas was perhaps inevitable in a formerly colonial context like India. Indeed, to begin with, the early *goyenda* stories in the late nineteenth and early twentieth centuries often endorsed the role of the newly introduced police force in British India, with few questions raised about the ethics of insurrection against colonial rule and how to resist power.[19] Tagore's parody 'Detective' (1898) initiated a critical look at the certitudes underpinning the genre at an early stage,[20] taken forward even more sharply in recent post-colonial crime fiction by authors such as Vikram Chandra (*Sacred Games*) and Ambai (*The Death of a Sarus Crane*).[21]

To turn to the stories included in this volume, Vaseem

Khan is one of the best-known writers in the South Asian diaspora in the United Kingdom and chair of the Crime Writers' Association. While his two series of detective fiction, the Baby Ganesh Detective Agency series set in today's Mumbai and the Persis Wadia–centred historical mysteries set in 1950s Bombay[22] followed the clue–puzzle template with a distinctive sense of humour and a subcontinental sensibility underpinning the narrative, his story 'The Librarian' is a departure into noir terrain. The first-person narrative about the travails of a librarian with a degree in philosophy centers on a sibling relationship, which turns corrosive in the wake of financial chicanery. The transformation of Mumbai society is mirrored in the depiction of the descent into fratricidal rage and the desire for untrammelled retribution on the part of a highly educated denizen of Mumbai caught up in a kind of intensified sibling rivalry that his philosophical training has not quite prepared him for.

RV Raman is the author of the Harith Atreya series of detective novels.[23] In 'King Phisher', he turns his attention to cybercrime, and the scam artists flocking to spaces like Gurgaon from small towns, riding the wave of aspiration ushered in by liberalization in the digital era. The transition from first-person narration to third-person narrative reinforces the sense of a bubble waiting to burst, as the personal situation of the protagonist comes to mirror the larger economic structures which facilitate his rise and precipitate his eventual fall. The parallel between the ethical hollowness underpinning the relationship the scamster/phisher king enters into and the prior deceptions initiated by him is sustained till the unexpected twist in conclusion.

Madhulika Liddle has established a niche for herself in

the domain of historical mysteries, with her Muzaffar Jung mysteries set in the time of Dara Shukoh.[24] In 'Society Murder', Liddle takes up a more contemporary subject. This story about a purported murder, set in the context of gated societies living in high-rise towers in the suburbs of metropolises like Delhi, is told from the vantage point of one of the domestic helpers, Munia. The vulnerability of the otherwise invisible class of servants is heightened when an unnatural death happens, especially for those with a past of migration with a minority identity. The unexpected turn in conclusion relies on an understanding on the part of the reader of the sociological significance of naming in a communally divided and prejudiced urban middle-class society.

Meeti Shroff-Shah is an upcoming young author whose Temple Hill series featuring crime writer Radhika Zaveri (set among the Gujarati community in Mumbai) have been well received.[25] 'The Baraat' upends clichéd assumptions about the great Indian wedding and its attendant rituals and spectacle in its depiction of the discovery of the death of the groom in question. The dark side to the marriage market and societal obliviousness as regards women's agency comes through in this edgy tale. In this feminist story, with its ironic echoes of recent achievements in the sporting arena, the perspective of the bride-to-be is revealed in conclusion. This debacle takes place in the wake of familial disregard for her choice leading up to the prospective nuptials, driven by status considerations and greed. There is a forthright disclosure of a determination to seize control of the direction of one's life, despite the asymmetrical relations of power in place, and a radical unsettling of assumptions about the traditional Indian *bahu*.

Arnab Ray has written several novels in the genres of horror, thriller and crime fiction.[26] In 'STRIDE' the focus is on the pathway of the protagonist from call-centres to ostensibly providing tools for cybersecurity, and the rackets in operation in cyberspace. The tensions resulting from the raid by officials from the cybercrime unit at one such enterprise disclose the psychological drift of one such operator, who seeks to mask her role using the acronym STRIDE. She is also acutely conscious of the eventual consequences of such an unwarranted 'Elevation of Privilege' for herself, indicating an awareness of a tenuous karmic balancing at work even in the shadowy world she inhabits.

Manjula Padmanabhan is an established presence in the domain of Indian writing in English, whether literary or genre fiction, and has previously engaged with crime in the city in plays like *Lights Out*.[27] In 'The Leopards' Leap Crime Fiction Workshop' she sets the action in a lodge in the Himalayas hosting a workshop for budding crime-fiction writers. This self-reflexive and satirical take on such conclaves in isolated settings (an ideal locale for a locked-room mystery in the cozy tradition) features an unreliable narrator, a seasoned journalist who finds herself being accused of the crime of murder by her fellow writers at the workshop. This biblio-mystery brings in a welcome touch of dark humour, also at the expense of the pretensions of some of the practitioners of the genre.

Tabish Khair is a well-known writer and critic who often traverses the boundary between literary and genre fictions. For instance, Khair initiated a creative dialogue with the tradition of Scandi-noir in his crime novel *The Body by the Shore*.[28] 'Murder by a Raised Eyebrow' is an interesting instance of a writer of literary fiction playing with the rules of genre, here upending the notion of the inevitability of justice being delivered at the end of the tale. The criminal lawyer who narrates the story takes up the 'Mohammad Murder' case, a seemingly indefensible position, whether for the killer or the attorney, given the 'facts' of the case, and already entrenched societal attitudes. In the process of unfolding the story, Khair launches an interrogation of pervasive inequities in Indian society, especially with reference to minority identity. 'Criminal' behaviour becomes a phenomenon determined by the asymmetrical relations of power that generate psychological tensions in relationships across the communal line, further aggravated by societal prejudice and the prevalent discourses militating against an acceptance of cross-border relationships. The ambivalences of the story come through in the candid revelation of the gruesomeness of the murder, and the acknowledgement of his own monstrous role by the defendant, even as sinister larger forces are shown to be at work implying complicity of all, including those like the actress who 'raise' their eyebrows at others.

Ajay Chowdhury's Kamil Rahman series has been received well in the UK and in India.[29] 'The Mermaid's Song' is a first-person narrative set in contemporary Mumbai. Told from the point of view of Alfred, a middle-aged, balding banker from Goa, the story has a dark psychological edge disclosed through ironic allusions to T.S. Eliot's 'The Love Song of J. Alfred Prufrock'. While Sub-Inspector Kamil Rahman does appear during the investigation, the emphasis is on self-delusions cultivated by the protagonist, and the resentment that drives his actions, especially towards the 'emancipated' and affluent exhibitionists with whom the story opens. Mumbai may be the city of dreams, but equally, the big coastal city may harbour a class of frustrated malcontents and voyeurs who nurse in secret the capacity for untrammelled violence, the story reveals.

Nev March has consolidated her presence as a writer of historical mysteries, especially her series featuring Anglo-Indian detective Jim Agnihotri, in the time of the British Raj.[30] Her story 'Out of Mercy', however, is set in contemporary suburban New Jersey, among diasporic Indian families in the US. This atypical story about the perils of online gambling addiction effectively explores the dark undercurrents of migrant life in the Indian community. The theme is topical and of the moment, and the offbeat point of view of the diasporic Indian policeman is captured with sensitivity, especially with respect to the ironic conclusion. This story is reminiscent to an extent of the hard-boiled crime tradition and the police procedurals of the mid-twentieth century in its critical exposure of the dark underbelly of the American dream, while retaining a specific anchorage in a diasporic Indian cultural context.

Tanuj Solanki has left his mark on the crime fiction field in India with his thriller *Manjhi's Mayhem*, featuring a formidable Dalit protagonist.[31] In his story 'Crime and Crime', Solanki turns his attention to the transformations afoot in Indian society in the wake of the opening up of the economy. The story addresses the psychological moorings of the youthful narrator, as he drifts from a conservative milieu to Gurgaon. The dark side to migration from the village context to the hyper-modern metropolis is explored in visceral detail, in the first-person mode. The narrator negotiates exile, abuse and the alienating conditions of the lowest class of workers in the big city, impelled from minor infractions into major crime along the way. Such inexorable implosion of moral codes seems to mirror the movement of society, especially in the mean streets of Gurgaon, even as new balancing acts are required of the protagonist in time on reaching a slightly more prosperous situation.

Anuradha Kumar has stretched the conventions of crime fiction in unexpected ways in her earlier work, as in the earlier novels set in Odisha (formerly Orissa) or the recent historical mysteries like *The Kidnapping of Mark Twain*.[32] Tangled human relationships between individuals belonging to often very different ethnic backgrounds are prominent in her work, even as the crisis triggered by the commission of crime or its likelihood precipitates unforeseen complications. In 'The Lamplighter', set in early twentieth-century Bombay, a drastic perturbation in the orderly passage of time seems to have taken place, even as clocks run awry across the city. The possibility of insurrection against colonial rule is one of the elements in the force field at work in the story, which also features a romantic subtext and the arrival of a renegade Romanov prince in the city of change, Bombay. Temporal shifts play an important role in the open-ended resolution of this tale about the attempted realization of submerged potentialities, whether 'criminal' or 'revolutionary', in time and space.

Anil Menon is a versatile writer who has experimented with literary as well as genre fiction.[33] In 'A Divine Madness', he takes a playful stroll across the history of ideas, with specific reference to the role medical science might perform in disproving the existence of God. This philosophical excursus in the form of a fictional meditation on parasitology, unfolds the experiences of Indian scientist John Janardhan, a researcher who unsettles the assumptions of the religious believers as well as the rationalists with his discovery of the role of the parasite *Neospora nicolai* in facilitating religious belief. In the process, this story stretches the boundaries of the crime genre in unexpected directions. While a murder certainly occurs along the way and the life of the protagonist is soon under threat from true believers in India, the focus is on recounting Janardhan's journey as a sceptical researcher whose claim generates an intellectual and cultural storm, in a tone of mock erudition. The story effectively works as a parody of both cerebral and visceral strands of crime fiction, with an undercurrent of black humour grounded in a regional (south) Indian sensibility pertinent to our times.

Salil Desai has been prolific as an author of crime and detective fiction, with nine books, whether novels or collections of short stories, out so far.[34] His character Inspector Saralkar also features now in a tele-series, with more likely to follow. His story 'Burden' is a grim and disturbing take on the ethics of care for the elderly, with the focus on a middle-aged man with an ageing mother who has suffered a paralytic attack. The resultant psychological stresses on middle-class families and changed attitudes in traditional Indian family spaces are disclosed ruthlessly in this story about impossible situations culminating in malefic, even nihilistic, choices. Care-giving in its various avatars is subjected to critical scrutiny in a scenario which culminates in a no-win situation for the protagonist Avadhoot.

Sumit Bardhan has published science fiction in both Bengali and English. His novel *Avarice* is a steampunk thriller set in colonial India.[35] His story 'In the Poisoned Entrails' engages with the realms of artificial intelligence and genetic engineering while extrapolating from contemporary trends at work, especially as manifested in the corporate and financial structures that are driving such technological innovations for profit. The conventions of the crime thriller are deployed here in a no holds barred depiction of the ruthlessness of corporate czars and their stooges as they devise new forms of indentured labour and slavery through 'scientific' means. Resistance, nonetheless, does take place, even if, at times, in unpalatable forms, as a balancing of forces ensues.

As we have seen, the genre of Indian crime fiction is thriving, not entirely surprising in the context of the many missteps and malaises in contemporary Indian society, whether in the big cities or the hinterland. These stories continue to refract the dilemmas and conundrums faced by many, whether those belonging to the burgeoning middle class or the subaltern classes afflicted by rampant inequality and indifferent systems of redressal of injustices in society, whether inherited from the colonial era or of recent vintage as a result of our relentless drift into mimicry of the worst tendencies in neoliberal capitalism as seen in the West. As a dark lens into the murky side of our present moment, Indian crime fiction offers the possibility of critique and the inference of more hopeful ways of being.

## References

1. Rishabh Suri, 'The Buckingham Murders movie review: Kareena Kapoor is the heartbeat of Hansal Mehta's slow-burn cop drama' in *Hindustan Times*, 10 November 2024. https://www.hindustantimes.com/entertainment/bollywood/the-buckingham-murders-movie-review-kareena-kapoor-slow-paced-thriller-might-test-your-patience-hansal-mehta-101726207537415.html. Last accessed 19 January 2025.
2. For a useful overview of the South Asian crime fiction scene, see Laura Brueck and Francesca Orsini, 'South Asian Crime Fiction' in Jesper Guddal, Stewart King and Alistair Rolls, eds., *The Cambridge Companion to World Crime Fiction*, Cambridge: CUP, 2022, 141–59.

3. Naman Ramachandran, '"Kohrra Indian Noir Series Is a Hit for Netflix, Powered by Experienced Crime Drama Team"' in *Variety*, 24 July 2023. https://variety.com/2023/tv/asia/kohrra-netflix-india-1235678520/. Last accessed 19 January 2025.
4. 'Introduction' in Tarun K. Saint, ed., *The Hachette Book of Indian Detective Fiction: Stories from the Subcontinent*, 2 Vols., Gurugram: Hachette India, 2024, 1–17.
5. For a detailed discussion of the noir tradition in the Western context, including novels and films, see David Lehman, *The Mysterious Romance of Murder: Crime, Detection and the Spirit of Noir,* Ithaca and London: Cornell Univ. Press, 2022.
6. The Newgate Calendar, https://www.exclassics.com/newgate/ngintro.htm. Last accessed 21 January 2025.
7. See William Godwin, *Things as They Are; or, The Adventures of Caleb Williams,*1794, retitled 1831, rpt. London: Penguin, 2005.
8. Charles Dickens, *Bleak House*, 1852–53, Ware, Hertfordshire: Wordsworth Classics, 1993, rpt. 2001.
9. David Lehman, *The Mysterious Romance of Murder*, p. 5.
10. Fyodor Dostoyevsky, *Crime and Punishment,* trans. Constance Garnett, first serialized in 1866, in 'The Russian Messenger'; also see https://www.gutenberg.org/ebooks/2554, accessed 18 January 2025; also Thomas Hobbes, *Leviathan*, Ch. XIII in https://www.britannica.com/topic/Leviathan-by-Hobbes. Last accessed 19 January 2025.
11. See hard-boiled fiction, Britannica, https://www.britannica.com/art/hard-boiled-fiction, last accessed 19 January 2025; also Dashiell Hammett, *The Dain Curse*, 1928, rpt. New York: Vintage Crime, 1989; also Raymond Chandler, *The Little Sister*, 1949, rpt. Harmondsworth: Penguin Random House UK, 2010; also Ross Macdonald, *The Chill*, 1963, rpt. London: Penguin, 2012; also Sara Paretsky, *Blacklist*, New York: Putnam, 2003; also Walter Mosley, *Blonde Faith*, 2007, rpt. London: Phoenix, 2009; also Henning Mankell, *The Fifth Woman*, trans. Steven T. Murray, 2000, trans. 2003, rpt. London: Vintage, 2009.
12. For a brilliant historical perspective on the epic, in which Romila Thapar underlines the significance of Draupadi's questioning of Yudhisthira's right to stake her in the game of dice, see Romila Thapar, 'The Epic of the Bharatas', in *Seminar magazine*. https://

www.india-seminar.com/2010/608/608_romila_thapar.htm. Last accessed 26 January 2025.

13. Richard Osman, *The Thursday Murder Club*, London: Viking, 2020; also David Barnett, '"Cosy crime" novels: Are they brilliant entertainment or "twee and insipid"?', *BBC*, 22 September 2023. https://www.bbc.com/culture/article/20230921-cosy-crime-novels-are-the-reading-choice-of-the-moment-but-are-they-brilliant-entertainment-or-twee-and-insipid. Last accessed 26 January 2025.
14. Maj Sjöwall obituary, The Guardian, accessed 19 January 2025; also 'Dashiell Hammett Hardboiled writer, communist fighter', in *Socialist Party*, Issue 151, September 2011. https://socialismtoday.org/archive/151/hammett.html. Last accessed 19 January 2025; also Dashiell Hammett, *The Maltese Falcon*, New York: Alfred A. Knopf, 1930, rpt. London: Hachette UK, 2007; also Maj Sjöwall and Per Wahlöö, *The Locked Room*, trans. Paul Britten Austin, 1972, trans. 1973, rpt. London: Fourth Estate, 2011.
15. Jane Ciabattari, 'Does Sigmund Freud still matter?', *BBC*, 22 April 2014. https://www.bbc.com/culture/article/20140421-does-freud-still-matter. Last accessed 23 January 2025; also Patricia Highsmith, *Ripley Under Water*, 1991, rpt. London: Bloomsbury, 2003.
16. Pamela Farber, 'Charles Baudelaire and his translations of Poe', at https://open.unive.it/hitrade/books/FaberBaudelaire.pdf. Last accessed 19 January 2025.
17. John Scaggs, 'Postmodernism and the Anti-detective novel' in *Crime Fiction*, New York: Routledge, 2005, rpt. 2009, 139–43; also 'The Eight Memes of the Postmodern Mystery – By Ted Gioia', in *Modern Literature*, 25 August 2018. https://modernliterature.org/eight-memes-postmodern-mystery-ted-gioia/. Last accessed 19 January 2025; also Paul Auster, The New York Trilogy, 1987, rpt. London: Faber and Faber, 2009.
18. Gabriel García Márquez, *Chronicle of a Death Foretold*, trans. Gregory Rabassa, 1982, rpt. New Delhi: Penguin, 1986; also Jorge Luis Borges, 'Death and the Compass', 1942, in *Collected Fictions*, trans. Andrew Hurley, 1998, rpt. Penguin: Harmondsworth, 1999, 147–57; also Peter Høeg, *Miss Smilla's Feeling for Snow*, 1992, trans. F. David, 1993, rpt. London: Vintage, 2012; also Seishi Yokomizo, *The Honjin*

*Murders*, 1975, trans. Louise Heal Kawai, London: Pushkin Press, 2019; also Keigo Higashino, *Salvation of a Saint*, trans. Alexander O. Smith, 2008, trans. New York: Minotaur, 2012.

19. For a critical account of early Bangla crime fiction, see Shampa Roy, *Gender and Criminality in Bangla Crime Narratives: Late Nineteenth and Early Twentieth Centuries*, London: Palgrave Macmillan, 2017.
20. Rabindranath Tagore, 'Detective', 1898, trans. Shampa Roy, in Saint, ed. *The Hachette Book of Indian Detective Fiction*, 238–48.
21. Vikram Chandra, *Sacred Games*, Gurgaon: Penguin Random House, 2006; also Ambai, *The Death of a Sarus Crane*, trans. Gita Subramanian, New Delhi: Speaking Tiger Books, 2024.
22. Vaseem Khan, *Midnight at Malabar House*, London: Hodder and Stoughton, 2020; also Khan, *The Strange Disappearance of a Bollywood Star*, London: Mulholland Books, 2017.
23. RV Raman, *A Will to Kill*, Noida: Harper Black, 2019.
24. Madhulika Liddle, *Crimson City*, Gurugram: Hachette India, 2015.
25. Meeti Shroff-Shah, *The Death of Kirti Kadakia: A Temple Hill Mystery*, New Delhi: Bloomsbury, 2022; also Shroff-Shah, *A Matrimonial Murder: A Temple Hill Mystery 2*, New Delhi: Bloomsbury, 2024.
26. Arnab Ray, *The Mine*, 2012, rpt. Gurugram: Hachette India, 2024.
27. Manjula Padmanabhan, *Lights Out*, New Delhi: Worldview Publications, 2020.
28. Tabish Khair, *The Body by the Shore*, Gurugram: HarperCollins, 2022; also Khair, *Jihadi Jane*, Gurugram: Penguin Random House India, 2016.
29. Ajay Chowdhury, *The Waiter*, London: Harvill Secker, 2021.
30. Nev March, *Murder in Old Bombay: A Mystery*, 2020, rpt. New Delhi: HarperCollins, 2021.
31. Tanuj Solanki, *Manjhi's Mayhem*, Gurugram: Penguin Random House, 2022.
32. Anuradha Kumar, *The Kidnapping of Mark Twain*, New Delhi: Speaking Tiger Books, 2024.
33. Anil Menon, *The Coincidence Plot*, New Delhi: Simon and Schuster India, 2023.
34. Salil Desai, *Murder Milestone: An Inspector Saralkar Mystery*, New Delhi: Fingerprint, 2020.
35. Sumit Bardhan, *Avarice: A Steampunk Thriller*, trans. by the author of Arthatrishna, Kolkata: Kalpabiswa Publications, 2023, rpt. 2024.

# THE LIBRARIAN

*Vaseem Khan*

I suppose the idea of committing murder first came to me at a party.

Don't get me wrong. This wasn't a family get-together, but rather one of those organizational affairs that one feels compelled to attend even when every fibre of one's being cries out in protest. Frankly speaking, I would rather have gone to a political rally, or a symposium on the agricultural impacts of export subsidies, but such is life. In truth, my attendance could not be avoided. I am the general secretary of the Mumbai Library Workers' Association. The title sounds grander than it is. There are not many libraries in Mumbai – far fewer in per head terms than any other city in India, and vanishingly small in comparison to other metropolises around the world. London, Paris, New York? They would have laughed me out of the building.

But I take what I do seriously. I grew up around books. Books made me the man I am today...I can hear my ex-wife, Radha, laughing. *The man you are today? And what exactly is that, dear Manoj?*

According to Radha, I am a failure. When she married me, I was a *man of prospects*. I had a degree in philosophy behind me;

an itch to pursue higher learning; and favourable connections courtesy of my industrialist father. I was one of those children of the mid-noughties, when India was shining (with a capital S), and money and ideas were flowing into the country. When it seemed that the superheated juggernaut of our economy would make all things possible.

Granted, many of those things have come to pass. India has achieved a degree of primacy in world affairs, as befits a nation housing fully one-sixth of the world's population. And that's before we count the multiheaded monster that is the Indian diaspora! Google. Microsoft. IBM. The only outfit an Indian isn't yet running is the American government. Give it time.

But progress has come at a price. I make no accusations. Perhaps this is simply how it must be when nations grow cognizant of their own power and hard choices become inevitable. When the exigencies of the *now* force a departure from the easy ideals of rhetoric.

Perhaps it would be easier for me to explain what I mean by tracing for you my path from naïve pseudo-philosopher to would-be murderer. After all, none of this would have happened had it not been for a throwaway comment made at that damned party.

*

My father left me more than his connections.

He left me a mountain of debt and a business empire dead on its feet.

When he died, my twin brother, Sanjay, who had garnered an MBA from India's top management school – while I was busy studying Descartes and Kant and Russell and Spinoza and

New Confucianism – which had just entered the consciousness of Western philosophy departments – found himself at the helm of our family concern, at the tender age of twenty-four.

He quickly discovered, to his, and our collective, horror that our father had been sheltering us from the truth. That is a kindly way of putting it. Our father had lied. In fact, he had been lying for a very long time, and to a great many people. In cahoots with his financial advisers and accountants, he had cooked the books for almost a decade, as the business had slumped slowly into the sea. What amazed me was how he had kept a charlatan's face on things. At home, he remained the upbeat man I had always known, the business titan whose handsome face had once graced *Business Today* and *Forbes India*, whose knack for spotting a market opportunity had led to some christening him an industrial Columbus, a man willing to take enormous risks to test uncharted waters.

Sanjay convinced us to stay quiet. He convinced *me* – with spreadsheets and the sort of business speak that sounds like the garbled language of an alien species – that I should leave it all to him; that, by some miracle of his MBA learning, he would save us from the bonfire of the vanities that had been lit beneath our family.

Sanjay was my brother, my twin, younger than me by mere minutes. We had never shared the umbilical closeness that twins are supposed to feel from birth, but for that I had always blamed myself. I was (notionally) older; I should have made more of an effort.

But Sanjay and I had always been so very different. In truth, he was my father's twin, rather than mine. Not that our father played favourites. He indulged us both. He would always joke, in that overloud way that came to be the signature of his final years, that Sanjay would be his successor – when the very concept of succession meant nothing to us – and I would be the one to carry forward his philanthropic ideals. My father was a generous man and had established, early on in his meteoric rise to success, a philanthropic division that had already become a household name in the country, doling out research grants and scholarships and no-strings-attached alms to charitable causes close to my father's heart.

I realize that I haven't said much about our mother. I will get to her in due course.

By now I was married. My father had picked out a bride for me – the daughter of a major business house. My initial reaction was to spurn his choice. I had just returned from my overseas study, my mind expanded in ways that my family could not possibly imagine. And yes, if we are making confessions, then let me confess that I had had my share of liaisons while abroad. Women – Indian and non-Indian – who opened me to all manner of possibilities. I had already decided that in this matter – the finding of a life partner – I must make my own choice and not kowtow to my family's wishes.

All that went out of the window when Radha came to visit us with *her* family.

What can I say? Beauty has a way of liquifying the strongest of ideals, of knocking us on our backs. But it was more than that. Radha had attended university to study literature. Radha loved books – mystery novels, yes, but books nonetheless. She was charming and demure and everything that a young man full of himself could possibly ask for.

And so we married, the last big occasion my father presided over before his untimely death. I say untimely, but the timing of his death was not set by some malign whim of fate.

My father shot himself.

The cracks began appearing almost straight away.

After my father's death, Sanjay took over the business and quickly discovered the mountain of debt – and borderline fraud – that was to be our legacy. To give him his due, he set to work with a will, locking himself away in our corporate offices, a newly built Nariman Point glass tower, soaring phallically above the Arabian Sea, that spoke not only to my father's vaunting ambition, but his penchant for the theatrical. He wasn't exactly a showman – not in the way we associate that particular label with some of the robber barons that have distinguished the Indian business landscape of late – but he was certainly a man who knew the worth of effective PR.

I offered to help. But Sanjay politely turned me away. My years studying the great philosophers had left me ill-prepared for the economic high-wire act needed to rescue our ailing commercial enterprise.

I felt chastened. Our father had left us both equal shares in the business, but his will had also directed that Sanjay be made CEO in the event of his death and that in all matters concerning the business, my brother's word was to be final. I had a share in the firm, but no say in its running.

You might think that this would be ideal for a man who had never seen his future embroiled in the tentacles of big business, but something strange happened. Vanity reared its ugly head. *I* was the older brother. I had a right to be consulted, if not placed in charge. But Sanjay – and his stooges on the board – cut me out so completely that I had not the slightest inkling of what they were up to until I heard some pronouncement or other in the *Times*, usually accompanied by a cheesy picture of Sanjay in his captain's armchair, wearing a two-thousand-dollar suit that he had had tailored in London or Milan or Paris – the same outfit would have cost him a fraction of the cost right here in Mumbai.

In short, my brother treated me like a child, a well-intentioned but naïve sibling who couldn't possibly be trusted with even the most basic commercial secrets lest he spill them to those plotting our corporate downfall. I confess, it stung.

And, as I was soon to discover, it wasn't just me feeling the pinch of pride.

*

In the two years that we had been married before my father died, I had never really been conscious of my wife Radha's ambition.

Perhaps I had ignored the signs. So lost had I been in the delirium that accompanied the early years of our marriage that it simply hadn't occurred to me to scratch beyond the surface. Radha was young, pretty, educated, and I loved her. What else did I need to know?

I expected us to proceed on the path that most couples in our situation followed. A few happy, honeymoon years, followed by children. We had the overwhelming advantages of our social class and the benefit of being cosseted by family wealth (or so I thought) allowing us to pursue careers as we saw fit, balancing parenthood with personal achievement.

But it turned out that I had misjudged my wife. Radha wanted more. She valued – *needed* – status. She had no use for a husband who did not live up to some grandiose expectation she had built up in her mind. We began to fight. Quibbling at first, and then full-blown rows. Always with the same theme: Why wasn't *I* running the business? I was the older son, after all. Why wasn't *my* face plastered all over the *Times*?

You have to bear in mind that I had kept from Radha the exact nature of our financial problems. She knew that something wasn't right, but she had no conception of the extent of the trouble we were in. Radha was sharp, but, like me, had never majored in finance.

I tried to reassure Radha that I was just as much a partner in the family business as my brother. It was simply that my expertise was being used elsewhere. To a certain extent this was true. By this time I had taken charge of our philanthropic arm. Not that there was much for me to distribute anymore, at least not from our own coffers. But our family name was still prominent enough to solicit donations via high-profile fund-raising drives, fronted by celebrity cricketers and actors.

My father's philanthropic passion had been literacy. He loved books. He *collected* books. His home office at our Cuffe Parade mansion was lined with expensive first editions purchased from around the world. My father loved the idea of himself as a bibliophile, if not the reality.

But the unintended consequence of his lifelong love affair with books was to infect his older son with a genuine passion for the written word. My time at university had gone a step further, underlining for me the power that words play in the destiny of humankind. After all, words are a philosopher's stock in trade. Gandhi freed India not by strength of arms but by outthinking the British. His philosophical renderings remain some of the most clear-thinking writings on human freedom yet committed to paper.

I took my role as helmsman of our philanthropic enterprise seriously. What I failed to appreciate was that my wife did not see me in the same noble light as I saw myself.

After a particularly vitriolic argument, my brother was forced to break us up. He then spent an hour trying to convince Radha not to leave the home.

For a while we patched things up.

But a few months later, my wife packed her bags and left for good. She had finally discovered some of the truth of our business woes. There was no way back.

Of course, I made an effort. Emissaries were sent. I swallowed my pride and begged her to return. To no avail. I appealed to my in-laws. I was rebuffed. By now our business plight had begun to raise a stink in the circles we moved in. My in-laws were horrified. I suspected that they felt they had been sold a bill of goods. In our country, hell hath no fury like a business family cuckolded.

*

But I digress.

My path to murder was predestined. Or so our astrologers would have you believe.

I disagree. There were many points along the way where I could have turned left instead of right. Fulcrums upon which the mass of my future might have shifted in another direction. For instance, the day my brother asked me to sign papers that he had had drawn up. 'I've found us a financier,' he explained. 'A loan agency willing to lend us the funding we need to turn this thing around.'

I frowned at him. 'Why are they willing to trust us when no one else will?'

'They specialize in cases such as ours,' said Sanjay. 'High-risk ventures.'

'You mean lost causes.'

My brother smiled wanly. 'We're not lost, Manoj. I know exactly where we are and how we can find our way out of this maze. You have to trust me.'

Of course I trusted him. What the hell did I know about corporate finance?

'There's just one catch,' he said. 'The funding cannot come to our main company. It has to be diverted through our philanthropic arm.'

'You want to use the funds for our charitable mission?'

'No. I want to use the funds to save our business. Your philanthropy outfit will loan the money to our business divisions. And, after we're back on our feet, we'll pay it back – with interest.'

'Isn't that illegal?'

'No. Charities invest funds all the time. For a return. It's how they manage to survive for longer than the initial bequest would allow them to. Believe me, brother, this is the only way.'

I didn't quite understand what Sanjay meant. I had no idea why the funding couldn't come through our company. But he spoke with such conviction, of matters that were hazy concepts to me, that I could do nothing but agree. After all, the future of our family was at stake. *My* future. And so, I signed the papers.

Two weeks later, Sanjay vanished.

⋆

I suppose, with hindsight, I should have seen it coming.

But I have always been a trusting soul.

Sanjay emptied the accounts of our charity – *my* charity – and left the country. I later discovered that the reason the loan couldn't have come into our company bank accounts was because those accounts had been frozen by the government's economic crime unit. We were being investigated for fraud. And my brother, my father's acolyte in all things, had decided to perform an act of corporate legerdemain that would have made my father proud.

He was last seen boarding a flight to Chile. He landed at Santiago Airport. And that's where the trail runs cold.

I, meanwhile, was visited by teams of government officials. And when I say visited, perhaps I reveal a talent for understatement. For months, the house was besieged. I was interviewed numerous times, by different wings of the government, accused of many different crimes. The papers that Sanjay had convinced me to sign provided my inquisitors with documentary evidence of my perfidy. *I* had accepted a loan into our family charity. *I* had then authorized transfer of those funds to an account in the Cayman Islands, an account beyond the jurisdiction of the Indian authorities.

Six months after Sanjay vanished, I was arrested.

At my trial, on the advice of my legal team, I pleaded guilty. I received a six-year sentence. My lawyers told me that the judge had been exceptionally harsh. Our family was being made an example of. Public perception of Indian businessmen was at an all-time low. Corporate misdeeds by several well-known industrialists had finally tested the government's patience one time too many, and I was being made a scapegoat for all those who – like Sanjay – had been smart enough to flee the country with their ill-gotten booty.

Three years later I was released, to return to the land of the living.

But if I had thought my troubles were behind me, I was mistaken.

*

People say that it is harder for a man who has been to prison to find work than it is for the proverbial rich man to find his way to heaven.

And, perhaps, this is true, certainly if the man in question were anyone but me. My father had left me nothing but a book of contacts. Most of them refused to take my calls. But one is all it takes.

By now, of course, everything had turned to dust.

Radha had divorced me. I had signed the papers without protest, sitting in my cell. There seemed no reason to behave truculently. Radha had cause enough to jettison me.

Our family home had been sold, the proceeds wolfed down by our insatiable list of creditors. Every item within the home had also been auctioned off, including my father's vast and expensive collection of books.

My mother had been forced to find sanctuary with a childhood friend, reduced to the status of disgraced dowager, living in a single room on the charity of a woman she had once considered her social inferior. When I went to see her upon my release, she refused to see me. I had no idea why she blamed me for the disaster that had overtaken us, but she did.

Of the real culprit, of Sanjay, there was still no sign. The

Chilean authorities had made a desultory effort to track him down – I imagined Sanjay's face on posters in police stations up and down the country – and had then lost interest. I did not blame them. What possible incentive had they to locate a runaway Indian fraudster?

I found temporary lodgings with an old school friend, a good-natured sort who had done well for himself in the publishing business. He offered me a job, as trainee editor, working on cheap, salacious romances. My heart curdled at the thought. But I needed a start, I needed money. I was just about to accept, when Lady Luck finally decided that it was time to smile upon me. For a change.

I was invited to meet with an old friend of my father's, a businessman who had been cheated by him, but who, nevertheless, had it within himself to forgive, if not to forget. His name was Ojha, and he was the man who had bought my father's book collection.

'I want to distribute this collection among our city's libraries,' he told me, when we met at his Bandra seafront mansion. 'And I want to build another library, in partnership with the municipal authorities, bigger than anything in the country. A library open to all. It will be my gift to the city.'

⋆

This then, became my life.

For the next eight years, I helped my benefactor to bring his dream to life. In that time, I rediscovered myself. I eventually moved out of my friend's home, and found a small apartment in Malad, a place where no one would recognize me, particularly now that I had grown out a beard and donned glasses. A poor disguise, but, by now, our family was dust in the wind, a cautionary tale of greed and hubris.

The great library was built, opened with fanfare, and I took my place as head librarian. In time, I became the general secretary of the Mumbai Library Workers' Association. I was content. Others asked me about settling down, a wife, children. I replied, with an enigmatic smile, that I was married to my books.

Years passed. Just after my fortieth birthday, I was invited to a party organized by the All India Library Collective. The party was to take place in Mumbai, and librarians from around the country were to attend. Following the party, a two-day symposium would be held. It was not a function I could avoid, as much as I hated such occasions. Aside from my work, I had grown used to a life of solitude, of avoiding others in my spare time. A lonely life you might say, but I had no desire to subject myself any further to the vicissitudes of fate. I had tried the other kind of life. Marriage and friends and all the rest of it. And it had ended in misery.

At the function I shadow-boxed around the periphery, making small talk. A man from Kerala took out his wallet and showed me pictures of his children. A woman from Bihar engaged me in a lengthy discussion about a neighbour who had behaved badly towards her and the declining state of basic good manners in the country.

I walked to the punch bowl and poured myself another glass.

As I turned, I came face to face with Radha. The floor fell away beneath my feet.

My ex-wife tilted her head. Age had only sharpened her beauty. She glowed. 'How are you, Manoj?'

'Radha,' I breathed. 'What are you doing here?'

'My husband has been invited to make a speech. He is the deputy chief minister of Maharashtra.'

A hand squeezed my lungs. 'I hadn't realized you had remarried.' I felt a fool as soon as the words left my mouth.

'We have a ten-year-old. Vijay.'

A ten-year-old. I realized that Radha must have remarried while the ink was still drying on our divorce. 'Well, I—I am happy for you.'

'Are you? Still the martyr, Manoj.' She shook her head, a mixture of pity and something cruel entering her eyes. 'You're a fool. I never got to tell you this before, there didn't seem much point...Your brother was a snake. That day, when he came to speak to me after we had argued, he tried to convince me to leave you. He claimed that he was besotted with me, had been ever since I had entered the house. He told me that I would have a better future with *him*, the son entrusted to run your family company. That you would always be little more than a glorified administrator. I refused him. I still thought I could bring you to your senses, convince you to claim your birthright, as the older son. How wrong I was.' Her lips tightened into a grim line. 'And you, fool that you are, blindly signed away your life to him.' She leaned in. 'How does it feel, Manoj? How does it feel to be such a fool?'

Her words stayed with me. They infected me, shattering the life I had built since leaving prison, destroying the illusion of peace I had erected around myself. The truth was that the rage I felt – towards Sanjay, my father, my mother and Radha, the whole damn lot of them – had only been hidden away, waiting to find release.

And now it did.

Two weeks later, I came to a decision.

I boarded a plane to Chile.

I will hunt down my brother. And I will kill him.

This is to be my life's mission. Perhaps it will take the rest of my life.

So be it.

But at some point, one has to draw the line.

# KING PHISHER

*RV Raman*

## I

Deception has always come easily to me. I am as much a natural at it as it is natural for my targets to be gullible. Even as early as in school, I found it far easier to fool my teachers or trap my friends than to solve a quadratic equation or to recall the names and dates of historical battles. There was little that innocent eyes, an open face and trembling lips could not achieve... short of scoring high marks in exams, of course.

But then how important are marks? Short of clearing a minimum threshold to avoid failing, they are just meaningless numbers. They are not essential for success, particularly when there are other less onerous – and lucrative – ways of making one's way in the world. Invoking trust, I've often found, goes a longer way than academic achievements do.

Surely, that does not come as a surprise, does it? Clearly, formal education is overrated. Grossly so. It doesn't teach life skills. Nor does it build monetizable capabilities, which we are forced to pick up elsewhere. The vast majority of what I was taught in school was indeed useless. It could be forgotten a day after the exams.

But that is not to say that the fifteen years I spent in classrooms were without value. Quite the contrary. Those years provided me a training ground for understanding and manipulating human behaviour, and they offered me invaluable opportunities to experiment.

As a result, by the time I graduated, I knew more about eliciting desired responses from my fellow humans and less about physics and geography.

But language, I realized pretty early on, was an entirely different cup of tea. Impeccable English is a passport to impressing people and earning their trust. As is the ability to speak Hindi in a refined and persuasive manner. Communication and the art of convincing others are the core skills I developed early in life.

Perhaps, I might have been good at psychology, had I formally studied it. Or maybe, I should have taken up writing, for I do spin a convincing yarn when the occasion demands it. Nevertheless, somewhere along the way during my 'education', I learnt to adapt and to modulate my voice so as to tap into people's insecurities, desires, and above all, their greed. I also realized that people became more open to my suggestions if I told them things they wanted to hear. So much so, by the time I turned twenty, I was quite well-equipped for the profession I would eventually gravitate towards.

Ah! I almost forgot to mention that the place I grew up in is a district in Jharkhand. A district named Jamtara. Does that ring a bell? It should now. But thirty years ago, when I came into this world as the fourth child to my penniless parents, Jamtara was not really known for anything. It is only recently that it has gained notoriety. More about that later though.

How my parents managed to educate me and my brothers,

I do not know. They must have raised the money somehow. It probably helped that both my brothers turned to repairing two-wheelers rather early in life. As soon as they were able, they dropped out of school to apprentice at roadside repair shops on the highway outside our town. Scattering nails and sharp pieces of metal on the highway ensured a steady stream of 'puncture repair' work for these repair shops.

My two sisters, of course, did not go to school. Education, my father believed, was not for girls. Their place was inside the house and out of sight of roving eyes. From a very young age, my mother taught them how to clean and cook.

And so, the lofty aspirations my parents had for their children ended up resting solely on one pair of shoulders: mine. They wished for their educated son to work 'in an office' and not on dusty roadsides as his brothers did. That suited me just fine for I hated getting my hands dirty. I am as fond of grease and grime as ships are fond of icebergs, especially the *Titanic*.

Fortunately, a white-collar opportunity came to me within a couple of weeks of my graduating. This was probably because many people in my town knew that I was fluent in English. So, much to my parents' delight, I landed a job that required me to sit in an air-conditioned office with a computer in front of me and a pair of headphones over my ears. All I had to do was wag my silver tongue.

⋆

It was a blazing hot day at the peak of summer when I walked into a renovated warehouse for my first – and only – interview. After much consideration, I had donned the cleanest of my three shirts and worn my only pair of decent jeans.

Ours was a small town where most families knew each other. Having heard of my proficiency in English and my ability to converse well, a local company had sent me a message, asking me to meet them for an interview. Jamtara's unofficial industry, I later learnt, was desperately seeking people who could speak well and impress unsuspecting victims over the phone. Doubtless, I was seen as a good fit.

I was shown into a small glass cabin that had a table, a telephone and two chairs. A minute later, a man who was a few years older than me walked in, sat on the opposite side and studied me silently. I stared back equally quietly, waiting for him to speak. I learnt later that his name was Nishant.

A few seconds later, Nishant broke the silence and told me, in English, that the company was engaged in telesales. They were looking for people who could call potential customers and sell them products or services over the phone. For that I needed to speak pleasantly and keep my cool in the face of rude customers. I would have to leave my pride behind at home. Would I be interested in such a job?

'Yes, sir, I would.' I nodded, speaking crisply. 'But I will require some details about what I need to sell.'

'Here is all the information you need,' Nishant said as he slid across a printed sheet of paper. 'Read it up in the next ten minutes. After that, you will have a chance to sell it over the phone.'

He gestured towards the phone on the desk and rose.

'Ten minutes,' he repeated and left the room.

The sheet had details of a health insurance policy and listed its advantages over other similar products. Five minutes were enough for me to absorb the details. I was confident that I'd pass the test, for the few sentences my interviewer had uttered suggested that his English was nowhere as good as mine. Besides, the insurance policy I had to sell was pretty straightforward.

Nishant returned shortly and took his seat. He pointed to the desk phone and nodded.

'Dial 233,' he said. 'When someone picks up the call, try to sell him the policy. Speak in English.'

It was a cakewalk. The person at the other end of the line, who presumably was another employee, was not particularly proficient in English. Judging by his reaction and that of the man across the desk, I was sure I had made a good impression.

'*Ab 234 dabao*,' my interviewer said after I completed the call. '*Phir Hindi mein policy becho*.' Dial 234. Then sell the policy in Hindi.

I repeated the routine in Hindi, which too was a breeze. Fifteen minutes later, I had an appointment letter in my hand. Nishant shook my hand and explained my emolument structure: I would get a fixed salary for working eight hours a day. Every additional hour will earn overtime, as would weekend work. In addition to the salary, I would receive a bonus for every call that converts into a sale.

Thus began my career, which I took to like a fish takes to water. Right from the beginning, it was clear that I was very good at this work. It quickly grew more remunerative when I began slipping in small falsehoods and exaggerations to improve my conversion rate. Once a sale was consummated, who cared whether I had lied or not? There was no record of what I told the customer, and I changed my name every day. If the customer was unhappy, I could potentially sell him a policy from another insurance company! There was no downside to this! My bosses happily agreed.

Things got even better in a couple of weeks. Seeing my outstanding success, Nishant gave me more insurance products to sell and asked me to extract certain additional information from my customers. He wanted me to get hold of their Aadhaar number, PAN, bank account details, date of birth and other sensitive information. How my company would use these, I was not told. But had a fair inkling of where this was heading. I played along.

A month later, the big boss of the company – Prabhod Sir – called me to his room. He spoke about my exceptional performance and congratulated me. He even treated me to a shot of whisky. Then, he popped the question.

There was an elite team in the company that did confidential work in a secure part of the office. They were paid far better and even partook of the company's profits. But I would have to be *very* discreet and *never* speak about my work outside the office. Would I be interested in joining the elite team?

It was a no-brainer. This was right up my street! By now, I knew how bank details, Aadhaar numbers and OTPs could be used – or misused. The profits, I knew would be nothing to scoff at. I accepted Prabhod's offer on the spot.

Thus began my career in phishing. I have not looked back since. Like I said, deception comes naturally to me, and I am pretty persuasive. The good thing about this line of work is that what you earn is entirely based only on your performance. It's up to you to monetize your abilities.

I had no so-called ethical reservations. We live in a dog-eat-dog world, and I would be a fool if I were to let sentimental considerations get in my way. Phishing was as good a line of work as any other. By good fortune, I had latched on to something worthwhile. I was not going to let it go.

★

The next five years in Jamtara were among my most eventful ones. It was a time when new-found money had begun flowing to me, enabling my family to move into our own house that was a permanent brick-and-mortar structure. My brothers opened their own bike repair shops, and good marriage proposals started pouring in for my sisters. My parents were delighted as their dreams began materializing. I too was thrilled that we had finally shed the manacles of poverty without having to dirty my hands with grease and grime.

At work, I began outperforming everyone else, including my colleagues in the so-called elite team. The ticket size of my hits began growing. Initially, a successful hit would yield a few thousand rupees. By the end of my first year, I was snagging 'phishes' or 'fishes' worth tens of thousands.

This is when Nishant's resentment of my success started growing apparent. We had been very friendly during my first year, but towards the end of the year, friction developed between us. He began grudging me my share of profits, which admittedly had grown larger than his. But then, Prabodh ran a meritocracy wherein profit shares were pegged to the revenue each person brought. The company had a robust system to track performance. My hits were larger and more numerous than Nishant's. As a result, Prabodh dismissed Nishant's protests. That sowed the first seeds of enmity.

Further, Prabodh made me a partner in the company along with himself and Nishant. I would now be sharing the profits along with them – something Nishant deeply resented.

Soon, my more successful phishes began yielding a lakh or more each. I remember emptying the bank account of a man who had just sold a plot of land. Seventy lakhs was our picking. I learnt a few days later, when the news hit the papers, that he had sold the land to fund his daughter's wedding. Did I feel a twinge of guilt? I probably did, but, as I keep saying, we all live in a dog-eat-dog world.

By the end of my third year, I had learnt quite a bit about hacking into computers and phones and about intercepting emails and financial transactions. Naturally, I began targeting businesses and corporates as that's where the big fish were. And for evacuating the pilfered funds swiftly, I set up a series of overseas bank accounts in places that offered the highest level of confidentiality.

One heist which I particularly enjoyed pulling off was a seven-million-dollar transaction. I filched a CEO's identity and sent an email to his CFO, asking him to transfer the money to a specific bank account. The foolish CFO executed the instruction faithfully and without verifying if the instruction was genuine.

That was when I earned the sobriquet 'King Phisher' – KP for short. It sent Nishant into a fit of jealousy. It took all of Prabodh's influence and expertise to handle the explosive confrontation that followed in his office. I realized that I had made a dangerous enemy. The fact hit home hard the next week in the most unexpected way.

I had finished the day's work and went to my parked car. I had just opened the door when I noticed something lustrous and colourful on the driver's seat. Under it was an irregular brown stain. Wondering what it was, I turned over the multihued object with my car key.

To my horror, it turned out to be the body of a small bird. As I turned it over, its head came away and rolled down the seat. A second glance at the dead bird showed that it was a kingfisher. Someone had decapitated the little thing and left it in my car. The message was clear.

I had no doubt as to who could have done this – Nishant.

Over those five years, while I had grown in leaps and bounds in my chosen profession, Nishant too had grown but in another way. In addition to phishing, he had gotten into extortion, blackmail and unsavoury forms of physical crime – all of which I abhorred. To the extent that Prabodh too became wary of him. A decapitated kingfisher was right up Nishant's alley.

Meanwhile, I had been messing about with crypto-currencies because of the difficulty to trace their ownership and movement. Which is why Bitcoin or Ethereum offered me anonymous ways to move out the money generated by my hits. In addition, I had discovered that the combination of ransomware and crypto was an unbeatable one. It was both safe and lucrative. I figured that Gurgaon would be a better base for these more tech-enabled hits. I decided to move there. In any case, I was wanting to put some miles between Nishant and me.

I gave up making small hits and left them to Nishant and his team, while I focused on the real big ones. Unfortunately, he regarded it as an insult and grew furious. The day before I was to leave for Gurgaon, he came to visit me.

'Good decision to move to Gurgaon, KP,' he drawled in Hindi as he played with a gleaming dagger in his hand. 'You can now catch bigger fish for us. Don't forget to remit the company's share of the profits within three days of a hit. Remember I, you and Prabodh are equal partners.'

He tested the cutting edge of his dagger on a paper-wrapped parcel he was carrying. It cut through the wrapping effortlessly.

'Don't think that you can go off and set up your own racket,' he went on as he sheathed the dagger and unwrapped the package. 'I'll be watching. Here, a gift for you.'

He stretched out his arm and gave me his 'gift'. It was a painting of a kingfisher in a gilded cage.

## II

If my initial five years in Jamtara had been very eventful, the next three years in Gurgaon were the most enjoyable ones. It was, beyond doubt, the golden period of my life, financially speaking. Not least because of the copious cash flow I enjoyed, but also due to the physical distance between Nishant and me. Glitzy Gurgaon, with its high-end restaurants, ritzy bars and swanky glass towers turned out to be the ideal place to enjoy life.

It was a place where I could socialize extensively without exposing my true self or letting people into my private world. Many were happy with superficial friendships that didn't ask uncomfortable questions. While most residents were honest, hard-working people, there were enough social butterflies and corporate climbers with whom I could rub shoulders if I seemed well-to-do and spoke well.

I invested in a wardrobe of branded clothing and accessories, bought a couple of club memberships and turned on my charm. My objective was to build a network that would help me rise socially. I might not be tall, bearded and muscular, but I could be as dapper as the next trendsetter when I wished. In addition to possessing a refined, clean-shaven face, I could speak flawless English. These qualities were sufficient for me to project the image of understated elegance that I desired.

To remain under the taxman's radar, I avoided luxury cars and bought a mid-range SUV and kept a driver. My symbols of wealth, like high-end watches, which were useful for my image, were not visible from a distance.

And so, I became a regular in Gurgaon's social circles as I graced parties and cultivated friendships with rich businessmen and corporate bigwigs. I knew that some of them would become my targets, and it was always useful to become acquainted with them and get to know their personal habits and idiosyncrasies. That makes it easier to plan a hit.

On the professional front, I took to the combination of ransomware and crypto as my mainstay, which turned out to be brilliant for me. This combination was anonymous and lucrative, and I could tuck away my earnings in places where neither the authorities nor my partners could reach. However, even as I raked it in from this new line of work, I continued to phish. I did so for two reasons.

First, I wanted to remain in touch with my original line of work. Second, I needed income that I could send to Jamtara as my contribution to the partnership I had with Prabodh and Nishant. I had no intention of letting them get a whiff of the ransomware business that I had built all by myself. So, I ensured that I contributed enough from my phishing business for them to not get suspicious.

Thus, the King Phisher continued to fish, but now in the great pond of Gurgaon, where there were unlimited number of fishes to catch. I began enjoying life to the hilt and my first two years there passed in a hedonistic daze. I truly had a ball.

It was only in my third year that I began to sense an inadequacy creeping up on me. It left a growing hole in my heart – a hole of unfulfilled desire. Let me explain.

When people asked what I did for a living, I couldn't very well tell them the truth. I had to be vague about it. I therefore told people that I was on my own – a catch-all phrase that could mean anything. If pressed, I would say that I assisted clients in marketing. That was as close to the truth as I could get. I had indeed started my career in telesales, for which 'marketing' was a euphemism.

But such an answer did not allow me to drop big names or the names of MNCs, which were a dime a dozen in Gurgaon. If I was not a big guy at an MNC or a known domestic name, I could not ascend to the topmost strata of the societal pecking order. A self-employed man without pedigree, however elegant, dapper and articulate he may be, was bound to be relegated to the second or third tier of the social ladder.

I found that I was not being invited to the truly sought-after parties. In the lesser parties, there would often be a small circle of guests who regarded themselves superior to the other attendees. These people didn't hobnob with me either.

Initially, I brushed it off. But slowly, it began growing on me, bothering me. I was far from being a pariah, but I was not a nobleman either. As I grew more adept at reading the subtle signs, it annoyed me that people didn't place me in the top social strata. I was not getting the recognition I deserved. That got to me.

Unable to make peace with it, I decided to go home and talk to my family. When I voiced my worries, my mother sat me down in front of her favourite deity picture and held my hand.

'You have come a long way, beta,' she advised gently in Hindi. 'A very long way; a lot more than anyone else in this town. You should be content with what you have achieved. Don't forget that we are small people. *Apni aukat mat bhulo.*' Don't forget your station in life.

Of course, she had no idea how I *really* made my money or how much of it I had stashed away in traditional and cryptocurrencies.

My siblings expressed similar sentiments while my father added his own angle: 'Don't overreach, lest you fall,' he said brusquely. 'Don't let greed into your heart. You have enough.'

As I left home to return to Gurgaon at the end of my visit, my mother held my arm and added, '*Koi acchi ladki ke saath shadi karlo. Bolo to mein dhoondoongi.*' Marry some nice girl. Tell me, and I'll find someone.

I travelled back to Gurgaon, preoccupied and troubled. I still couldn't shake the feeling that I was not getting the recognition I deserved. I had as much money as the next fellow at any party and I was not thirty yet! How many self-made thirty-year-olds in Gurgaon had done as well as I had? How many forty-year-olds? Every rupee I possessed had been earned by me. How many scions who were born with silver spoons in their mouths could claim that? Surely, I deserved better! I was *not* second best!

Over the next few months, my craving for recognition only increased. I tried distracting myself with entertainment and immersing myself in other substantive things. But the yearning gradually grew into an obsession. I made several lucrative heists during those days, but none of them gave me satisfaction. A fixation took hold of me.

I was left depressed at the end of each hit – what had I *truly* achieved? Yes, I had made some more money, but in the eyes of the world, I was still the same second-rate fellow who had hit his social glass ceiling. I was not getting the respect my achievements warranted. I grew restless...was I not good enough for them?

However, it didn't take me long to recognize the crux of my dilemma: As long as I was 'on my own' in some vague sort of business, I would not rise socially. But, I could also not reveal what I actually did for a living. I was stuck.

The way out dawned slowly on me. If I were to satisfy my craving for recognition, I would have to give up cybercrime, take up a legitimate line of work and do well in it. Which meant that I would have to start all over again. Not to mention give up my copious cash flows. Truly, I was between a rock and a hard place.

My response to the quandary? I began drinking myself to sleep every night.

*

It was a little after my thirtieth birthday that things began turning around. I was at one of those parties that take place around Diwali, when I met several people for the first time. Curious, I soon found myself in a group of go-getters who had opinions on everything under the sun. Only two of us in the group listened more than we spoke – me and a quiet young woman.

Losing interest in the loudmouths, I struck up a quiet conversation with the young woman. As we chatted, I discovered that she had just moved to Gurgaon to take up a job as a product manager at a start-up tech company. As that was an area of interest to me, we got talking about technology and its profound impact on day-to-day urban lives.

I soon learnt that this soft-spoken woman was not only adept at using technology, but also had a good handle on human behaviour, especially that of her customers. We had a good chat and parted with neither of us taking the other's phone number. I went home, and she was out of my mind.

Until two weeks later, when I ran into her at a mall. Divya had just moved into a flat and was buying kitchenware. As I had gone there to buy some glasses, we bumped into each other. With her kitchen not in working order yet, I invited Divya to my club for dinner.

We had begun meeting regularly, when Cupid snuck up on me and shot his little arrow. The clouds that had gathered due to my obsession parted and sunshine lit up my life. I had always considered myself a hard-nosed and unsentimental professional who had no time for mushy stuff. But even the toughest of us is tripped up when the time comes.

I began viewing Divya differently. She was pleasant to look at without being gorgeous. And she was pleasanter still to talk to, which I really liked. She was neither gregarious nor shy, and preferred to blend into the crowd, like many quiet people do. In many ways, I found her to be the kind of person I was trying to be – one of understated elegance.

To say that the two of us hit it off would be a gross understatement. In no time, I got emotionally entangled for the first time in my life.

But unfortunately, I couldn't take matters forward for a very good reason: I couldn't very well tell Divya what I *really* did for a living and where I got my money from. I couldn't say that I was a cybercriminal. If I did, she would walk out of my life, and I'd lose the only girl I have ever cared for.

There was only one way out: I had to quit crime and find a respectable job. Money wouldn't be an issue – I had tons of it. Enough for the rest of my – our – lives. The quickest way to change colour, so to speak, was to buy a small business.

Ideally, it should be a business that dealt with technology and cybersecurity. That was a domain I understood, and it was also an area Divya could participate in. We would have a neat little business of our own.

The only catch was funding the purchase. While I had enough money, it was all illegal income that the taxman knew nothing of. Only a small part of it was in 'white', and a large portion of my hoard was in cryptocurrency, which I couldn't use to buy a business in India. While I could pay for a part of the purchase legally, I would have to take out a loan for the rest.

Once I got myself a business, I decided I would propose to Divya.

The next month was the busiest I have ever had in my life. As my mother always said, honest and sincere work never goes unrewarded. I shortlisted three businesses in the next two weeks and clinched an in-principle deal with one of them in two more weeks.

All of a sudden, I realized that I had not indulged in cybercrime for a whole month! A sense of relief and optimism swept over me. But a phone call from Prabodh reminded me that I had one more thing to do before I could cut my links with phishing. Even as the bank was processing my loan application, I dashed to Jamtara to chat with Prabodh and Nishant.

'Congratulations, KP,' Prabodh said when I told them that I had quit cybercrime and would be taking up something legal. 'I'm genuinely happy for you – you have taken a step that I have long wanted to take. I've had enough of crime and the fears that come with it. But it is too late for me – my only option now is to retire quietly. But you are young, KP. You can start anew and rebuild your life.' He shook my hand warmly and patted me on the shoulder. 'I wish you the very best. Good luck!'

Prabodh's unsought approval and encouragement touched me. For the first time since I've known him, I bent down and touched the older man's feet, asked for his blessings, which he gave unreservedly.

But Nishant's reaction was different.

'Fine,' he said brusquely, his features cast in stone. 'If you want to change lines, it's your business. As a Jamtara boy, you will always have our good wishes.' However, the hatred in his eyes was unmistakable. 'But don't forget that we know enough about you and your activities to get you a one-way ticket to jail. All your secrets are known to us. As long as you don't squeal on me, you will be safe. Rat on us, and you are done for.'

As I made my way home, I knew in my heart that this wasn't the last time I would hear from Nishant. His hatred for me ran too deep for him to sit back and let me prosper unmolested. Fortunately, I hadn't spoken to him about Divya.

I pushed away unpleasant thoughts and opened my mind to happier ones. I was now elated that I had cut my ties with cybercrime and looked forward to a clean future. Now, I had the all-important thing to do.

As soon as I returned to Gurgaon, I proposed to Divya. She accepted.

An hour later, the bank approved my loan application. Before the week was over, I had inked the deal to buy the small cybersecurity firm.

I was truly convinced that God wanted me to turn over a new leaf.

*End of excerpt from King Phisher's abandoned autobiography.*

## III

The next few weeks passed in a pleasant daze for KP as he divided his time between the love of his life and the cybersecurity firm he had acquired. When he was not at his new office, coming to grips with his new business, he was at home with Divya, who had the flexibility to work from home. At his suggestion, she had partially moved in while she still retained her flat where she spent a couple of days a week.

By mutual consent, they agreed not to enter the other's room when they were working from home. As a product manager, Divya dealt with product plans and other sensitive items that she was contractually obliged to keep confidential. This arrangement suited KP well for he desperately needed privacy to wind down his former ignoble occupation and withdraw from it completely. And most importantly, he needed to reorganize and consolidate his financial assets into a few large holdings. The last thing he wanted was for Divya to get wind of his former life and his sullied earnings.

Neither of them had yet told their families about the other, opting to get to know each other a little better before publicizing their relationship or formalizing it in any way. After all, they hadn't known each other for very long. Besides, Divya felt that she needed to prepare her mother for the announcement.

A couple of weeks later, KP's quiet state of euphoria was rudely disturbed by the unexpected ringing of the doorbell. Opening the door, Divya found herself confronted by two uncouth men. She called out to KP.

'Who are you?' the apparent leader of the men asked her roughly before KP could come.

Simultaneously, he put one foot inside the threshold,

preventing her from closing the door. He studied her with keen interest.

'None of your business,' she shot back. 'What do you want?'

Before the stranger could respond, KP arrived at the door and gently pulled her back as he put himself between her and the men.

'Nishant!' he gasped as he recognized the visitor. 'What brings you here?'

'Can I come in?' Nishant growled. 'Surely, I am not unwelcome here?'

His stony gaze was fixed on Divya as he spoke. Feeling uncomfortable, she turned around and went to another room, with the newcomers' eyes following her.

'Sure,' KP replied with his heart growing heavy. 'Please come and sit.'

'So, the kingfisher has a new mate?' Nishant asked as he took a seat.

'Just a friend,' KP commented non-committedly before changing the topic. 'What brings you here? How can I help?'

'Oh, I was just passing by and thought I'd look you up.' He placed a flat package on a table. 'Another gift for you...lest you forget our arrangement.'

KP did not need to open the package to know what was in it...another painting of a caged kingfisher.

Mercifully, Nishant kept his visit short even if his eyes kept darting to the door of the room Divya was in. He voiced veiled warnings a couple of times and then rose to go. The purpose of his visit – to remind KP of his warnings – had been accomplished.

As soon as the front door closed behind Nishant, Divya came out of the room.

'What an unpleasant man!' she griped. 'What did he want? He seemed to know you.'

KP had his answer ready.

'He is an example of the occupational hazards one faces while dealing with cybersecurity. Don't worry about him. In my profession, I have to deal with all kinds.'

'Not your friend, then? He tried to act familiar with you.'

As KP shook his head, Divya noticed the package Nishant had brought. She picked it up and opened it.

'Ooh! What a pretty bird!' she exclaimed. 'Lovely colours, no? Pity it's in a cage.'

KP remained silent as she unsuspectingly put down the painting and went to her room.

*

Nishant's visit left KP unsettled and insecure. He became acutely conscious of the power the former now wielded over him, including the ability to destroy his happiness at will. All Nishant had to do was to tell Divya about KP's past. Being far from honourable, Nishant might well resort to blackmail once he realized KP's position. What should KP do then?

For a moment, KP considered taking a drastic step. No sooner had the thought crossed his mind than he dismissed it. He shouldn't compound his crimes with more serious ones.

The best thing for him to do was to expedite matters with Divya and conduct the wedding as soon as possible.

Which meant that he had to tackle what he considered to be the biggest hurdle in Divya agreeing to marry him: take her home to Jamtara to meet his family. While he himself appeared suave, his siblings and parents did not. His brothers ran motorcycle repair shops – a far cry from his cybersecurity firm. They hardly spoke English. How would Divya react to his unsophisticated family? Would she be shocked? Would she call off the whole thing?

There was only one way to find out: take her to Jamtara.

He broached the idea to her the very next day.

'I've been meaning to ask you myself,' she said with a nod and a smile. 'A long weekend is coming up later this month. That might be a good time to go.'

'Of course! Good idea!'

'And if we are going all the way to Jharkhand, let's also visit one of the wildlife parks that you have been talking about.'

'Brilliant!' he enthused. 'Let's do that.'

'Done!' She pumped her fist. 'I'll make the bookings at a resort.'

*

To KP's surprise and delight, their visit to Jamtara went far better than he could have hoped for. Divya took to the small town as if she were born to it. Which was when KP recalled that her parents were from an obscure town in Uttar Pradesh. She seemed very comfortable with his siblings too, who seemed to look up to the city girl. His mother welcomed her with open arms and treated her like a princess. It was apparent that she thoroughly approved of Divya. KP's father, as was his wont, was gruff and laconic, but was blown over when the elegantly attired girl touched his feet and sought his blessings. Divya had brought gifts for the entire family and they, in turn, reciprocated heartily with what they could afford. KP's mother cooked an elaborate meal for Divya.

Before KP knew it, the brief, one-day visit came to an end and he found himself in a car with Divya, heading towards the wildlife park.

The next forty-eight hours were spent in a veritable time warp far removed from the bustle of civilization. They lounged about in cosy timber cottages that were surrounded by a forest, which mobile phone networks seldom penetrated. While Divya's BSNL phone picked up an occasional weak signal, KP's mobile didn't detect even a trace. But he didn't mind it at all as he spent a delightful two days with Divya in splendid isolation.

When the happy sojourn came to an end all too soon, he reluctantly entered the car to begin his journey back to Gurgaon.

★

His mood had improved quickly, and elation had returned by the time they reached Delhi. Whistling gaily, he got off the taxi and rode up the elevator to his apartment. Divya had got off at a metro station on the way to visit a friend. The only thing marring his upbeat mood now was his mobile phone – it still wasn't connecting to the network. He had called it from Divya's phone only to get a 'switched off or unreachable' message. He decided to deal with the problem the next morning.

After taking a relaxing shower, he poured himself a drink and started up his laptop to catch up on his email. Seeing that there was very little on the work front, he switched to the email ID he used for his financial matters and downloaded those emails. He was greeted by a surprisingly long series of beeps – he had received numerous messages.

He opened the first one and stared at it. It was from one

of his banks and was a debit advice for ninety-odd lakhs. The amount had been transferred to an unfamiliar bank account. The balance remaining in his account was ₹5.23.

The next message was for an even larger amount that had been transferred out from one of his illegal overseas bank accounts. That account too had been emptied. With mounting panic, he scanned the dozen-odd emails from his banks. All of them were intimations of outward transfers from his accounts.

All his bank accounts – both Indian and foreign – had been emptied over the weekend. A major chunk of his wealth had been usurped.

With clammy hands and trembling fingers, he opened the remaining emails, which were from another set of sources – his cryptocurrency holdings. Within a minute, his worst fears stood confirmed. His stashes of cryptocurrency too had been cleaned out. And given the nature of this asset, there was no way to determine who had stolen them.

In any case, he couldn't report this theft or go to the authorities – over ninety-five per cent of his wealth, if not more, was illegal and ill-gotten. All that was left in his personal balance sheet was the multi-crore loan he had taken to buy the cybersecurity firm. How he would now pay it back, he had no idea.

Abruptly, a part of the puzzle fell into place – so that's why his phone had not been working! The thief must have cloned his SIM card when he was in Jamtara. How stupid of him to have not suspected it!

But who had done this to him? Nishant? That didn't seem right – Nishant was not smart enough to pull off such a complex 'techie' thing. Besides, the thief must have had access to his laptop and phone to steal his credentials unnoticed.

A moment later, an agonizing thought seared his heart and ripped his soul. An involuntary sob burst out through his mouth. He leapt up and ran to Divya's room, where he ran around like a madman, opening cupboards and drawers. They were all empty. She had moved out of the flat. Nothing of hers remained.

Other pieces fell into place. That's why she had got off at a metro station...to vanish. She was the only one who had access to his laptop and phone, and all his credentials that he had stored there. She had systematically stolen them before engineering a visit to the wildlife park that had no network coverage other than BSNL. Her final act was to clone his phone and empty his coffers.

The King Phisher had been phished.

*

Clearly, everything she had told him was a lie. He wondered what her real name was and where she hailed from. In his heart, he knew that he would not be able to trace her.

He had wanted to jettison crime and lead an honourable life. Now, that was not likely...not as long as he had the huge loan to repay. There was only one way out now: return to cybercrime. That was the only thing he really knew.

# SOCIETY MURDER

*Madhulika Liddle*

Four flats to a floor. Twenty floors to a tower.

Two lifts per tower.

That is if you don't count the servants' lift.

It isn't called that, of course; that would be politically incorrect. It would be incorrect to even suggest that 'domestic help' (yes, that is what they *should* be called now, not 'servants') should have a separate lift. Instead, the 'Others' lift – that's what it's labelled, in both English as well as Hindi – is set apart from the other two, which are supposedly for 'Guests'. If visitors to the towers are guests, then why, wonders Munia, does the guard at the bottom of the tower have instructions to direct delivery men, couriers and repairmen to use 'Others'?

It is no business of hers. She knows her way around. She is known here.

Munia comes to a halt almost as soon as she enters the cramped lift lobby at ground level. She has been on her phone all this while, talking to her daughter Reema, making sure she's reached the polytechnic safe and sound. Even past that distraction, she had heard the muted hubbub of many voices and had half-wondered what was happening.

Now she sees, and it brings her up short. She mutters a

quick word of goodbye and hangs up, shoving the phone into her capacious jhola before moving forward.

The lobby is full. A seething, simmering crowd milling about in front of the lifts. There are maids, and an assortment of uniform-clad workmen: gardeners in green overalls, housekeeping staff in maroon, a couple of security guards in navy. There is a man carrying a large, scruffy backpack with the logo of a quick-commerce company, and two others, both from courier companies: all three restive, the quick-commerce employee pelting one of the guards with urgent questions.

Besides all these people, there are the residents, and they make up the bulk of the crowd. Early-morning walkers, a couple of them with dogs. A group of middle-aged mothers, most of them still in their nighties, back after seeing their school-going children off at the bus stop. A little group, men and women, mostly white-haired, fiery dots of vermilion on their foreheads and little plastic bags of puffed rice and crystal sugar in their hands.

One of the other maids – Khushi, who got Munia this job, and who works in two flats in this tower – breaks free from the melee and comes hurrying to Munia. Her eyes are bright, her voice brimming with excitement. 'What do you know,' she says, grabbing Munia by the elbow and steering her into a corner, 'there's been a murder!'

⋆

The dead man is Mr Chopra, who lives – *lived*, that is more accurate – all by himself in #803. He was a widower, his wife having died in a car crash three years earlier. Whether they had had offspring or not, it was unknown; nobody ever came visiting. And given that Chopra Sahib was such a recluse – rarely venturing outdoors, not even to the society's park or to the shops – nobody had ever heard him talk about any children. He kept to himself, a single servant attending to all his needs. Sohan cooked and cleaned, did the shopping, watered the plants, ran whatever errands were needed.

Sohan has been on leave the past three days: his grandmother, many miles away in his village, had passed away. So, he had to leave Chopra Sahib to the tender mercies of a hurriedly appointed temporary substitute, a neighbour of Sohan's. Rehaan has no experience as domestic help, but he was desperate for a job; Sohan was desperate for a substitute, and Chopra Sahib cannot manage on his own. Sohan spent fifteen minutes telling Rehaan what had to be done and how, and judiciously omitted a mention of the chores that could wait a few days. Also judiciously, he had a chat on Chopra Sahib's behalf with the next-door neighbour's maid and arranged for her to come over to do the cooking.

Over the past couple of days, Supriya has made it a practice to arrive at Chopra Sahib's after finishing her morning's chores next door. She rushes in at around 8 a.m., quickly brews tea, fries eggs, and makes toast. While Chopra Sahib eats, she rushes around making lunch and dinner: a big batch of rice, a big batch of dal, two vegetables. By 9.30, Supriya is out, yelling to Chopra Sahib that she is going. Supriya is a busy woman, working in five different houses through the day; she has no time to waste.

Which is why, this morning, after ringing Chopra Sahib's doorbell and not getting an answer, she has become increasingly impatient. She has banged on the door, yelled loud enough to have curious people emerge from the flats next door. Including the people she regularly works for. The man, known universally as Sudhanshu Bhaiya, is an avid gym-goer and fancies himself quite the muscle man. He leans one heavily muscled shoulder into Chopra Sahib's apartment door, and just a few shoves later, the door bangs open, the latch on the inside torn clean off its screws.

They step in, and there, sprawled on the dining room floor, they find Chopra Sahib, dead as a doornail. Flat on the floor on his back, his face contorted in pain, a pool of congealed blood under his head. There is blood everywhere; in fact, so much of it that Supriya has to rush out again so as not to vomit all over the scene of the crime.

For that is what it is, unmistakably. A crime.

*

Bhabhi – her name is Mitali Gupta, but to Munia, she is Bhabhi – works from home. Her schedule is flexible, so she has the time, but more importantly the inclination, for gossip. She also has good friends among the neighbours. Some of them do not work; some, like Bhabhi, work mostly from home. At any rate, today they have all set aside other considerations, all other demands on their time and energies. It is a day like none other.

Munia has been a little late today, but Bhabhi isn't complaining. It's expected, given the excitement in the building, in the entire society. The police were already in Chopra Sahib's apartment when Munia arrived, and their comings and goings and restrictions on movements within the tower had entailed a temporary embargo on people using the lifts or the stairs. There are constables now stationed outside Chopra Sahib's home, and another in the lift lobby downstairs. Though the lifts and stairs were opened up once the body had been taken away by the cops, Munia has only been able to come upstairs to Bhabhi's place by around ten. She is on her haunches, sweeping, trying to hurry, telling herself that even if she is a little slipshod today, she will make up for it tomorrow.

The doorbell rings.

Bhabhi hurries towards the door, calling over her shoulder for Munia to carry on with her work, which is a relief. On most days, Munia is expected to leave whatever she's doing to attend to the doorbell.

Today, Bhabhi doesn't want to miss any chance of a possible snippet of information. Whoever's come might have something to offer, some nugget of juicy gossip.

She is right. It's Sujata, a friend who lives in the next tower. With her is her mother-in-law, who is visiting these days, and who was one of the temple-goers Munia had noticed in the lift lobby.

'Mataji was there, right there,' Sujata says in an awed whisper, even before they've sat down, even before Bhabhi can offer chai or coffee. 'I had to bring her along, no?' She grins triumphantly.

Munia is now mopping, moving from room to room, so she can hear only brief snatches of the conversation. 'The police are being so close-mouthed. All puffed up and pompous,' Sujata sneers. 'What's wrong with telling us what happened? We have a right to know.'

But the police haven't said anything. Which, of course, leaves everybody free to speculate.

The door was latched on the inside, even if it wasn't locked. So, the murderer must have got in through a window? Or a balcony? Bhabhi is a devoted watcher of suspense thrillers and can see loopholes, clues, red herrings – things that the police are *sure* to miss.

'Balcony?' Sujata scoffs. 'Arre, how will anybody climb up to the balcony, so high? And a window? That's even more absurd.'

Both Bhabhi and Sujata turn to Sujata's mother-in-law. This is why she has come, after all: as the one with the insider's viewpoint, the one who *knows*.

Mataji, sipping delicately at a glass of nimbu-paani, pushes her spectacles up a beaky nose and pats the austere grey bun at her nape. 'Somebody cracked his skull,' she says authoritatively. 'I was there in the lobby when they took his body out, you know.' No, she clarifies in a tetchy sort of way when asked; she did not see the body herself. They had covered it up. But she overheard one of the policemen saying it to another.

'Have you seen this Rehaan?' Sujata says in a gleeful whisper to Bhabhi. 'All heavily muscled, one of those biryani- and kebab-eating types. He could have crushed Chopra Sahib's head without batting an eyelid.'

Munia continues to hear bits and pieces of the conversation as she works, but she's too busy to pay much attention. When she leaves, she says, as usual, 'I'm going, Bhabhi.' But Bhabhi just nods in an abstracted sort of way and waves her away. Sujata and Mataji are still around, all three women with their heads together.

*

The next flat, the second of three homes where Munia works, is a young couple's. They have moved in just six months ago. Newly married, and from what she can tell, young people who lead a very hectic life. Their home is invariably messy, and they host parties very often. Munia dreads coming in to clean their home on a Monday; it takes ages to clean up after one of their weekend dos.

This has been the usual sort of weekend, it seems. The young woman has already left for her office – Munia has only rarely seen her home in the mornings, only on Sunday, and once when she was ill – but her husband is home, looking groggy and unshaven when he opens the door to Munia. The smell of coffee wafts out from the kitchen. Munia goes about clearing up, picking cushions off the floor and placing them on sofas, picking up empty glasses and paper plates from tables, bringing some semblance of order to the room before she starts sweeping. The man pours his coffee into a big mug and slides the balcony door open. Steps out, his phone in one hand, the mug in the other.

He has been on the phone, chatting while drinking his coffee, for at least five minutes when Munia, sweeping along the inside of the balcony door, hears him say: 'It's these slum-dwellers, you know. That great big sprawl right beside our society, just outside the walls – you see them, don't you, every time you drive in at the gate? – it's them. Bloody beggars.' He takes a gulp of his coffee. 'I mean, it's all very well to say the poor deserve our sympathy and all, but, sorry, that's just bullshit. These buggers aren't poor. They steal electricity, you know, by tapping into our wires. They have coolers in their windows! And dish antennas on each roof!' He spits, the anger pulsating from him in waves that Munia can sense even through the glass separating them.

'Criminals,' she hears him say as she moves away from the door, deeper into the room. 'I can bet anything the murderer is from that slum. This Rehman, or whatever his name is. Temp. They wouldn't have done even a background check on him—'

*

The third home where Munia works is at the far end of the housing society. She has to go there only in the afternoon, after lunch. Between then and now, she has a little free time, a couple of hours during which she usually scurries home across the road to attend to chores. But today her friend Khushi grabs her arm just as Munia is going out the gate. 'Oye, Munia, off so soon? Come, let's go have chai before you leave.'

There's a chaiwallah at the corner, his rickety *thela* with a huge soot-stained aluminium *patila* constantly boiling on it. The tea, in thick bluish-green glasses, is hot and sweet and milky. Khushi pays for her tea; Munia pays for hers. This is an indulgence, a little treat for themselves.

'They're going mad there, no?' Khushi remarks. She and Munia have taken their tea and walked ten paces to stand under a nearby tree, far enough from the chaiwallah to not have him eavesdrop on their conversation. 'All they can talk of is the murder.' She blows on her tea and uses a fingernail to push away the thin skin that's formed on the surface. 'Every single house I've been to today, that's all I've heard. Who killed him, why, when, how.' She slurps. 'I wanted to scream, "Let the police decide that! Who made you the cops?!"'

Munia nods but says nothing. Khushi is quite capable of carrying on a one-sided conversation. She is a born raconteur, delighting in entertaining her audience.

Now she mimics some of the more interesting statements

she's heard today. Her voice rises to a high whine as she copies Verma Aunty, president of the society's Resident Welfare Association, the RWA: 'Mark my words, this is all because Chopra Sahib didn't take due care. You cannot just bring in whoever you want to work for you. There are procedures. We have rules!'

Pooja, her daughter-in-law, who is always out to needle Verma Aunty: 'If the rules can be broken so easily, they need to be changed, no?' Her voice silken, sophisticated. The 'no' in English, of which Khushi, of course, knows only a handful of words.

Paresh, the guard on duty in the tower. His eyes narrowed, his nostrils flared, his voice a sibilant whisper: 'I told the cops, this Rehaan is a bad one, I had my eye on him from the first time I saw him. And where is he today, eh? Where?' Khushi waggles her eyebrows and looks so ridiculous that Munia cannot suppress a giggle.

This Paresh looks down on them, on the 'jhuggi-wallahs', the slum-dwellers. He lives in an LIG flat – a low-income group housing scheme construction. A proper house, cement and bricks. Pukka. He is higher up the pecking order than the likes of Munia and Khushi, and he knows it.

'Do you know Chachi – the one who lives behind my place, the old woman with the polio leg? – she tells me she knew Paresh when he was a teenager and lived here, quite close to Chachi's,' Khushi says. 'He was one of us.'

Munia raises her eyebrows.

Khushi nods. 'No love lost there,' she says. She drinks down the last of her chai and waits for Munia to finish hers. 'Who knows what really happened,' she says, as they walk towards the little cluster of shacks where both of them live. 'I only hope this doesn't spark off all sorts of nonsense for us.'

She doesn't explain, but Munia can guess. An incident like this – if Rehaan *is* responsible – could have uncomfortable repercussions for the domestic help in the society. The RWA could become stricter about whom they allow in; they could enforce all sorts of rules...Munia shudders, suddenly realizing what this could mean. She could lose her job.

What makes it all the more frightening is that it might happen even if Rehaan isn't responsible.

*

The police are going about their own investigation, though they are not – in the SHO's words – 'in a position to divulge any details' yet. They have questioned some people in and around Chopra Sahib's tower. They have taken Sohan's phone number and will presumably speak to him. They have, or so goes the gossip, admonished the RWA's office-bearers, leaving Verma Aunty seething.

Who knows when the police will discover who killed Chopra Sahib, or why; in the meantime, the RWA is taking steps to prove its worthiness. To cover its ass, as Sudhanshu, Chopra Sahib's neighbour, puts it.

The RWA has decided that it has to investigate this sordid business on its own. Why wait for the cops, who – as Verma Aunty says, completely off the record – will probably push this under the carpet because there's nobody to bribe them to hurry up and find Chopra Sahib's murderer. No heir wanting the case closed, no grieving offspring or widow to push for closure. Besides, the corruption of the police is legendary. They will not do anything if they aren't going to get anything out of it.

The RWA, to start with, have decided to question all the domestic help. One by one, each of them has been called to the club house, where Verma Aunty and the other top brass of the RWA have set up shop in a small office. Here, four of these members of the RWA sit lined up behind a large desk, trying to look as formidable as they can, presenting a picture of justice-loving righteousness that they hope will awe or frighten their questionees into divulging the truth.

Munia's turn comes shortly after she returns to the society that afternoon.

'Do you know Rehaan?'

Munia shakes her head.

'How come? Doesn't he live in the same village as Sohan?' That is what these people call the slums when they're trying to be polite: villages. To Munia, the word 'village' implies fields and clear skies. Birdsong. A slow, uncomplicated life. All that she left behind years ago in her desire to make a better life for herself, for her daughter.

She shakes her head again. 'Sohan doesn't live near me,' she replies. 'I have only seen him now and then here, never outside the society.'

Verma Aunty looks disgruntled. 'And you did not phone Rehaan to tell him to stay away?'

Munia blinks, puzzled. 'I don't know him,' she says. *How can I phone him if I don't know him.*

'Someone here has phoned him, or tipped him off,' one of the members of this committee explains. 'Telling him, no doubt, that the murder has been discovered and that he should stay away.'

Munia shrugs. She does not say anything.

*

Chanda Taiji lives in one of the ground-floor flats, with its own little garden outside. This is the only house Munia visits in the afternoon, because this is where she does work that extends beyond the usual sweeping-mopping-bathroom cleaning routines of the other two homes. Here, she is expected to dust, to water the plants, to wash the garden path and clean the flowerpots. Chanda Taiji has green fingers. Where others may be said to be house proud, Chanda Taiji is garden proud; there is no other word for it.

Today, though she is hovering about while Munia does her chores in the garden, Chanda Taiji is not pottering about among her plants. Wilted flowers droop on their stems, a caterpillar makes its ponderous way along the leaf of one of her prized crotons. All Chanda Taiji can talk of is Chopra Sahib's death.

'But why...' she says, after Munia has apologized for arriving late and Chanda Taiji has brushed it aside, because she knew the RWA secretary was questioning domestic help, 'why would Rehaan murder Chopra Sahib? You don't just go around killing people for the sake of it.'

Munia, training the hose on a row of flowering plants, has no explanations to offer. All she's heard so far amongst the rumours whizzing about the housing society is that Rehaan has murdered Chopra Sahib. People have said that the very fact that Rehaan has not been seen since the previous evening is a testament to his guilt; he is absconding because he is the culprit. The general consensus about motive is that Rehaan burgled Chopra Sahib's home. Was caught in the very act of stealing, and so, in desperation, killed Chopra Sahib to avoid being caught.

Munia, after a bit of thought, ventures this suggestion in a timid little voice.

Chanda Taiji shakes her head. 'No,' she says. 'My son is in the police, you know. Not here in Noida; in Delhi. But he knows people here. He has friends among the cops here. I telephoned to ask him.' She looks briefly smug, pleased at being privy to information that is not known to everybody, not even the pompous Verma Aunty. 'Nothing was stolen from Chopra Sahib's, not as far as they can tell. At any rate, the CCTV cameras in the tower showed nobody emerging from Chopra Sahib's flat after Rehaan had left for the day.'

Munia is not very interested. She is thinking right now only of the work she must finish before she hurries home to complete all the chores that await her there. Will her daughter be home on time? The buses are so unreliable, so liable to run late. Reema is usually home by six every evening; let her get even half an hour late and Munia begins to fret. Munia has had enough stress for the day. Today, at least at home, everything should go like clockwork. No unpleasant surprises, no tension, nothing to add to the exhaustion and worry that is swamping her.

'They think Chopra Sahib was killed sometime near midnight,' Chanda Taiji says, oblivious of Munia's indifference. 'They are yet to do the autopsy – they have doctors, you know, who examine the body and just on the basis of that, they can tell when he died and how – and once that's done, they'll know for sure.' She smiles cheerfully, a rather macabre expression given the circumstances. 'And Rehaan was gone long before that.'

She wags her woolly grey head as she bends down, somewhat absent-mindedly, to pinch off some seed heads from a pot of basil. 'I don't understand why they're trying to pin this on Rehaan,' she says, more to herself than to Munia. 'I mean,' she adds after a moment, 'I suppose I can guess, but it makes no sense. You have to have something logical to pin onto a suspect, you know.' She crumbles the seed heads in her fingers and lifts the fragrant handful to her nose, sniffing appreciatively if without really registering any of it.

'The police will sort it all out,' she says confidently.

★

Reema is home, and just that little fact is enough to help Munia breathe a little easier. Mother and daughter say hello to each other, and then get busy with their respective chores – Reema, especially, to study. It is imperative that she study, get a good job. Do well, never have to work in people's homes for a living. Munia has all her hopes pinned on Reema.

It is only when the two of them sit down for dinner that Munia tells Reema about all that has been going on at the housing society all this day. The gossip, the speculations, the outright accusations. 'Chanda Taiji says the police will sort it out,' she finishes, unconsciously parroting the woman's words.

'Sort it out!' Reema repeats, with a snort. 'Pin the crime irrevocably on this Rehaan? The people who live in that society only *think* it's him and *say* it's him; the police will be able to cook up evidence to *prove* it's him, even if he had nothing to do with it.' She shakes her head in a resigned sort of way. 'That's all they know how to do.'

She is too outspoken for her own good. Munia tries to shush her.

'No,' Reema shakes her head stubbornly. 'If you keep quiet, people think you're scared, because you've done something wrong. Not because you're too nice to oppose them.' She tears the last roti in halves, handing one half to her mother and taking the other for herself. 'If, as your Chanda Taiji says, Rehaan is not guilty, he should come out of wherever he's hiding and let people know he didn't do it.'

Munia does not express her disagreement, but she knows that if she were in Rehaan's place, she too would stay away, would lie low. They can only accuse him behind his back; they cannot actually throw him to the hounds if he's not there.

*

There is news, and from an unlikely source. Supriya, the young woman who works at Sudhanshu Bhaiya's home, and who had been cooking at Chopra Sahib's while Sohan has been away, had shown some initiative: she has telephoned Sohan of her own accord and has shared all the gossip with him. The police too had taken his phone number the previous day, but they don't seem to have phoned him yet. 'Sohan says that's probably because they don't think they even need to talk to him in order to accuse Rehaan,' Supriya announces to a small but eager audience of maids when they meet just inside the society gate the next morning.

Sohan seems pretty sure that Rehaan has not murdered Chopra Sahib. Supriya repeats his words: 'He's a gentle fellow. He wouldn't harm a soul.'

'You've met Rehaan,' someone says to Supriya, 'haven't you? The few times you worked at Chopra Sahib's recently? He was there too.'

Supriya looks doubtful. 'Ye—es,' she admits, 'but how can you really know what somebody's like just because you've been in the same house for a few minutes? He would be doing something else, I would be in the kitchen, rushing through my work. I barely even remember what he looked like.

'In any case,' she adds, 'when Sudhanshu Bhaiya broke open Chopra Sahib's front door, it was latched from the inside. Rehaan couldn't have killed Chopra Sahib and then gone out the front door, latching it on the inside.' She glances triumphantly around, though this is not something she has deduced; Sohan has said this, and there are others among those around – Khushi, in particular – who have already pointed this out too. What with Chopra Sahib's flat being so high up, there really is no other way in or out of the house other than the front door. Munia remembers hearing the same thing the previous day, when Sujata and her mother-in-law had come to Bhabhi's home while Munia was there.

'If he's innocent, then why isn't he showing up?' Munia overhears one of the women say as they disperse to go to their respective flats to work. 'There is something fishy about all of this. I tell you, Chopra Sahib paid for his gullibility with his life. How can you just take on someone like this, without checking?' Munia is walking a few steps behind the woman and her friend, and the words drift her way, a little garbled now and then, but fairly audible.

'I worked for Chopra Sahib, once, many years ago,' the woman continues. 'When he first moved here, and before Sohan came to work for him. Such a gullible man I've never met. So easily taken in. I wouldn't put it past this Sohan to have been behind the murder. He knows the ins and outs of the flat, after all, and he must know where any valuables are hidden. It's easy to bring in an accomplice who will help you do the deed, while you have an alibi.'

*

In the two flats Munia works in through the morning, things are much quieter than they were yesterday. People are back to work, the excitement has fizzled out. Bhabhi, at the first house, is sitting at her laptop and working. In the second house, the man is again on the balcony drinking his coffee and chatting on the phone, but Munia gathers, from the conversation, that he's talking to one of his parents, perhaps; there's a deference in his voice and the talk is all domestic. Relatives, some uncle they have to visit, the upcoming engagement of a cousin.

Life has moved on.

On the surface, at least. Verma Aunty and her lot at the RWA aren't giving up so easily. Questions have been raised about their competence, and they will not rest easy until they have got to the root of the matter. Verma Aunty is now going from house to house, asking people for their opinions, seeking suggestions for improving the security of the society. Putting in what she calls 'further safeguards' to make the society more watertight.

'We have to make sure we're only letting in people we can completely trust,' she says, addressing a random group – a woman, a teenager and her pet dog, and a maid with the toddler of the family she works for – who happen to be waiting for the lift along with Verma Aunty. 'Everybody has to be vetted. Every single domestic worker,' – she looks pointedly at the maid – 'must have their documents verified from the police. No coming in to work however and wherever you please.'

The lift pings, the doors slide open. 'These Bangladeshis,' Verma Aunty says, to no one in particular, 'will learn that they can't come and invade our country from the inside anymore. We are patriots, we will be an army defending our Bharat Mata!'

The maid with the toddler is known to Khushi, and it is through her that they come to know of this latest diatribe. 'Bangladeshis!' Khushi says, shaking her head in mock disbelief, when she tells Munia about it as they leave together at noon that day. 'As if there's anybody Bangladeshi here!'

'There is, actually,' Munia says. 'Sumati and her family migrated from there, I heard. And a couple of others. They're from Bangladesh.'

'Sumati is Hindu,' Khushi says, giving Munia a bleak look. 'And you know as well as I that that's not what they mean. They don't even really mean "Bangladeshi". Muslim. Muslim is what they mean.'

Munia knows it too, has known it from the moment she has heard of what happened. Has known it since well before, when Khushi got her here and helped her get her first job, with Chanda Taiji. It was Chanda Taiji who had not just taken on Munia but had also made a few suggestions to help her establish herself here in the city. A widow, alone, with a daughter to bring up, Munia would have found it difficult on her own, but Chanda Taiji, while not offering any monetary assistance, had offered her sound advice. Advice that has stood Munia in good stead.

★

That afternoon, a police jeep arrives at the housing society. Verma Aunty and her clique are hurriedly summoned to the club house, where the investigating officer speaks to them. It is not a long meeting; he leaves within fifteen minutes of having arrived. Verma Aunty, looking oddly thwarted – odd, because she has just discovered that the case has been solved, and should therefore be relieved, not upset – sends out a WhatsApp message to the society group.

The autopsy report has come. Chopra Sahib's head has been bashed in, not by a muscled, biryani-eating Rehaan, but by the edge of a marble tabletop, against which he collapsed after a massive heart attack that killed him. And Chopra Sahib's phone, which has been in police custody since yesterday, was turned on last evening only for the cops to discover that there had been seven missed calls from Rehaan. They called him back, only to discover that he had been trying to contact Chopra Sahib to let him know that he would not be able to come in to work. He had been hit by a motorcycle and had fractured his leg. The cops got his address without letting on who they were, or how they had got hold of Chopra Sahib's phone; a head constable was sent to his home, along with the security guard Paresh, to identify the man. Sure enough, there was Rehaan, his left leg in a plaster, hobbling painfully around and bewildered at the sight of these unexpected visitors.

He was questioned, and it has become amply clear that he knows nothing of Chopra Sahib's death.

Chopra Sahib has not been murdered after all. Not by Rehaan, not by anyone else.

In the afternoon, when Munia arrives at Chanda Taiji's home, there is a lightness in her step, a radiance in her face. Chanda Taiji, opening the front door, smiles at her. 'I told you,' she says, 'it would be all sorted out.' Munia shuts the door behind her and Chanda Taiji says, 'Muneera Begum can safely go on being Munia; the chances of being exposed have abated, haven't they?'

Munia, heading out to the garden, nods back happily.

# THE BARAAT

## *Meeti Shroff-Shah*

*A baraat is a grand pre-wedding procession that follows the groom to the bride's home.*

The groom has been shot. But nobody seems to have noticed. The baraat band is so loud that even the groom's great-grandaunt whose hearing failed more than a decade ago, is tapping her foot to the beat of the music's vibrations. The shehnai players are intent on making their presence known. Too often, they feel they've been relegated to the sidelines by the brash and flashy trumpet. But no more. The three of them have collectively picked today to be the day they outplay the showy bastard. Behind them, the lone cymbals player knows that he was an afterthought, that he has only been included because the band leader plays teen patti with his father-in-law and owes him two thousand rupees. He is expressing his gratitude by clanging the metal discs with all his might. Rest, respite and rhythm be damned. The newest member of the band, the maraca player, is young and inexperienced and has let his shakers be snatched away by one of the groom's friends who is now rattling them as proof of his great love for the groom. But no one in the band, not even the trumpet and the shehnais put together, can match the decibel levels of the dholak players who are spurred on by something far more powerful than the need to be heard. The groom's maternal cousins are waving fans of hundred-rupee notes in front of their faces, the more deafening the *dhab dhab* of their dholaks, the faster the notes fall upon them. These cousins travelled from a neighbouring town and arrived late to the baraat. This flashing of money is their way of making up for lost time, and also of establishing their position within the hierarchy of the baraat. Their clout rising, or so they believe, in direct correlation to the denomination of the currency notes they shower. This, of course, has rubbed the groom's cousins from his father's side, the wrong way. Refusing to be out-thundered, they've dipped into their gunny bag of firecrackers and lit up a string of a thousand ladi bombs in one big, ear-splitting blaze.

It is the groom's college mates from Delhi who have brought the gun along. An SAF Carbine 2A1 and many bottles of expensive imported liquor. They want to show the small-town bumpkins how city slickers do weddings. They pass the rifle amongst them, taking turns to fire shots into the air. Not aiming at anything in particular, unheedful of where the bullets fly, their concentration devoted to the Jack Daniel's balanced on top of their heads. Arms outstretched, they're trying to dance without toppling the bottles, a mating ritual from their fine city's many fine bars, which they hope will attract the groom's many comely sisters.

The sisters should have noticed the stain of deep crimson spreading fast across the front of the groom's cream-and-gold sherwani, seeing that they are standing closest to his horse. But they haven't removed their dark glasses, despite the late hour of the evening. They're busy pouting in front of their phone cameras, focused on capturing at least a dozen 'hawt' pictures for their Instagram accounts: #weddingswag #whoisnext #hitchedandhow #bhaikishaadi; they've all agreed to use the same hashtags.

Under ordinary circumstances, the groom's mother would have been his best bet. Besotted as she is with her only son, today she wouldn't have let him out of her sight had it not been for the pandit who is running late. She's having a minor panic attack in one of the cars behind the groom's horse, making frantic calls, trying to arrange a backup pandit one moment, and yelling at the delayed pandit, the next. A part of her is afraid that the wedding might not go ahead as planned, another, petrified that it will, and she'll lose her son forever. She's consoling herself with what the arrival of the new daughter-in-law will mean. No waking up at five for the milkman. No tea and hot parathas ready at eight. No lunch tiffins packed before nine. She can palm it all off on the new bride. Isn't that the point of having a son? Besides, hasn't she done it all, ever since she stepped foot into her husband's house? Now, she tells herself, it is her turn to take it easy, to sit in the temple all morning with her friends, should she so wish. Of course, there's the small matter of her daughter-in-law's job. Something high up in the railways that she got through the sports quota, that begins at nine a.m. sharp. But surely, that can't be *her* problem. The girl will just have to learn to work around it.

As things are, nobody on the groom's side notices when he slumps face forward on his horse. Nobody except the horse, that is. But the beast has been traumatized in any case, what with the gunshots and firecracker explosions. Nobody pays it any heed when it jumps and whinnies some more. It is finally some children, young cousins of the bride, who point to the groom and yell. They have been entrusted with the job of stealing the groom's shoes which they must hold onto, as custom demands, till the end of the wedding and return only in exchange for an envelope of cash. They've been watching the wedding procession approach the bride's home, their eyes fixed on their prize. They notice the groom fall and not rise again, and find it strange enough to tell the grown-ups, but no one pays any attention to them.

Now that the baraat is so close to the bride's home, the groom's side have put their petty differences aside and come together in an amplified show of strength. The dancing, the drums, the revelry have all been turned up a notch, this time for the viewing benefit of the bridal party who are standing at the gate to receive them. Some of the men from the bride's side join in the dancing in a bid to move the baraat along. But the groom's side have clear instructions to not enter the gate of the bride's home until they receive a signal from the groom's father.

The bride's side sends out servers holding platters of scented facial napkins and cool drinks. There are tall glasses of rose sherbet with floating chia seeds and fluorescent green floats, thick and frothy with vanilla ice cream. The groom's side accept the drinks gratefully, and yet they refuse to cross the perimeter of the bride's compound where chairs have been laid out in neat columns for the wedding guests.

Someone, the bride's aunt most likely, in the chaos that ensues it is never really clear who it is that finally sounds the alarm, but someone thinks to offer the groom a drink and finds the horse's saddle bedecked with maroon velvet and gold zardozi but entirely bereft of its rider. The groom has fallen off the horse and is sprawled on the ground, eyes wide open, one hand still clutching the fake, ruby-studded sword and scabbard at his waist, in no need of a cool drink. In no need of anything ever at all.

When the groom's father hears the news, he doesn't quite register it. He is in the midst of a spirited negotiation with the bride's father, wrangling one last addition to the dowry. The Bajaj Chetak and the Galaxy S22, along with the two lakh rupees in cash, which was their initial demand have already been delivered to their home. But the groom's uncle has given the groom's father the idea of the last-minute ask. Something substantial but not so exorbitant that it puts a spanner in the works. The groom's father is now asking for a new, two-door Voltas refrigerator, without which he has decreed that the wedding procession will not cross the threshold of the bride's home. The bride's father, who has already taken out a loan to pay for this wedding, is wringing his hands. He finds this last-minute wrangling unfair and dishonourable, but of course he wouldn't – couldn't – dare call it such.

Someone announces again that the groom is dead, that he has been shot, that he is lying on the ground in a puddle of his own blood, and this time the groom's father pauses mid-sentence and blinks. 'What?' he says turning around. 'What?' as if he has completely lost the ability to comprehend speech.

There is an immediate exodus from the room. The groom's uncles lead his father towards the body, stumbling, staggering, as quickly as the stunned man can manage. The bride's father follows behind slowly, alone, shocked, but embarrassed to admit that despite the terrible tragedy, his very next thought is about the great expense he has incurred. He's worrying about his debts, wondering what he can salvage and where he must cut his losses. The sarees and jewellery, he knows the women will be able to reuse. The decorator has only been paid a twenty-five per cent advance for the red and gold fairy lights and the scalloped strings of marigolds, roses and jasmine on the roof. Surely, he won't expect a full payment now? The catering costs form the bulk of his problem. The caterers have set up a makeshift kitchen in the backyard of his home and have been cooking since the previous evening. The food, including the five kinds of milk-based sweets that the groom's mother insisted upon, is ready, and the guests, most of whom have been in attendance since the morning, will have to be fed. The bride's father doubts the caterer will be empathetic to his plight. Not now when he has already started frying the lamb-meat balls, the chilli-cheese cigars, the hara-bhara kebabs and the other welcome-starters which the groom's uncle had clearly specified. He curses his luck, then his own daughter, who, he is sure has wished this upon them.

As the groom's family surrounds his body, as his mother howls and throws herself to the ground and as his sisters attempt to contain her, unmindful for once, of the mascara streaking their cheeks, the bride's father catches his son's eye. He knows exactly what the boy is thinking, because he has been wondering the same thing himself. Is next week too soon to retrieve the Bajaj Chetak and the rest of the dowry from the groom's house?

The bride's brother doubts the groom's side will hand everything over easily. He doesn't like the look of the groom's uncle and is sure the man will make trouble. He carries chairs outside for the groom's side, and while they all wait for the police to arrive, he decides he'll take a few of the neighbourhood boys with him. A little show of power to be enhanced only if required, by hockey sticks and metal pipes from the boot of the car. But no guns. Hell, no guns for sure. He looks over pityingly to where the groom's friends, the ones who fired the gun, stand in a far corner in a stunned and terrified huddle, unable to meet anyone's eye. The cortisol and adrenaline coursing through their brains has bamboozled any remnants of intoxication. They're done with blaming and blasting and berating each other for firing the fatal shot. Now they're silent, spent, desperate that the cops take them away before the groom's family thinks to look for them.

The bride's mother sends someone over with bottles of Bisleri and a wad of tissues for the groom's family. As much as she is aghast at how the night has unfolded, and at all the stories about their ill fortune that the neighbours are sure to spin in the coming months, she is, if she were being honest, also secretly relieved. She's heard a persistent rumour about a dowry death in the groom's family, something tragic about his uncle's daughter-in-law on his father's side and has been tormented by worry. But in the face of her husband's blind fervour to see his eldest daughter married, and without any way of substantiating the story, she had contented herself with praying to the gods. Now, she wonders guiltily if it is *her* prayers the gods have answered. And whether this answer is really the solution to her problems. The bride, her eldest girl, is twenty-seven. She's not a beauty, no, that much the mother herself admits. But she's efficient in the kitchen, good at sports, has won many medals in fact, and is soft-spoken and demure despite the well-paying railways job. But twenty-seven is still a frightening place for an unmarried girl in their country. Like standing on the precipice of a future without prospects. The bride's mother wonders what tonight means for her eldest daughter, and for the one after her. Her youngest is fairer and prettier but has just turned twenty-five.

The bride's sister, however, suffers from no such ambiguity of feeling. She has dealt with the groom's leers ever since the engagement was announced. And just yesterday, at the mehendi ceremony, she had to smack his hand away when it 'accidentally' touched her breasts while she bent to serve him pakoras. He'd apologized of course, but he'd also winked and licked his lips, and she'd had the urge to pour hot oil down his shirt. As she rushes about to tell the decorators to dim the lights and the caterers to cease cooking, she is happily relieved at the turn of events. Her mood darkening only slightly when she overhears some of the neighbours gossiping. The Sharmas, who share their left wall, are speculating if tonight's tragedy is the result of bad karma. Whether the bride's family is finally paying for cutting down the hundred-year-old jamun tree between their houses, so mercilessly. The Kumar women who live across the street, cluck their tongues. This is ancestral wrath, they whisper. The bride's father didn't feed any Brahmins during shradh this year, and now he must bear the consequences. The Kumar women have long felt that the bride has a chip on her shoulder about her hi-fi railways job and are glad she'll come down a notch. Maybe now, she'll accept the invitation to their next satsang, they feel. Irritated with stories being spun about her family, the bride's sister curses and walks away. She wonders if someone has told the bride what has happened and considers running up to check on her sister. But the police van has just driven up their street.

The inspector gets out of the car, pulls his pants over his massive belly, spits betel juice on the ground, wipes his tobacco-stained lips with his sleeve and proceeds to survey the scene in an unhurried manner. This is not the first wedding in this town where someone's been shot during the baraat, though, perhaps, he concedes, this is the only time where it has proved fatal. They are received by the bride's brother who gives them a brief gist of the sad saga. While the police doctor takes the groom's pulse and pronounces him dead, and his mother thumps her chest in a fresh round of tears, the constables secure the area, taking the groom's miserable friends into custody and forbidding everyone else from leaving, as if anyone present would voluntarily miss even a moment of the proceedings. The inspector summons both families into the bride's house for questioning. The bride is brought down to the living room, where she sits between her sister and mother, hands tightly clutched in her lap, nails digging into the palms, eyes downcast, her face ashen beneath the rouge of the bridal make-up. There isn't much to say. All the mandatory questions are asked and answered by the various men. And the bride is reminded of another such gathering only a month ago when the groom's family had first come to see her. There had been questions then as well. Did the girl know how to cook and sew and clean? Did she have a degree, a job, a salary? Were jobs through the sports quota permanent? What about her work hours? Would she be able to balance work with the responsibilities of her new home? Then too, her father had answered on behalf of her while her sister served the guests ginger tea and chaat. Then too, there was one question no one had thought to ask. Despite the sports quota job, despite the medals on the walls, no one had wondered about the sport she played. Every other accomplishment forever eclipsed by her ability to make round rotis. Since no one asked – not then, not now – they never found out that she'd been a shooter in the 50m rifle category. Had they known, they'd probably have wondered whether the bullet that went straight through the groom's heart had really been fired by the drunk-dancing bozos outside. But since they didn't, she didn't feel the need to tell them about how the groom had tried to force himself on her on the terrace on the day of their engagement ceremony. And how, when she'd pushed him away, he had sneered, shown her a picture of his girlfriend, and told her that all anyone could ever want from her was her dowry.

It will probably be a week or so before the police realize that the bullet that killed the groom didn't come from the gun they have in their custody. Lawyers will get involved, the groom's friends will be let out on bail until the investigation proceeds further and the police will come back to the bride's house, scratching their heads. But by then the banyan tree in the bride's front yard will be devoid of its red and gold fairy lights, the marigolds, roses and jasmine will have turned black and brittle in the bin, and the gun that killed the groom will be lying safe and sedate, at the bottom of a lake. The police will search a few rooms, talk to a few neighbours and ask some more questions. But by then the smell of gunpowder will have long faded from the bride's hands, along with the deep maroon of her henna.

# STRIDE

*Arnab Ray*

'S-T-R-I-D-E—STRIDE.'

'You mind telling us what this is?' the man asked as he slapped the paper onto the table with force.

I sat on the opposite side, leaning forward with my shoulders hunched in a submissive manner.

'Nothing, sir. I was making some notes for an IT certification exam. That's all. Nothing important.'

'Let us be the judge of that,' the woman said, arching an eyebrow lightly, positioning her shoulders sideways as if she was looking for the perfect angle for a selfie.

'STRIDE is an acronym, ma'am,' I replied in my best good-girl-front-bencher voice. 'It is a mnemonic to be more accurate. STRIDE is a Microsoft threat modelling approach, a conceptual framework for understanding and modelling cybersecurity threats.'

I realized I was regurgitating what I had memorized. I needed to explain it.

'It's like a map for thinking about hacking into computers.'

'Don't act over smart,' the woman snapped. 'I belong to the cybercrime unit; I know very well what STRIDE is. The question is, why did you write this down on a piece of paper and tape it in your cubicle?'

'As I said, ma'am, I take notes for concepts I have to brush up on before my exam.'

'You are criminals here, every single one of you. Stop acting cute.'

She was right. I was a criminal, just like everyone else who worked at the New Horizons IT Park Building Number Five. Floors one and two housed legitimate IT consultancy firms with real clients, but anyone who pressed the elevator button for a floor from three to fifteen was either there to deliver food or to scam someone out of their savings.

I looked back across the table, and across the table, they looked back at me.

If there's one thing criminals understand, it's to avoid saying more than what a police officer asks. It's human nature to want to fill silences, take control of conversations, show off, or be accommodating, but that's how you can end up incriminating yourself.

However, if this wasn't a cop and I was not a criminal, I would have shared more about STRIDE.

The first letter 'S' stands for Spoofing. It involves pretending to be someone you are not.

That's our bread and butter.

We are fake 'customer service executives', slipping into the skin of your bank, computer vendor, power company, and sometimes, even the government, to scam you out of your money.

You don't call us; we call you.

We're the ones sliding into your life with smooth voices, offering to purge the malware that's crawling through your computer or notifying you about fraudulent transactions on your bank account. We are not always nice, though. Sometimes, we come with threats, too. Outstanding arrest warrants have been issued against your name for back taxes owed, which will all go away only if you go to the nearest store, buy some Apple gift cards, and send them to us because, apparently, that is how many people expect their governments to work.

'Good morning, sir. I am calling from Microsoft. There seems to be a virus on your computer. Can you please download this app so I can troubleshoot remotely?'

Now, I can install malware and watch everything you type on your computer, including the passwords to your bank, email account and Amazon.

'Good morning, madam. I am calling from Bank of America. We take cybersecurity very seriously here. To ensure that you are speaking to a genuine Bank of America customer representative, I will be sending a text message to your phone. Please click on that.'

That text message has a link to a website that is very much like the page of Bank of America, except that it is not. Once you have entered your password there, I will have it.

'How are you doing today, Mr Smith? You will be getting a code on your phone from our system. For security purposes, can you please read it back to me, so I can be sure I am speaking to the right Sam Smith?'

I am basically getting you to read back the OTP that your bank sent you. Once you tell me that, I have your second factor of authentication.

I am now *you*. I can now do what you can do: transfer money out of your bank account, buy iPhones in bulk, and apply for credit cards in your name.

So, there you have it. My job description. I impersonate people to people and then impersonate those people to other people.

For profit.

In the call-centre world, where I once used to work, doing customer service for companies in the USA, spoofing was a way of life. They gave us foreign personas, with names like Sally and Sam, voices polished to a faux American sheen. Accent correction, they called it. They crafted our characters as carefully as they scripted our lines, forcing us to wear masks that concealed who we really were and where we hailed from. 'Cold in Detroit today, isn't it, sir?' I'd say, hiding the truth behind the curtains of my fabricated identity. 'Did you catch the Yankees game last night?' I'd spin the lie, but it was never a crime.

Not then.

The companies we worked for were legitimate, and we were legitimate, outsourced customer service providers. The only things that were not legit were our names, accents, locations, and the phrase 'customer care' because no one really cared about the customer.

Spoofing. Yes. It is always the first link in the chain.

'Are you not ashamed?' the man asked. 'Educated young men and women cleaning out the life savings of people halfway across the world.' He shook his head in disgust. 'What do you people do this for? An iPhone? An Audi? A Hermès bag? For god's sake, these could be your parents or your grandparents, left without money for their treatment or for their rent.'

He looked at my identity card, and my name on it.

'Do you have no conscience, Sonali Sengupta?'

Since he has taken my name, I took his. Of course, not openly, for he was a cop and I a criminal, but in my mind.

Nandan Salgaonkar.

He wasn't the type of cop you typically see at traffic

intersections, chewing paan and waving his wooden stick. This man was from a central government agency, some important acronym that investigates high economic crimes. I would have guessed it was the CBI, but I know it wasn't. Perhaps it was the Enforcement Directorate, but I'm not sure. Regardless, it didn't really matter. He looked like he had been cast straight from an Amazon Prime web series – lean and wiry, wearing a safari suit that hugged his bulging muscles in all the right places. He had a moustache that he believed projected intensity, but the way I saw it, made him look more like a backup dancer in a Telugu macho song.

'Since you brought up my conscience, let's talk about yours, Nandan sir. Singhania, who owns my company and many others operating out of IT Park, ensures that payments to the police are made on time, along with performance-based bonuses during Diwali and Christmas. Yes, I admit that I am a criminal, but at least I engage in it with honesty. I am a criminal who does criminal things. On the other hand, you are a cop and, most likely, are on the payroll of criminals. By raiding our business and eating into our time, you are turning on the very people who ensure that your EMIs are paid for on time. If this doesn't make you ashamed, I don't know what would.'

Of course, I did not say this out loud. I am not crazy.

Nandan Salgaonkar was attacking my integrity. Which brings us to the 'T' in STRIDE: Tampering. An attack on the integrity of a computer. Hackers tamper with your computer and install viruses or backdoors, corrupting what was once reliable. The laptop you once trusted may no longer function in your best interests, much like a person who has lost their integrity will not do what is right.

Think of that word for a second. Tampering. A microcosm

of the real world. We distort the truth and turn it into news. We manipulate justice to turn it into laws.

God damn it, I once had a conscience. I once had my integrity.

At those call centres where I started off, I was just 'Sally', 'Mary', or 'Anna'. I would clock in, clock out and follow the damn script like a puppet on a string, forcing a smile as I greeted angry men and women with a hollow 'good morning' and an even hollower 'thank you for your business.' They yelled at me from half a world away, cursing me for things I couldn't control – damaged goods that arrived late as if I were the one responsible. And when they weren't blaming me for that, they tore into my accent or my very existence – curry bitch taking American jobs. And yet, I wore the mask of a smiling, obedient worker, clutching on to my integrity like a life raft in an ocean.

Till they closed the call centres down, transferring our jobs out to Malaysia, Vietnam and Bangladesh. All those bastards now taking Indian jobs.

'Sir, none of the associates here are as wealthy as you might think,' I said, adopting my old call-centre polite voice. 'They are small-town men and women who commute for hours each day on local trains. This isn't just for extra income; it is necessary for their survival. For us, it's a matter of taking care of our families, even if it means doing so at the expense of others.'

'You have a way with words, Ms Sonali,' the woman said. 'I wouldn't expect anything less; you are the manager here, correct?'

Ah, the woman. She introduced herself as Arpita Thakur, the head of cybercrime. Her make-up and lipstick were flawlessly applied – not too heavy, so she didn't look like an overdone cake, but just enough that no one would mistake her for someone who didn't care about her appearance. I could have been her if I had made a few better life choices or if my father had. However, no matter which path I had taken, I would never have been able to pull off the 'professional look' quite as well as Arpita Thakur was.

Raids in the IT Park are such a rarity that when they do occur, we're usually given a heads-up. It's almost charming how swiftly we spring into action – records vanish, power cords are unplugged, and external hard drives walk out through the service entrance to find a cosy, temporary home in the trunks of cars parked far, far away. Naturally, most staff members are asked to enjoy a little unexpected unpaid vacation at home. All of this is just part of the elaborate dance: Singhania, with his knack for charming the local police and government officials, operates in this little paradise without a care in the world. And when a raid finally happens, we know it's just the opening act in a negotiation for higher cuts. Some new babu must have been transferred in, and he wants a bit more than what the last one had settled with.

In this place, crime is just a tango, where both sides of the law glide gracefully in sync, exchanging knowing glances and entwining their fingers together.

But today was different. Arpita Thakur and Nandan Salgaonkar had burst in without notice, accompanied by what felt like a small army. It's not that we don't have security – we do. We have guards and closed-circuit cameras monitoring the perimeter. This has been the case since a few years ago when a scam-buster channel on YouTube, based out of Germany, with five million subscribers, sent a package that exploded upon opening, releasing an industrial-strength stink bomb and unleashing hundreds of rats that scurried into every corner.

However, a security perimeter designed to guard against pesky YouTubers would not hold back a central agency, who had come in black SUVs and were carrying guns.

Once inside, they aimed for maximum shock and awe. We were instructed to step away from our terminals as guns were brandished. One of the younger associates, known for his hot-headedness, attempted to speak up. He received a hard, open-palmed slap directly to the mouth. He was bleeding from his lip the last time I saw him. Everyone from the entire floor was packed into the common area, standing close together like commuters on a crowded bus during rush hour. No one was allowed to leave the room, and it had now been four hours since the raid began. Requests to use the restroom were met with harsh rebukes, and if the request came from a woman, permission was granted reluctantly, accompanied by various threats.

As the manager on duty, I was summoned to the room we referred to as the 'boardroom'. This room had glass walls on two sides and flat-screen monitors on the other two. It served as the nerve centre of our company, where we tracked daily metrics for all operations and watched cricket games. The police had set up their operations there. They brought in equipment, and the two leaders of the raid were questioning me about the employees, asking when we had hired them, and their names and addresses. Their line of questioning then shifted to me, focusing on what they had found on a piece of paper.

STRIDE.

'R', the third letter, stands for Repudiation. Hackers aim to avoid accountability for their actions. For example, when money is transferred from a grandma's account in Wisconsin, she will never know who is behind the transaction. This is where our adversaries, the YouTube scam busters, come into play. Their stated goal is to expose our anonymity. To quote their motto, 'Let's make these Indian scammers famous.'

To be precise, they don't use the word 'scammers'. They say 'scum-mers'.

See what they did there?

They are good at what they do – the YouTube vigilantes. They infiltrate our networks, activate our webcams, obtain our names and addresses from our files, and publish them, throwing us into the eternal memory of the internet.

If any of us ever try to go straight, we will likely not survive a prospective employer's Google search.

That's what makes the 'R' so important. Repudiation allows us to deny our actions. We can deny them to the police, to our families, and even to ourselves.

That's why this raid seemed different. The cops were unconcerned about where the stolen money had gone or who we had scammed. They were not here to return the funds to their rightful owners.

They were not here to shake down the Singhanias either. If they were, they would be collecting evidence to establish the money trail to them.

Instead, their singular focus was on us, the employees of this scam centre. They were reviewing our access logs and employee records, including our login and logout times. They had also collected all our mobile phones, both personal and work devices – and piled them together. At first, I thought they had taken the phones to prevent us from communicating with the outside world, possibly because they were raiding other scam operations. However, I began to have doubts.

For the first time, I noticed a gentleman who had

accompanied the raiding party. Until that moment, he had not spoken a word or shown any identification. He was dressed in a simple white shirt that had taken on a grey shade after way too many washings and a discordant set of nondescript brown trousers, one size too big, a balding man in his fifties whom I would have called 'uncle' if others weren't already referring to me as 'aunty'. This man stood quietly in the corner of the boardroom, observing everything while smoking a cigarette. Typically, smoking isn't allowed inside the building, and even criminals abide by the rules. However, today was different.

He caught my gaze and that seemed to trigger something in him. He stubbed the cigarette out on the expensive carpet – and walked towards the table where I sat with my interrogators.

As he approached, Nandan and Arpita stood up. 'Go outside and make them unlock their phones,' he instructed with a tired nod of his head. There was an economy of movement in whatever he did, almost as if he felt that those around him were not worthy of his energy.

From the look on her face, it was clear that Arpita wasn't thrilled about being abruptly dismissed – like a cat who's just discovered its favourite chair is now a dog bed. Still, she complied with his request, shooting me a glance that said, 'Oh no, we're definitely not done here!' Meanwhile, Nandan seemed like a pro at being a human puppy; he scurried off quickly, tail wagging like he'd just been told there were treats involved.

The man spoke a single word.

'Ask.'

'Ask what, sir?' I replied.

'You have questions. I can see them in your eyes.'

'I'm sorry, sir, but I don't understand.' However, I did understand; I just felt the need to keep up the façade.

He remained silent, letting out a sigh. It was clear he was silently asking me to stop acting dumb.

Yet, I didn't ask any questions. Instead, I stated, 'You're not here to raid us, not in the way one raids a scam centre; you're looking for something or someone.'

He said nothing, but I could make out a smirk at the corner of his lips.

Reaching into his chest pocket, he brought out his pack of cigarettes.

'Do you smoke?' he asked. I used to, but not anymore. I shook my head in response with a 'No.'

'A month or so ago, you had a party here. In it, Mr Vijay Singhania said something out loud that he should not have said.'

It's time to introduce the Singhania family. When someone mentions 'Singhania' without specifying a first name, they are referring to the patriarch, Vikramraj Singhania. If that name conjured up, in your mind, a villain from an 80s Hindi movie – complete with a white dinner jacket and trousers – it's because Vikramraj Singhania fits that archetype. As for the other family members, they use their first names along with their last names. There's Ajaypratap Singhania, the eldest son of Vikramraj, the Mumbai socialite and movie producer. Then we have the middle daughter, Madhuri Singhania, who is reportedly the proxy part-owner of two major T20 cricket franchises and is married to one of Ahmedabad's biggest diamond merchants. Finally, the youngest sibling is Vijayraj Singhania, or Vijay, the Maserati-driving crypto-king and underboss of the scam call business.

Three weeks ago, we achieved our annual quota – the target revenue set for twelve months – in just seven.

To celebrate this accomplishment, Vijay, came to the office to host a party.

Vijay Singhania's parties are well known for their extravagant wildness, celebrity guests, top-notch liquor, and even some illicit substances.

However, those glamorous celebrations were reserved for his circle. For us, his employees, the event consisted of cold pizza, which he had chosen to host on a Tuesday when the restaurant offered a buy-one-get-one-free deal. In his defence, he did spring for booze, but of the bottom-shelf type. In a display of camaraderie, Vijay Singhania did what leaders often do to demonstrate their leadership: he drank the same cheap liquor that the men were drinking.

The nasty stuff hit him faster than the expensive stuff, I suppose. Before he realized it, he began saying things he really shouldn't have. He kept mentioning that he had five million US dollars in Bitcoin stored on his phone. This wasn't just a casual comment; he repeated it several times. He went so far as to stand on the big central table, swaying from side to side, and shouted it out for anyone who would listen. He didn't just talk about it. For effect, he pulled out his phone, opened an app, and showed everyone the actual amount.

'You peasants, you make money for me. Me. Who am I? I am the Big Daddy, baby, I am the Big Daddy. If you want to see how big this Daddy is, come on, gather around. This is what I made off you, not the full amount; no, you boys and girls, don't make me this much; don't kid yourself, but then I put it in crypto. Bazinga. Five million dollars. So, if you want to complain about the work and the commissions, go ahead. That's what people do when they're small. They whine like babies in diapers, hoping to catch Daddy's attention. But Daddy here, he doesn't care. His baby is this, his digital wallet. I could replace the lot of you with fresh faces, and I will be as big a Daddy as I always was.'

Information Disclosure. That is the 'I' in STRIDE. When the hacker learns things that they should not know. It is the revelation of your secrets, the crown jewels, the fact that you have five million dollars in one place.

I know where this is going.

'So, he lost his Bitcoin?' I asked.

The man reached into his pocket and took out a cigarette.

'Last evening, Mr Singhania found out that his money was all gone. Someone had hacked into his crypto-wallet and stolen his Bitcoin. As you can well understand, the most likely suspects are in this room.'

Now, it made sense. Singhania had set the police on us. Not just any police, but the best of them.

'You have been here for the longest. You hired everyone. Who do you think did it?'

'How was he hacked?' I asked back.

'We don't know. He never clicked on anything or did anything stupid. We think it's a highly sophisticated cyberattack. I am not a technical person, but people are working on it as we speak to find out how it was done.'

'We aren't technical people here either. Some of the guys like to call themselves 'hackers', but they really aren't. I've been in this business for years, and I've seen many come and go; none of them are the toppers of their classes. We read from scripts and use software developed by others. The people who fall victim to us are mostly those who don't know better –

grandfathers and grandmothers. It's like taking candy from kids, and Vijay Singhania is anything but a kid.'

'Yes, he is the Big Daddy.' The man was now lighting his cigarette up with an ornate lighter from the 70s. 'Wasn't that what he said that day?'

I stayed quiet.

'We will find out who did it. Of course, we will. Five million dollars is no chump change, but more than that, it is the reputation of the Singhanias that's at stake. They are the lions in this den, and lions do not have their cubs eaten by jackals. I am not saying someone here did it; they could have, but they could have also passed the information on to hackers on the Dark Web. We're not just turning this place inside out; we have agents at your homes seizing your computers. We will examine every message you have sent or received since that party. As I said, I will find out, and then Mr Singhania will administer justice.'

Taking a puff from his cigarette, he asked, 'So let me rephrase. Who here in this office, do you think, has the motive to steal from the boss? Who, in this building full of anonymous cowards, has the daring to pull this off?'

'I suppose I am the person with the biggest motive here.'

'Go on, tell me more.'

'I have helped build the business into what it is today. You might not think highly of what we do, but we are hugely profitable. I wrote the scripts the operatives use now. I made things more efficient than they were. I created and designed many of the scams myself. But, when I went to Singhania, the big man, asking him for what I thought I was owed, he said that the role I wanted, that of being the boss, was what he wanted to give his son on his eighteenth birthday. I was better off where I was, as the line manager.'

He hadn't exactly referred to me as a 'line manager'. What he had actually said was, 'You have served as a caretaker for my business. I truly appreciate all that you have done. However, let us be realistic about your role. You are a nanny – an excellent one at that – but still a nanny. You are not the mother. This business is Vijay's inheritance, and it will eventually pass on to him. As a word of advice from someone with experience: you are nearly fifty. It's time to slow down, take care of your child, and prioritize your happiness. Leave the pursuit of glory to the younger generation. As a token of appreciation for your hard work, I will increase your commission by twenty per cent. Does that sound acceptable?'

Denial of Service – the 'D' in STRIDE – occurs when a hacker consumes resources, preventing legitimate users from accessing them. For instance, making a million requests to download a file can block others from downloading theirs. This type of attack reflects greed, wanting more, even when it's not needed, to ensure that others can't have it.

Singhania did something like that to me. He denied me what I was owed, even though he didn't need to. It's not that I wanted Vijay's money; I wanted the respect that comes from being acknowledged for running the business, something that I felt I was owed.

'Yes, that gives you the motive,' the man said, exhaling smoke contemplatively in my direction. 'But it doesn't give you the daring. You're not the type to take risks.'

He looked at me with a level of contempt I can't imagine anyone showing me in my years on this planet.

'This may seem strange to say to someone running a criminal organization, but this is about as risk-free a business as there can be. You scam people half a world away, facelessly.

Singhania ensures that the local police cannot touch you. Your business model relies on human gullibility and deference to authority. Stupidity and meekness: there's plenty of that in the world. Your market size is infinite. You claim to have built this place, and that may well be true, but it's not a risky business in the same way that selling drugs or committing burglary is. Legitimate IT consultancy firms that bill their customers for fraudulent hours take more risks; at least they could be caught in a thorough audit. You take absolutely none.'

He stubbed the end of his cigarette on the edge of the mahogany table as the ash crumpled down over the edge.

'But that's not even the whole story. People who are truly daring don't just ask for what they deserve; they take it. With the knowledge and experience you claim you have, you could have competed with the Singhanias, but you chose not to. You remained an employee, not out of loyalty, but out of timidity.'

I opened my mouth to say something, but the man spoke over me, and I dropped quiet.

'You're the kind of person who might create an anonymous account online to criticize your employer, but you wouldn't confront them directly in competition. You'll complain about the system but won't make any changes to it. You will shout at your spouse because of what happened at work, but you won't shout at your manager. Mr Vikramraj Singhania did name you as his primary suspect, but I disagree.'

'He suspected me?' I asked incredulously. 'He mentioned me as a suspect by name?'

'He was giving you too much credit. I've done my research on you. You are a fifty-year-old woman with a husband and a child in college. You have lived in the same place for thirty years, your definition of extravagance is a dinner with your family at a nice restaurant, and your idea of getting ahead in life is signing up for more IT certifications.'

He picked up the piece of paper with 'STRIDE' written on it, crumpled it into a ball, and threw it at the waste paper bin. It landed perfectly inside.

'You believe that the world rewards those who are better. You believe that there is a notion of cosmic justice, that the universe is fundamentally meritocratic. Have more certifications, demonstrate knowledge, and do more, and you shall be rewarded. However, the universe doesn't work that way. It favours only those who take risks. Big risks, the all-or-nothing risks. It favours the young. It favours the impulsive. It favours those who see an opportunity and seize it. Smart, yes, but ruthless. They do not think about the downsides, they do not second-guess themselves, and they are not afraid of failure and ruin. So, is there anyone here like that, a wolf that you believe is hiding in sheep's clothing?'

I pursed my lips shut and sat, leaning back into my chair.

'We will, of course, be investigating you just like everyone, going through your phones and your home computers, but if you could point us in the right direction, and something tells me you pick up on things others don't, then we do not have to turn so many lives upside down. The quicker this is over, the better for all of us.'

He was right. I do pick up on things others do not. And I do believe that there is cosmic justice, that things right themselves in the end.

He was wrong. It was me who had taken Vijay Singhania's inheritance.

I won't spend the money. I refuse to take the risk. The

Singhanias and their hired watchdogs will be monitoring me closely for the rest of my life, scrutinizing all my receipts and statements. If their suspicions turn into certainty, I know the lengths they can go to, and I fear for my safety and my family's well-being.

I want to return some of the money to those from whom we took it. However, that could also result in me getting caught. Sometimes, the risk of doing something good can be greater than the risk of doing something wrong. So, yes, I will continue to live my life as I always have, and the money will remain in the digital ether. I will find solace in knowing that the Singhanias will not be able to spend it either.

So how did I do it?

After Vijay Singhania's performance on the table, he had to be taken to the restroom to puke out the mushroom pizza. He should have had the chicken. Enough time for me, the person escorting him there, to use his face to unlock his phone. Once I had spoofed his identity, it was a matter of seconds of loading malware onto his phone, tampering with its integrity. He was puking and swearing throughout, so of course, he did not see me doing any of this, allowing me to, you got it, repudiate my actions. The malware sent me his Bitcoin-wallet password and OTP the next time he logged in, and that was the information disclosure part. I could then log in to his wallet and clean him out. And now he will never see his money again, and that will be the denial of service. Of course, I set it up so that the malware auto-deleted itself from the target phone. All traces of my activity were removed from my devices a long time before they burst into our homes and our offices.

But wait, that is just the S-T-R-I-D part of it. Where is the E?

The 'E' stands for Elevation of Privilege.

It is the finishing touch, the coup de grâce, the line drawn between what is right and what is wrong.

We live in an orderly world where everyone has a designated role and specific permissions – defining what they can and cannot do. The workers work, the rulers govern, and the wealthy accumulate riches.

But what if a worker desires to rule? The only way for them to achieve that is by breaking the rules.

This, in essence, is elevation of privilege. It's the insidious act of usurping authority, of controverting the natural order. Sign up for the free account, and break into the premium layer.

Elevation of privilege is not solely about malicious intent; it also stems from the inherent human desire for power and control. This ambition drives us to climb the social ladder, seek recognition, and yearn for authority over our own lives – and, perhaps, over the lives of others.

What I do is wrong. I will be served justice for it. Someday, somehow, I know it will happen.

When I gain access to the bank accounts of helpless individuals who have harmed me in no way, I am acting against the flow of privilege. This is not an elevation of privilege, but rather, the opposite.

I may have been doing the S, T, R, I and the D, but never the E.

But when I broke into that brat's digital wallet, that was right.

Now the 'E' was there, in harmony, with the other alphabets, defining the moral code by which I may not live but aspire to.

The piece of paper I look at every day before starting my work.

S-T-R-I-D-E—STRIDE.

# THE LEOPARDS' LEAP CRIME FICTION WORKSHOP

*Manjula Padmanabhan*

Nestled within a cloud-mattress, under a silken razai, I woke to a room in darkness. What had punctured the warm bubble of my sleep?

Loud thumping.

*Wake up, WAKE UP!* screeched a voice at the door. *THE COOK'S BEEN MURDERED!*

'Wha—?' I croaked, my voice froggy with sleep. I must have heard wrong. To leave the delicious warmth of my bed was an intolerable torture. Nevertheless, I pulled on my fleece-lined dressing gown, thrust my feet into fake-fur slippers and stumbled to the door.

Broad daylight. Chunks of snow hurtling down out of a grey sky. Madhvi Dhillon, her hair wild and uncombed, a bright pink parka over her lace nightie, was screaming, 'The COOK! MURDERED! Come to the COMMON ROOM!' She sped away, continuing to scream, 'Oh my GOD, oh my GOD!'

I threw on some clothes and hurried to the main building. Thc central structure was built onto a steep slope. The main entrance to the building was on the top floor. It led onto a mezzanine with a glorious two-storey viewing window through which Nanda Devi and all her fellow peaks could be seen in all their glory. Today of course there was only fog and snow.

A curving wooden stairway led down to the spacious and cosy Common Room, ringed with bookshelves. I took the path that skirted the cliff, entering directly into this lower space, warm and brightly lit.

The bokhari, a wood-burning space heater, was roaring and the electric samovar of tea was steaming on the counter that separated the Common Room from the cafeteria. Madhvi was there, still wearing her parka and negligee. So were Sugar Kara, Harsha Lalwani and Zinnia Batlibhoy – all fully dressed. They were all four huddled together on the huge scuffed-leather sofa that defined one corner of the room. They were each hunched over the mugs in their hands, looking miserable.

Our hosts, Manoj and Chetna – Mango and Chutney, as they were fondly known – weren't present. They'd told us they'd be away for one night midway during the retreat. They assured us that their excellent cook, Peter, was perfectly good at managing on his own.

But he was gone, according to Madhvi. And so was Leena Rodrigues, the glamorous supermodel writer, who was the star of the group.

I took my seat in the spherical armchair opposite the sofa and waited only a couple of minutes before saying, 'Look—'

'Shut up,' hissed Sugar at once. She had bushy black hair and gold rings pierced through her eyebrows. She wrote steamy adult crime fiction in which there was never any suspense. The victims were always men, and the murderers were always women for whom intercourse was a bloodsport. 'You slept through the whole thing!'

'Rubbish!' snorted Harsha, not looking at me. 'How could she? She must have done it! After all, her room is closest to the you-know-what—' she trailed away.

'No, what?' I asked, feeling stupid. The accusation was too ridiculous to be worth even denying.

'Scene of the crime!' Harsha exclaimed. She was wearing a bright blue phiran, woollen salwar and thick-soled boots. She was the oldest in the group, with the largest number of novels under her belt. Fifteen to be exact. All highly popular, all involving the same diminutive female detective, who worked as an *ayah* for a middle-class Delhi family by day, while solving crimes for the police at night. She claimed that her books were responsible for making the word *ayah* socially respectable again. 'Naturally, Miss Purity Patel, hack reporter for the *Evening News*, denies all knowledge of the situation!'

My name, of course, is Purini, not Purity. But they had slapped the nickname on me when we all met, four days ago.

Madhvi – Mads, for short – said to me as if reciting the multiplication tables, 'The cook's been murdered. Leena's gone missing. Our host's stranded in Almora by the snowstorm. And...and—' She made a gesture of helplessness with her hands, 'we're just sitting ducks!'

This made no sense to me. 'Sitting ducks to whom?'

Zinnia turned on me like a smooth, shiny snake, her grey eyes flashing and black ringlets shaking. '—to *you*, of course, you twit! Can't you recognize the most classic pattern in all of cri-fi?' She made a disgusted sound, '—*keh*!' and turned her head away. She was, it has to be noted, extremely lovely, even at seven in the morning in the midst of a blizzard, with a murderer possibly on the loose.

Sugar said, imitating Mads's sing-song voice, '—a group of people...stranded together...in a remote location...with a dead body in their midst!' She lifted her mug. 'Cheers!'

I glanced around frowning. 'But – *where's the body*?'

'See how she's playing innocent?' This was Harsha again, addressing the others.

Mads said, 'The morning tea hadn't come. So I went there. To the kitchen-pantry – the door was shut' – now she clutched her forehead – 'and...and when I opened it, there was blood *everywhere* – and the tracks pointed directly to your room—'

She began to heave with dry sobs. Mads was the only one of the participants with an actual connection to violent crime. Her father had been a police–pathologist. She'd grown up hearing about cases and criminals. Her books were all about crooked politicians, dead paramours and political rivals drowned in canals.

'But no body?' I asked.

'No!' Sugar shouted at me. 'No, you fool – you know very well it wasn't there – because you're the one who must've dragged it out of the pantry!'

'Why me!' I asked, hotly. 'And I didn't see any tracks just now when I came out—'

'OF COURSE YOU DIDN'T!' screamed Mads, her voice reaching hysterical pitch again. 'It's all covered up by the snow!'

I was completely nonplussed by the extreme hostility being expressed towards me. 'Look – I know you lot think that I've got no right to be here – but surely that doesn't mean that I, automatically, become the murderer?'

Four pairs of eyes stared stonily back at me. Clearly, they *did* think that. 'Because of what – I'm a journalist? Not a published author? That makes me the murderer?'

Sugar cut in, her voice dripping scorn, 'If you were a real writer, you'd know that the killer is always the odd one out. I mean, nine times out of ten.'

'It doesn't have to be obvious,' said Harsha. 'For instance, if this was a novel, the casual reader would not notice that you are different to the rest of us.'

'But this *isn't* a novel,' broke in Zinnia. She'd grown up in Sydney and had an irritating nasal accent. Her novels were always about immigrants being harassed by racially motivated murderers. 'And of course we all knew, even before we got here, that you'd be a sore thumb. I mean—' she looked around, '—I even complained to Mango. What's the point of a genre-specific workshop if one person does NOT belong? But he's too nice to understand the stresses and strains of living in today's competitive, cut-throat world. He said I'd come to see things differently once we'd all spent time together.'

I said, 'You're discriminating against me for no reason at all. I'm a crime-writer too—'

'—not like us!' she cut in. 'We're *professionals*! We've got books in print and even a fan club or two!' She meant, of course, Leena and Harsha. The others' books, including her own, were too unorthodox to be popular. 'You made a name for yourself writing about a serial killer! And you almost got killed because he escaped from prison as a result of your reportage!'

'Wrong!' I riposted. 'My reporting is the reason he went *back* to prison after his escape! And anyway, I'm supposed to be writing a report about this workshop – that's why I'm here! It was meant to be a secret – a combination of promo for the retreat and for each of you.' I looked at them through narrowed eyes. 'There's no point keeping the secret when you're all being so mean. It's going to be quite a feat for me to write anything positive about any of you now—'

Mads took over. 'What have you done with Leena?' She was sitting forward and staring closely at me.

'What would I have done with her?' I snapped. 'I haven't seen her since last night!'

Harsha said to the others, 'See? She never answers straight!'

'Plus, her eyes flicked to the left,' said Mads, also to the others. 'Classic sign of someone telling a lie.' She turned back to me. 'This morning, when I saw the track through the snow, leading towards your room, I screamed so loudly that any normal person would have leapt out of bed. Then I came running back to wake up the others and told them what had happened. That's when we all agreed that it had to be you who did it—'

'But WHY!' I fairly screamed. 'WHY would I kill Peter? What's my motive?'

'To get rid of us,' said Sugar, coldly. 'Because you're jealous. Of our success. Starting with Leena. Last night, as we all know, she was very drunk. You offered to walk her back to her room, which is on the other side of the kitchen block. Once you were alone in her room, you must've strangled her, using that scarf that you admired so much last night—'

'—just because I admired her scarf, I've become a strangler?' I was getting really upset now.

'Obviously, we can only guess as to the sequence of events,' said Mads. 'We believe that Peter must've come to deliver Leena's hot-water bottle, just after the strangling was over. He would have knocked on the door, before coming in—'

'—no!' I interrupted, 'he'd never enter her room without permission!'

But she swept on. '—that gave you time to hide behind a curtain. Whereupon he came in, found the body and ran right out again – realizing that a killer was on the loose. He'd have gone to the pantry, where he must've left his cell phone. You had no choice but to run after him and kill him before he made the call, using one of his own big knives. After which you dragged him out again, past your own room, threw him over the side of the cliff – and went to sleep! Cool as the serial killer you are!'

'Oh my *God*,' I said, half-laughing as I got to my feet. 'That plot is so crude and idiotic that only one of you would have thought it out! Come on...let's go to Leena's room right now to disprove your ridiculous theory—'

'Not on your life!' screeched Zinnia. 'None of us is leaving this room until Mango and Chutney come back!'

'Be reasonable,' I wheedled. 'They won't be back for hours! If we go out right now, you'll at least see how wrong you are!'

'Not a chance!' said Sugar. 'We'd have to be mad to go out in a blizzard with a murderess by our side – why, you'd just kick us off the edge of the cliff the first chance you got!'

'In fact, you'd best sit down right now,' said Mads, leaning forward as if planning to stand up. 'You're a cornered rat, after all. This is when all murderers are at their most dangerous—' A confused expression crossed her face however, and she didn't stand up.

'You're all completely bonkers!' I yelled. 'How can I possibly murder all four of you, all by myself? And how would I get away with it?'

'Easy,' said Harsha, putting her mug down suddenly. A strange expression came across her face too. 'By putting poison in the samovar. It's always set up the night before, and it only has to be turned on in the morning.'

'But you've all been drinking that same tea,' I said. 'And you're all still alive—' I stopped abruptly, realizing that the other two authors were sitting very still, though I could see that their eyes were moving and their lips twitching.

'Yes,' said Mads, putting her mug down too, speaking slowly but distinctly. 'We're alive, but none of us is able to stand up... except for you.' She was looking up at me. 'Which means that you must have used that date-rape drug in the samovar. It doesn't kill the victim, but they become immobilized.'

'—but the four of you were the last to leave the Common Room last night!' I cried. 'I've not been in here since then! Check the CCTV footage – you'll see that I'm telling the truth!'

'Who knows!' said Mads, really struggling to speak. 'Perhaps you came back here after throwing the cook off the cliff and—' She couldn't go on.

'Oh, for goodness' sake!' I exclaimed. 'On the one hand, even if I wanted to carry out such a macabre plan, it's only the blizzard that makes it possible! Surely you don't think that I could fix the weather to suit my dastardly plot?'

'Ha!' said Harsha, forcing herself to speak. 'You've just admitted it was your plot!'

'But it was *not*!' Like a bell, a voice speaking from somewhere above all of us slashed through the demented discussion.

And there was Leena, quite alive and splendidly well, standing on the mezzanine balcony above the Common Room. She was dressed in a form-fitting black outfit, with a silver-fox fur collar, scarlet high heels and her hair cut in glittery blue spikes. She was in her mid-fifties but her skin had the enamelled patina of the uber rich. She was as elongated and thin as a praying mantis, with great long legs and long bony fingers. 'What a bunch of complete ninnies!'

She began a languid descent down the curving stairs. 'The idea that the great Leena Rodrigues could be strangled to death by a mere pipsqueak journalist is already ludicrous. Huh! Do you people have no understanding of scale? Of the hierarchy of characters – not just in fiction, but in life?'

She had reached the floor. Her voice was a contralto purr shot through with a twist of honey: mesmerizing. 'No, my silly pets! It's not just that it did not happen in the cartoonish way described just now! What I'm trying to reveal to all you amateurs is that even in real life things do not happen in that boring way. People like me are simply too...too...consequential to just collapse and *die*! And that too, at the hands of an ordinary little nobody such as this poor dull thing, dressed in a fleece-jacket and fake-fur slippers!' Meaning me.

Leena's books are all about fabulously wealthy people, living their diamond-encrusted lives whilst being preyed upon by a never-ending army of avaricious relatives and manic ex-lovers. The books were utterly devoid of any content deeper than the always-plunging necklines of their heroines. Who, of course, always solve the crimes shortly before falling into the arms of their immaculately handsome, rich and worldly-wise lovers. Yet, such is the seductive power of wealth, that just reading about olives dipped in gold satisfies the appetites of very empty people.

I watched as she coiled herself, like a glittering black anaconda, into the easy chair closest to the bokhari. The four others had by now fallen into a helpless state. But I, even without the drug, was hypnotized by the sheer glamour and poise of the woman.

I had to force myself to stammer out the question that had to be asked. 'A–all right then, Leena! Whose blood was in the pantry?'

'Why, the cook's, of course,' said Leena, shortly.

'All right, but then who attacked him?' I persisted.

She shrugged her magnificent shoulders, causing the shimmering fur around her throat to ripple like the pretty little creature that had died to provide it. 'The leopard.'

'What!' I exclaimed. The spell of her glamour was broken with a single swipe. It was such an idiotic response. 'But the pantry door was shut! Leopards don't break into buildings, pick up their dinner and close the door behind them!'

She regarded me with steely confidence. 'You weren't there. I was. I saw it happen.'

'Leena,' I said, 'are you saying you followed Peter back to the pantry?'

'Wait till you hear what really happened,' she said, glowering. 'It'll make all your childish stories turn to sawdust in your mouths.'

She leaned back, utterly at her ease. 'What none of you know is that that lecherous fool has been pursuing me ever since we arrived here! Each time he brought my hot-water bottle he'd beg and plead to let him massage me – *yech*! But last night, seeing that I was a little tipsy, he actually tried to take advantage of me. Imagine! Yes. He did. I literally had to beat him off, using the steel heels of my shoes to whack him. Then I threw him out of the room and locked my door!'

I stared at her, speechless. 'Go on,' I said.

'A short while later, I heard that horrible sawing sound. Remember? We heard it the night before? Well, I heard it again last night. As everyone knows, that's the sound a hungry leopard on the hunt makes. Which is when I thought of the foolish man, who must have by now limped back to his pantry, perhaps bleeding because of the way I had thrashed him. And I felt sorry for him.'

She gazed at me, with her magnificent kohl-lined eyes, as if daring me to contradict her account.

'Go on,' I said.

'So, I took the big, heavy fire extinguisher that we all have inside our rooms, and I crept out towards the pantry. I could hear a terrible snarling going on. The next thing I knew, there was the leopard, with its jaws clamped around the throat of the cook, dragging the wretch out of the pantry. Blood all over the place.'

There was a brief silence, during which the only sound was the bokhari, hissing softly.

'Then what happened?' I asked.

'Well, obviously, I had to save the man, even though he had attacked me earlier! Using the fire extinguisher, I hit the leopard hard, but it also caught the idiot cook on the side of his head. I suppose I may have shattered his skull. The leopard let go with a ferocious howl and in the next instant, it turned towards me, growling hideously! Its tail was lashing from side to side! And it swiped repeatedly at me with its fearsome claws! It was an absolutely terrifying sight.'

She was acting her words out as she spoke, her face animated and the long nails of her hands flashing as she swiped the air.

'Go on,' I said. There was a faint sound coming from somewhere above, but I didn't dare look up.

'I knew I shouldn't run from the beast, because it can easily overtake me. So instead, I backed away slowly, always keeping the fire extinguisher between me and it. All the way back to my room, I kept it at bay until – finally! I could leap inside and slam the door shut.' She took a long, shuddering breath. 'After that, I completely fell to pieces. I could barely walk; I was so shocked and was still trembling. I crawled to my bed, took a giant dose of sleeping pills and fell into a coma.'

Barely had she finished, when, from the mezzanine floor came a man's voice. He couldn't clap because his left arm was in a sling. '*Wah, wah, wah,*' said Peter the cook. His head was heavily bandaged, covering the left eye. He was pleasant looking, a short, stocky young man. He had the thick, straight, black hair and almond eyes of the hill tribes. He was wearing black jeans and a shiny white nylon jacket. Still generously spattered with blood.

'Wonderful performance, madam,' he said, in Hindi. 'Wonderful. Good thing I didn't die, huh? Or else how would we know that Madam is not only a famous writer but also a great actress too?'

Beside him stood a hefty-looking man wearing full khaki gear complete with monkey-cap. He looked like a military policeman from the nearby army recruitment camp. Behind them both were a couple of men who may also have been military types or perhaps part of an ambulance team; it was hard to tell. They were dressed in heavy winter clothing, their faces wrapped in brightly coloured woollen mufflers.

I wish I'd taken a picture of Leena's face at that moment when she looked up. The lustrous skin dimmed, the cheeks hollowed out, the eyes bulged from their sockets and the lips drew back in a feral snarl. '*You*—' was all she could say.

Here's where I reveal that I am, or have been up till now, what is known in cri-fi circles as an unreliable narrator. But that's over now.

The first part of the story was the reverse of the one Leena told us: *she* pestered *him* for a 'massage'; *he* refused, *she* attacked. Then he made his escape from the room and got to the pantry.

This next bit is partly speculation.

She, no doubt writhing with humiliation whilst still very drunk, decided there was no choice: she had to get rid of him. To shut him up. To save her reputation. So, creeping out to the pantry with her trusty fire extinguisher in hand, she opened the door when his back was to it and really did hit him with it. From behind.

He fell like a...well, like someone who's been dealt a fearsome blow to the head with a blunt object. She may have had the idea of hauling what she thought would be a dead body to the cliff's edge. But he may have hit the side of his temple on the edge of the counter as he went down. Whatever the case, he began to bleed profusely. The sudden shocking sight of blood must've sobered her right up. And she returned to her room.

The time was a little before 11.45 p.m.

That's when I entered the picture. Completely unaware of the earlier part of the drama, I got up, wanting a fresh bottle of drinking water. There was always bottled water to be had in the pantry. All the rooms have porch lights, which we can switch off voluntarily from inside the room, in the interests of conserving energy. So, turning on my porch light, I stepped out and saw, to my shock, Peter lying face down on the stone-flagged path. A few feet from my door.

Behind him, on the still lightly falling snow, was a trail of blood and the pantry door wide open.

Horrified, I ran to him. I was vastly relieved to find that he was alive though terribly groggy. I went back inside my room, grabbed a towel to hold to the wound on his temple, then helped him up, and into my room. I had a bottle of brandy and gave him some, but he was in a lot of pain. Clearly, he was going to need medical attention.

So I called the local ambulance. There's a country clinic nearby and they know the Leopard's Leap Retreat very well. They readily agreed to come – because the blizzard, though forecast, had not yet begun. I helped him climb the short incline that led up to the front of the property. Before we went up, I locked the door to my room and made sure that I shut the door to the pantry firmly. It was never locked, because guests need to have easy access to snacks and water.

Peter told me what had happened while we waited for the ambulance. We both agreed that confronting Leena, particularly while Mango and Chutney were away, would be very messy. His word against hers, her money against his lack of it.

By then the ambulance had come. I told him to go get himself fixed up, but that, when he returned, he must bring a policeman with him.

We both realized that there may be a protracted period during which the blizzard would make movement and cell phone communication impossible. Already, we could not get through to Mango and Chutney, in Almora.

I went back to my room, fretting over the best course of action. Unable to decide what to do, I remained fully clothed but got into bed, thinking that I might as well try to get some rest.

The next thing I knew was that Mads was thumping on my door and shrieking. I pulled on my dressing gown for appearance's sake when I went to the door. The moment she'd gone, I tried calling Peter, on his phone. But by now there was no service. I could only hope that, with daylight, Peter would somehow be able to return, accompanied by the police.

I understood that I and the other four writers were potentially in grave danger. There was no saying what Leena would do if she felt trapped. CCTV footage showed, when we checked afterwards, that she'd gone in and out of the main building a couple of times around 5 a.m., before anyone else had woken up. The camera is only at the entrance, not inside so we can't be sure what exactly she did while she was in there.

The other four rooms are attached to the main building. No one can say what she may have contemplated, in those early hours, all by herself.

Since her arrest, she's remained out of sight and incommunicado. No admissions. No apologies. Since there was no actual murder, perhaps a few mouths will be shut up with money and no more will ever be known.

Two small mysteries can be cleared up now, however.

One, it was she who dissolved the date-rape drug in the tea of the samovar. It was a clever idea. By keeping all five of us literally paralysed, she could either force us or bribe us to accept her version of events. Too bad for her, I arrived too late to drink the tea. Or else, who knows? The story may have had a very different ending altogether.

The second mystery is more interesting. You recall how Mads claimed she saw tracks leading to my room from the pantry? Do you recall wondering why, if she saw tracks, she didn't mention any sight of blood outside the pantry?

The answer to both is: the leopard! We all knew, from hearing the sawing sound, that the resident leopard was indeed in the vicinity. It was perhaps calling to its beloved. Or cursing its fate, having been stuck out in the cold on a snowy night. Or who knows what.

But the point is, it was close by. It smelled blood. It waited for all the activity to die down. And then it stole up to the door of the pantry, smelled carefully all around, smelled the blood under the snow, on the flagstones and...licked it clean.

Mind you, this is mere conjecture. I have no idea whether leopards are so fastidious or whether this one would even bother to dig the snow aside to look for the blood on the path. And if it wasn't the leopard, then I have no idea why Mads saw marks in the snow, leading to my room.

I just like the idea of the silent spotted predator, crouching close to all the action, perfectly hidden. Watching clumsy humans traipsing back and forth. Its whiskers twitching.

Hungrily.

# MURDER BY A RAISED EYEBROW

*Tabish Khair*

It was the way you looked at me, your eyebrow raised and arched, that I could not forget. People have looked at me in different, harder ways. A successful lawyer gets used to looks of interrogation, scepticism, disbelief, distaste, anger, repulsion. And with this case – the 'Mohammad Murder' case as the papers love to call it – I have received more than my share of such looks. I have also received verbal abuse and threatening letters. You would have noticed that I have gone off social media. Once, I was assaulted outside my office, by a disturbed young man demented further by the media coverage of the case. I would have suffered serious damage if two junior colleagues, both Hindus, unlike me, had not come to my rescue. But all of it was nothing; I had more or less expected it when I took up the case. What I had not expected was your look.

We go back such a long way, all the way to that small town – Phansa. Who has even heard of Phansa? – and that ordinary school from which only two students emerged into national prominence: you as an actress known for her uncompromising roles, I as a leading criminal lawyer. And, strangely, we stayed in touch, all through our struggling years, all through our later successes: my famous cases and TV appearances, your National Award for playing the role of an unwed, single mother and that Cannes nomination for your supporting role as a widow who refuses to wear white. Yes, all through your three divorces, and my one marriage, and then the death of my wife from cancer almost a decade ago, we stayed friends. We always understood each other, no matter what the tabloids wrote. We never questioned – no, we never doubted – each other's integrity. That is why your raised eyebrow hurts.

I had gone to the party only because I had heard that you would be there. I no longer go to parties. Partly it is because I am going to turn sixty in a year, and I had my gall bladder removed three years ago – you know because you had made time to fly over to be with me at the hospital – and partly because I am tired of answering questions. Why had a Muslim lawyer like me, known for his agnosticism and his secular stance, accepted the 'Mohammad Murder' brief? How could I even think of defending that obvious criminal, one who had repeatedly confessed? That monster who had not only killed his beautiful girlfriend but butchered her into pieces, stored in his fridge? And always the laughter and scoffing (in polite society), when I give my reply: 'He is not the real murderer.' Or sometimes I might say, 'He is not the only murderer.' I have learnt not to say more, even though my statement always provokes a howl of protests. This time though, you added your raised eyebrow to that howl. And something like a wave of guilt or shame, an immense tide of loneliness, washed over me, and I left the party as soon as I could.

Why do they even call it the 'Mohammad Murder'? His first name is not Mohammad. His name is Mohammad Ashfaq Hussain; we are not Americans or Europeans, we know this means that his name is actually Ashfaq. But it is *always* the

'Mohammad Murder' case in the media. Though even that was not the reason I took the case. Many decades ago, I stopped trying to correct people. Only lunatics, or perhaps writers, bang their heads against stone walls. I will tell you how I took up the case, and then you might understand why.

## 1.

It was a regular July evening. Remember how humid it gets in Delhi around that time? Almost as bad as your Mumbai. It had not been raining, but the moisture was draped like a wet blanket over all of us. As I stepped out of my air-conditioned office, tiny beads of perspiration broke out on my face. While I was wiping my face with that large florid handkerchief that I carry and that you always make fun of – 'Aha, Akram, I can see you still carry our hometown in your pocket!' – I heard my name shouted out in a breathless voice. It was a voice that I recognized. It belonged to a minister from a neighbouring state, who spent much of his time in the capital, trying to make it into the National Cabinet. I would have readily avoided him if I had seen him coming. I would have ducked into an alley! But the minister sahib – I will call him Masterji, as he was known before he entered politics – and his SUV, engine running, were right in front of me, and I was stranded on the curb. Had I even made it to my car, I could have perhaps jovially waved and accelerated away.

Masterji extracted his considerable girth from the back door of the SUV – cars honked behind us, but his security men in another black car waved the traffic on – and engulfed me in a large embrace. He is known to hug people. After I had surfaced from the folds of his flesh and his attar-scented loose kurta, he remarked to me that he had come this way just to see me and that I was leaving my office earlier than usual. I gave him the reason: I was going to meet some friends at a restaurant in Khan Market. 'Come, Akram Ansari ji,' he said, addressing me formally by my full name, 'I am going that way too. I am supposed to inaugurate some cultural function-vunction at IIC. We can talk along the way, and my men will drop you back.'

There was nothing I could do. I acceded to fate.

## 2.

The interior of the SUV was plush with real leather, which was rather surprising as it also contained enough pictures, medallions and statues of various gods, and the sacred cow-mother, to stock a small temple. A bhajan was playing, faintly, and the air conditioner was running on full blast.

Inside the SUV, other than the driver and a security guy on the front seat, there was an elderly couple – oh well, at least a few years older than us – in the back. I joined Masterji in the middle row, where there was more leg space. At a signal from the security man, our SUV and the security car revved abruptly into the traffic – causing some more timid honking – and proceeded towards Khan Market. It was then that Masterji gestured towards the couple in the back seat: 'Sri Mohammad Rahmat Hussain and his respected wife. Hussain ji is a retired government engineer.' He emphasized 'government'.

I glanced at them and nodded a greeting. The man was thin, bearded, with the tell-tale gatha – a thumb-sized dark spot in the middle of the forehead, which the religious flaunt as a sign of praying regularly, forehead against the praying rug, and which I suspect many create by rubbing repeatedly. The woman was veiled, but her face covering was pushed back; her face was plump and less austere looking than that of her husband.

'I was bringing them to see you,' Masterji added. 'They are from my constituency, and I help all from my constituency, regardless of caste or creed.' This second sentence was spoken partly for the sake of posterity, I am sure, and partly perhaps to explain to me why two religious Muslims were in his car, for the man was not known for his good opinion of Muslims. His political career largely depended on a careful harnessing of suspicion at Muslims.

'See me?'

'You don't read the newspapers anymore, Advocate Sahab. Too busy, too busy with your famous clients, but we poor servants of the public have to stay abreast, ha ha,' Masterji responded jocularly. 'You don't even know who these people are!' Then he added, after a pause, 'They are the parents of Mohammad Ashfaq Hussain.'

Yes, I had read of Mohammad Ashfaq Hussain. The case had been on the front page of every newspaper and the cover of every magazine for a week now. It had been debated loudly and repetitively on talk shows. Mostly, the news started with the latest take on the incident. A young Muslim man, in his mid-twenties, working as a fashion photographer, and his Hindu girlfriend, slightly older, an aspiring model and actress: they had been living together, which was not so unusual in some circles in Delhi, even though such an inter-religious pre-marital relationship might have invited a mob in Masterji's state. What was unusual was that the woman had disappeared: Ashfaq had told friends that she had left him. This had not surprised the friends since the two had been bickering often these past few months. Except that no one had heard from her in a while. Then, she was found almost a month later, chopped into bits, and strewn in different places outside the capital. That's when it hit the headlines. Those bits led the police back to Ashfaq. Some remaining bits and pieces were discovered in the freezer and refrigerator in the barsaati that the two were renting. It was an open-and-shut case, as the investigating officer put it.

There was no way I was going to take it.

I said so to Masterji.

Masterji laughed.

'Busy, busy, busy,' he guffawed. Then he turned towards the couple and added, 'See, Hussain ji, I told you that Advocate Akram Ansari Sahab no longer takes on such cases.'

'Sir,' said that man at the back, 'it was you who suggested Advocate Sahab's name.'

'Yes, yes, I did. You know why, Advocate Sahab?'

I waited for him to provide the answer, and he obliged.

'Because we are a democracy. We are a nation built on law and order. And these people, these people who are from my constituency, have not been able to get anyone to represent their son. It has been in the news. When I was told of this, I sent my secretary to them, and I said, I don't care that you are Muslim, I don't care that your son is a murderer, I don't even care that you are from my constituency, but I care about my great nation and the law of my great nation, and the law says that everyone is entitled to a lawyer, a good lawyer.'

He paused, perhaps expecting me to clap. In the silence after his speech, the man at the back mumbled, 'Thank you, thank you, sir.'

Masterji resumed, 'And I said to them, didn't I, Hussain ji, that I will get you the best criminal lawyer in the country, and one from your own faith too...What's wrong? Why are we stuck here?'

The questions were addressed to his driver, who replied that there was some kind of wedding procession on the road.

'Get it cleared. We are already thirty minutes late.' Then he turned to me and explained, 'I am the chief guest.'

The security guide grumbled something into his mobile, and a couple of security men jumped out of the other car and marshalled the procession to one side of the road. Masterji sat there, looking deeply offended. It was only after we had passed and were rolling smoothly down the road again that Masterji returned to his topic. He did so in a circuitous manner.

'Why are we the greatest democracy in the world?' he enquired and paused for an answer.

'Largest population?' I offered.

He waved that answer away and looked at the couple behind us.

'Free elections, sir?' the retired engineer suggested.

'No, no, no,' said Masterji. 'We are the biggest democracy in the world because everyone is equal here. You, me, him, her, my driver, Brahmin, Rajput, Dalit, Hindu, Sikh, Muslim. All equal.'

He regally surveyed us for signs of agreement, which we provided.

'And why are all equal?' This time he did not wait for us to answer, having decided that we could not do his catechism. He provided the answer himself. 'We are equal because our law, our courts treat us as equal. For this, I need hardly remind you, Advocate Sahab, everyone needs to be fully defended in our courts.'

'Oh,' I replied, 'I am sure Hussain Sahab will be able to find lawyers to plead his son's case...'

'What lawyers? Some two-piece fixer whose degree is as worthless as his cardboard bow-tie! No, no, no, Advocate Sahab, that won't do in our great democracy. Even though I am as appalled as the rest of the nation at what their son did, I have promised them the best lawyer I can get them...'

It was then that the woman in the back, the mother, spoke up. She spoke in a loud, angry voice, 'It was not the poor boy's fault. That shameless girl forced him to it.'

That was when I decided to take the case. I have heard such voices and statements before. I know where they come from. Those were the kinds of voices I was escaping when I left Phansa; no, we were escaping when we left Phansa. But, of course, they are not confined to small towns, as both of us have since discovered.

I looked back at the couple, the father so prim and correct in his religiosity; the mother incensed less on behalf of her son and more because her son had chosen a woman totally different from her. I felt a tinge of pity – yes, pity – for the boy. I wanted to meet him. I knew then that he was not the only murderer. I am not saying his parents had encouraged him to kill the poor woman – they were not that kind of people. They were narrow but righteous. They were bigoted but proper. And I knew that they were culpable. I shrank away from them, as you would shrink away from a monster. I wanted to defend the boy. I wanted to defend him not for the crime he had committed, but from the charge of being the only murderer. His parents were murderers too. Passive murderers.

I was naïve then. His parents were not the only passive murderers.

## 3.

The youth, Ashfaq, turned out to be as I had imagined him. He had not been mistreated in custody. His case was too visible, and, in any case, the police already had everything they needed: evidence, body, or pieces of it, motive, witnesses (not to the murder but the circumstances around it), even an initial confession that had later been retracted as 'obtained under duress'. But days in custody affect a normal person: he looked haggard, sleepless, and his clothes were dirty and crumpled.

Despite that, he was a handsome young man, and his body had obviously been shaped in gyms. I was expecting that. And just as I had thought, he was a man without a single idea of his own. I suppose he had never read a book, nothing more than cheap thrillers in any case, and film and fashion magazines. His idea of the world had largely come to him through his smartphone. When he spoke, I heard so many other voices, and it was only after some time, in his weakest moments, that I heard a whisper of his own voice.

Popular culture and films and fashion spoke through him: 'We were so much in love, like Laila and Majnu... When I first saw her, she was wearing exactly the dress that Alia Bhatt is wearing in the "Love You Zindagi" song...My love for her drove me to desperation...'

Then his mother spoke through him: 'She never understood the meaning of decency...Why did she have to flirt with every man in every party?...Family background matters...Her family has bad blood and no traditions...My mother warned me: they are not even good Hindus...She was a girl who knew how to attract men like me. She had me wrapped like a strand of hair around her finger, she did!'

And finally, his father: 'I should not have stopped going to the mosque after high school...I am trying to perform regular namaaz again now in my cell, though there is hardly space for a mat...Cultural and religious differences matter, I should have listened...Finally, it is all in the hands of Allah: he decides whatever happens.'

And then, very rarely, that whisper, which he did not even know as his own voice: 'Sometimes I wonder if things would have turned out different if we did not have families and friends around us...I wake up many times at night and feel for her in bed.'

## 4.

One day, the police inspector who had escorted him, handcuffed and chained, as if there was any place he could escape to, came to my office. His men had locked Ashfaq into the van that they used to bring him and were waiting downstairs. He was direct with me.

'I want to tell you that you should not waste your time on that boy,' he said. He was a big man, with a huge tilak on his forehead, and it was obvious that his sympathies were not with Ashfaq.

'I am just doing my job,' I replied.

'You are a famous lawyer. I have googled you. We have discussed it.'

'We?'

'Me and some other friends in the force. We have discussed it, and we are following the case. I suppose everyone in the nation is. We can see that you are pushing for a verdict of homicide.'

'It was a crime of passion. It was not planned. He tried to hide the evidence later on.'

'It does not matter what he tried. We know what happened. We know who he is. These boys think they can toy with the honour of our women, and then toss them away like, like, a piece of trash. So, my friends asked me to tell you...'

'Who are your friends?'

'Does not matter. My friends want to tell you that the boy should hang, as soon as possible. All you can do is get his sentence commuted to life, maybe 15 years or 18 years...'

'That is what I intend to do. I don't believe in capital punishment.'

'Who cares what you lot believe in...Let me explain what my friends want to tell you. If the boy is just sentenced to prison, he will die there. And he will die horribly. We will make sure he suffers a hundred times more than that girl did before he dies. It is best for him, and you, if he dies quickly, on the gallows.'

He turned around briskly and walked out.

It was then that I realized that the list of murderers was longer than I had imagined. It was not just the boy's parents.

Don't join that list of murders, my childhood friend. Even a raised eyebrow can murder in our world.

## 5.

The case was expedited. In a country where cases linger on for years, decades at times, the 'Mohammad Murder' case got quick dates, and the judges turned up on time, and no judge was transferred at a crucial moment. Of course, I tried to delay the process. That is what a good defence lawyer with a weak case does: the more time that lapses, the more gaps and inconsistencies appear in the case, weakening it.

But this time I knew that it would not have worked. Even if I had delayed the case for a decade, it would have made no difference to the judgement. The boy had already been tried and condemned. One part of me was even relieved when the judges – first in the high court, where we lost within six months, and then in the Supreme Court, to which we appealed – smiled patiently at my pleas and requests for adjournments, and mostly rejected them, or gave me a date only a week away.

Interestingly, the only person who wanted my case to fare better than it was faring, apart from my juniors who were working on it with me, was Masterji. He called almost every other week. He suggested ways – sometimes clever ones – that I could apply to weaken the case of the state prosecutor. I was surprised. Had I misjudged the man? Had the media misreported him? He had always been portrayed as a Muslim-baiter in his state, and here he was trying to help a Muslim man who had clearly killed his girlfriend.

But the heat was on me, and I did not give it too much thought. The threats had increased. Then there was that assault. My guard was on the other side of the car, and if my colleagues had not grabbed the demented young man and wrenched the iron rod away from him, he would have done some damage. I was gradually ostracized from society, even as I took to the media, initially to sow doubts about the police narrative of cold, premeditated murder, but increasingly to spread the net wide enough: to implicate others, everyone, all of us, in the boy's homicide.

When I repeated (Objection, Me Lord!) what the mother had said to me – 'My son was a chaste boy until that siren lured him away from us' – I wanted to point an accusing finger at all the mothers of sons in the land. When I interrogated the father – 'If he had not taken to drinking with that woman and her friends, if he had only prayed as I had taught him, this would not have happened' – I wished to accuse all fathers. When I prodded friends and acquaintances of the couple into accusatory remarks – 'She was too sophisticated for that country hick', 'He had a temper, but then Muslims are a meat-eating people with quick tempers', 'Ice and fire do not mix', 'He deceived all of us with his glass of wine: essentially he was a fundamentalist', 'She was not a woman I would've married; dated, yes, but not married' (Objection! Objection!) – I was not accusing anyone other than the speakers...and millions more like them.

But it was lost on the world out there. It was lost on everyone. I was just seen as the cynical, cunning lawyer, at best, and even something much worse, much worse, as I was yet to discover. I should have realized that the day you raised your eyebrow at me.

## 6.

I was too busy to seek you out or even email you after that evening. Your raised eyebrow haunted me, but I had no time to think about what to say to you, how to say it. Actually, I did not even, then, fully understand why your raised eyebrow haunted me.

It all became clear only after the final judgement a week ago. It went the way everyone had wanted it. The boy was sentenced to death. We filed the usual clemency pleas and legal objections, but there was nothing more that I could do, and I left those formal matters to my juniors. Partly because I was tired – I had no wish to even see the boy again, fraught and shallow, guilty and not-guilty – like much of the rest of the nation. But mostly because I read an item on an inner page of a paper about Masterji's election campaign. It drew my attention, because there was a photo of Masterji thundering into a sea of microphones on a dais.

You see, I had been too busy to notice that campaigning had been going on for a couple of by-elections to the Parliament, and Masterji had quit his MLA seat in his state to try to upgrade himself to a Member of Parliament at the national level. If he managed that, he would obviously have a better chance of making it as a minister or deputy minister at the national level. Both the constituencies were in his state, and, as such, the Delhi papers had not been giving the by-elections too much coverage. But now voting was just two days away, and I caught a news item reporting a speech by Masterji.

This is what the news item quoted him as saying: 'Some people are not to be trusted. Look at what that boy did. He looked like Salman Khan, didn't he? Suited–booted. They say he even drank liquor. You know what he did. He lured one of our women and then chopped her to bits. And look at who defended him: the biggest criminal lawyer in the country they say, a man who claims to be an atheist, a man who says he does not practise his own religion. But, when you scratch the surface, you see his real colour. It is green. He defends a cruel murderer because his real colour is green. Not green-white-saffron, just green. Remember that. Remember: some people are not to be trusted.'

I wearily folded the paper and put it away. 'Another murderer,' I muttered. Or maybe I said, 'Et tu, Brute.' You always laughed at my penchant for literary clichés.

Yes, it makes sense. That is when it started making sense. Remember, we had read of the scapegoat in school? Where was it: history, literature, sociology? What subject? I remember the line: The scapegoat is, by definition, not innocent.

Of course, the boy has to hang. What other option do we have? We cannot hang an entire nation, can we? Come to think of it, you cannot even raise an eyebrow at an entire nation, for it doesn't exist except in our collective imagination, and that is the imagination in which the boy has to hang.

It was then that I understood why your raised eyebrow had disturbed me so much. You would never vote for someone like Masterji – I know that – but the nation, one of those many imaginary nations that always demand blood sacrifices to turn and stay real – Masterji's nation had entered you. It is not just that I had lost you. It was worse than that. You were not aware of it, but I had enabled Masterji and his nation to breach your defences, your decency, your innocence. Was this why Masterji had wanted me to take up the case? I was complicit. I was complicit in turning you – and I am sure thousands like you – into murderers as well.

Now I understood why I had felt so guilty and lonely – lonelier than after the death of my wife – when you raised your eyebrow at me.

# THE MERMAID'S SONG

*Ajay Chowdhury*

*'There will be time to murder and create'* – T.S. Eliot

An unreal mist hangs over the city like a liar's promise as I push my way into Churchgate Station after the IMAX movie at Eros. The drizzle clings to my clothes. Its cold fingers crawl down my neck. Fuming, I grab the last seat in the train carriage, my mind simmering with frustration. The harsh fluorescent lights cast a sickly glow over the faces of the tired commuters. A scent of stale sweat and cheap perfume permeates the air.

Above the noise of the train, Esra's voice still echoes in my head, each word a sharp reminder of my failures. Why do I always submit to her diktats? Let her pull me into watching films I hate? Compel me to do the things she decides are best? I clench my fists, feeling the bite of my nails. I must assert myself. Make myself heard. Show her she's not the boss of me.

I don't get women. Never have. Intimacy is a foreign language to me. An indecipherable code. She says I'm lucky to have her. And she's right. Let's face it, I'm not exactly god's gift. Can't do easy banter. Can't...

'Alfred. Look!' Esra's voice is a hook, yanking me back to the present.

In the middle of the compartment, next to the exit, a young woman wearing a short black leather skirt over fishnet stockings, blue top and a red scarf is locked in a passionate embrace with a man in a suit. Actually, embrace doesn't even begin to describe it. This is virtually public fornication. His hands grip her bottom possessively. Her mouth devours his face. The carriage is awash with shocked glances and lascivious grins. A woman in a *Cats* T-shirt opposite them is goggling at the spectacle, holding up her phone to capture the performance.

'Bloody hell! Get a room!' Esra whispers.

'Maybe they're in love,' I mumble, suppressing a pang of envy that twists in my gut. I've declared my feelings for Esra countless times. And has she reciprocated? Not a chance!

The train squeals to a halt in Dadar. The lovers disentangle. The man gets off the train as the woman blows kisses after him.

We rattle off again.

The Cats woman approaches our mini-skirted enthusiast. Whispers something in her ear. They laugh.

And then...

What? No!

The leather-skirted girl starts kissing the Cats woman as fervently as she had the guy!

What. The. Hell.

The carriage holds its collective breath as we watch the show, agog.

'Oh my god! This is insane!' says Esra. 'Is she drunk? A prostitute?'

'Maybe they're a throuple?' I say, my voice barely above a whisper. My mind racing with possibilities.

That term entered my lexicon B.E. Before Esra. A time when I'd given up all hope of being part of a couple, let alone a multiple of one. A thousand right swipes. The occasional coffee meeting. The scent of perfume. A bare arm on the table. Glazed eyes looking over my shoulder. The quick excuse.

Then one day, there was Esra. A connection I'd never experienced. Finally, someone who made me feel worthy.

So what if she pushes me every once in a while? Everyone needs a little push sometimes. I can be a bit lazy. Unmotivated.

The train stops at Bandra. Our two mysterious exhibitionists jump out.

'Let's follow them!' says Esra, suddenly. 'I want to see where they go.'

'Are you crazy? We can't...'

But five minutes later, we're outside the station. A pulse beats in my neck. My shadow trails the couple as they stroll, hand in hand, through the half-deserted streets. Snatches of their conversation drift back to us. 'I got tickets for the exhibition at the Jehangir Art Gallery of his early sketches for the Sistine Chapel...'

'Stay back, they'll see you,' mutters Esra.

I slow down. My palms are clammy with nervous sweat. 'I can't believe we're doing this. It's stupid.'

The women turn onto St. Leo Road. The mini-skirted one retrieves keys from her handbag. They disappear into an apartment building called Olympia. Lights flicker to life in a ground-floor window.

I tiptoe to peer through the bars. Something brushes my leg. I stumble, my heart leaping into my throat. A yellow cat. I bend to pet it, but it shoots me a disdainful look and sashays off.

That's when I see it. Her scarf. She must have dropped it. Pashmina. I nuzzle the soft wool. Pocket it. Turn to leave.

'Wait,' says Esra. 'Let's see if the other guy joins them.'

'This is ridiculous. I'm tired. Can we please go home?'

As usual, Esra prevails. We wait under a pool of light created by a jaundiced street lamp that is attempting to beat away the darkness. Insects bang against the bulb, their clicks providing a counterpoint to the roar of the vast, indifferent sea a few streets away. I shuffle restlessly for half an hour until the Cats woman re-emerges. Heads to the end of the street. Turns onto Perry Road.

'Now can we go?'

But Esra is Esra.

'Just wait...'

*

Esra is unusually subdued by the time we finally stumble into my Andheri flat an hour and a half later. I shower and sit on my bed, staring at the scarf.

'Why do you think she did it, Esra? The man and the woman?'

Silence. Then, her voice, soft and contemplative. 'Maybe she was unhappy. Like you, she was searching for something more. One person wasn't enough. She needed two. Maybe they complemented different sides of her personality? After all, aren't we all complex creatures?'

Her words make sense. A twisted kind of logic that only Esra can provide. She is my guide. My compass. But do I really need her as much as she says I do?

I fold the scarf and nestle it in my bedside drawer.

I can't sleep. My mind's jangling with unanswered questions about this bizarre evening. My agitation builds like a pressure cooker. This must stop.

Now. I can do it now!

'Esra.'

'Yes?'

'This isn't working.'

'What isn't?'

'This. You and me. I have to end it.'

'What do you mean?'

'Just that. You've got to go.'

A soft laugh cuts through my gloom. 'And what'll you do then?'

'I don't know. Find someone else.'

'Who's going to want someone like you?'

Her words slice through me, sharp and cruel. I curl into myself, doubt gnawing at my insides. Is she right? But how do I stop her from running my life?

'Don't talk to me like that. It's not on.'

'I'm sorry, but I've got to be cruel to be kind, Alfred. It's the truth. You're a stick-thin, balding, middle-aged banker. Can you honestly see yourself finding anyone else? Do you even remember how lonely you were when I came into your life? Shireen had just walked out on you at Tipsee Monkee when, as usual, you had said the wrong thing. You're lucky I was there. That I felt sorry for you. And didn't mind your weirdness! Do you want to go back to that?'

'I don't know,' I mumble.

'Stop being ridiculous. Go to sleep.'

Is she right? How do I stop her from ruining my life? She's not good for me. I need to act.

*

Two days later, the newspaper runs a story of a woman found strangled in Bandra.

'Esra, look! It's her!'

'Oh, my goodness!'

Alia Datta. Twenty-nine. Corpse discovered by her girlfriend, Shanti. The woman in the Cats T-shirt!

'If this Shanti is her girlfriend, who was the guy?' I ask.

My fingers fly over the keyboard as I google Alia Datta. Standard social media fare. Cocktails. Dinners. Pretty friends. Worked at a law firm in Bandra Kurla Complex. Then, a face catches my eye. A lawyer in her company. Shyam Davar.

'Look!' My voice rises with excitement. 'It's the suited guy that Alia Datta was kissing on the tube!'

'Maybe.'

'I'm sure it was. Shall we tell the police?'

'Why?'

'Because he could be the killer! It's possible he went to Alia Datta's flat after we left. The police can bring him in for questioning.'

'I'm not sure we should get involved. Remember what happened last time?'

But a fire has been lit inside me. 'That was different. I really think we should tell them.'

'You always get carried away, Alfred. It's a bad idea.'

'You don't always know best. I'm calling them.'

'Oh, just do what you want, then. But leave me out of it. And don't mention we followed them.'

'I'm not an idiot.'

As I dial, a thrill runs through me. For once, I'm taking control. I'm doing something that matters.

*

Three nervous hours later (Was Esra right? Have I screwed up again? Am I the loser she says I am?), the doorbell's shrill ring shatters the silence, sending my heart into overdrive. Two men are at my door.

'Mr Alfred?' says the older one.

I've put on my best suit to ensure I make the right impression. Hopefully the look says 'responsible, community-minded civilian'. I force a smile, praying it doesn't look as fake as it feels. 'Yes.'

'I'm Inspector Naik and this is Sub-Inspector Kamil Rahman. You say you have some information regarding Alia Datta's demise?'

Show them your sober, reliable side, Alfred. I try to control my excitement as I launch into my carefully rehearsed story, omitting our stalking adventure. My voice sounds distant, alien. 'It was Shyam Davar kissing her on the train. Before the other woman – Shanti – started to kiss her as well. She filmed them. Check her phone.' I pull up Davar's profile on my laptop, the screen's glow harsh in my dim room. 'Look. He's a partner specializing in wills and estates. Suspicious, no?'

Their faces remain impassive. Unreadable. The silence stretches. Oppressive. The room suddenly feels claustrophobic. The ticking clock on my wall becomes deafening, each second a countdown to... What? Sub-Inspector Rahman looks around my flat. For some reason, I feel ashamed. Why? I have no reason to. It's neat and tidy. So what if it's small? This is Mumbai. Property is expensive. His eyes flick to my bedroom door. 'You were alone when you saw this on the train?'

A bead of sweat trickles down my back. 'The train was packed. Everyone saw.'

'You live alone, Mr Alfred?'

'I do.'

What's he getting at? There's no way he can know about Esra.

'And your occupation is...'

'Manager at Kotak Mahindra Bank.'

Inspector Naik's voice cuts through the room. 'Alfred? That's an unusual name? Anglo-Indian? Goan? Christian?'

Prejudiced bastard. 'Goan. It wasn't a crime the last time I checked. Nor was being a Christian.'

'No. Of course not.' He licks a finger. Thumbs through his notebook laboriously. 'You contacted us a year ago about your neighbour? The one who lives downstairs?'

My stomach drops. 'That was a misunderstanding.'

'You thought she was dead?'

'She had a cat. It came up to my flat. Mewing. Hungry. I gave it milk. Banged on Shireen's door. There was no answer. I thought something had happened to her. So, I called the police.'

The room seems to shrink with each passing second. He stares at me. I'm liking this guy less and less. 'The police broke the door down and she wasn't there?'

'Correct.'

'And she came back from holiday a day later to find her

door broken down?' He gives me a contemptuous look. I want to punch him.

'She was actually very good about it. Said it was touching to find neighbours looking out for each other in Mumbai. I was being a good Samaritan. As I am now. Are we done?'

After they leave, I slump against the closed front door, exhausted.

'Well?' I whisper into the empty air.

Esra's voice floats back. 'Nice job.'

Doubt gnaws at me. 'I'm not sure they believed me. Should we investigate Davar ourselves?'

'Why?' Her tone drips with scepticism.

'If we find something incriminating, we can tell the police. People like that need locking up. Those two cops were useless. We can do a better job.'

'I'm not sure...'

'Come on! You're always saying I should get out of my comfort zone.'

A pause. 'All right. But on your head be it.'

'We'll find a way,' I insist, a manic energy building inside me. 'Predators like that should be put away for ever.'

*

I call Davar's office the next day and ask for the last appointment of the day to discuss 'an inheritance issue'. All day at the bank, I can't concentrate. Anticipation pulses through me as I walk towards Café Coffee Day outside his office in The Capital building in BKC. Hoping he'll leave when he realizes I'm a no-show.

Time ticks away endlessly. The barista gives me an odd look. I smile benignly at her.

'There!'

Davar emerges from his office in the same grey suit he'd worn with Alia Datta. I look around for an auto to follow him in case he gets into a car, but luckily, he walks. We follow him discreetly for fifteen minutes until he enters an upscale block – Signia Pearl – in a quiet road off Avenue 3.

'Now what?' asks Esra as I stare at his building.

'He's a partner with a posh flat. Alia Datta is a junior employee living in a tiny studio. This is a textbook case of the power imbalance that leads to sexual harassment. He was scared he'd be exposed as a #Metoo pervert. That's his motive for killing her. The police will get it. All we need to do is hand them the evidence.' I hope Esra's proud of my feminist take on the matter.

She ignores it. Says reasonably, 'Why the public display on the train then? Wouldn't he want to keep his affair quiet?'

'He knew he was going to off her and wanted a last grope before...' I make a slitting motion across my throat.

'With no proof, the police won't act.'

'I just said that we would get them the proof,' I say irritably. Why doesn't she ever listen?

'How?'

'Be quiet. Let me think, will you?'

As I'm formulating strategies, Davar opens a window overlooking the street and leans out, looking this way and that.

An idea strikes. 'His flat's on the ground floor. We could climb in there. But we need to lure him out of the house without him closing the window.'

As I think about how to do this, Davar shuts the window. Moments later, he emerges. We trail him as he goes into the underground garage, where he hops into a parked red BMW and drives out.

A plan forms. 'I know what I have to do.'

I go up to the front door and ring the bell to his flat. No answer. Good. He doesn't have a maid or anyone else living there. My plan will work.

*

The following day, I dial Davar's office once more. Apologizing profusely for the missed appointment, I secure another meeting for the same time.

We return to wait outside his office.

It plays out the same way.

I don't show up for the meeting. He emerges at six, visibly irritated. Marches homeward. Opens the window.

This time, I'm prepared and have everything I need in my rucksack.

Ensuring the coast is clear, I go into the garage, shatter the windscreen of his car with my hammer, setting off a blaring alarm. Adrenaline coursing, I sprint up to his building. He answers the bell. Confirms he owns a red BMW. I relay the faux emergency, and we remove ourselves as he rushes out in pursuit of the phantom vandal.

We scramble through his window, landing in a well-kept room. Plush carpet. Large double bed. Red silk bedcover. Is that where he romped with Alia? I force the thought away from my head. Time is an enemy, and I have no clue what to look for. Photos adorn his bedside table, showcasing him with two kids. No trace of a woman's belongings. I rummage through his stuff. Nothing.

In the fancy bathroom, I shrug off my rucksack. Sift through his clothes hamper. Just dirty T-shirts and underwear. Yuck.

'Divorced,' I mutter as I take photographs of the laundry before sealing the clothes-basket and stowing away my phone.

Esra whispers, 'The door!'

The lock turns, resulting in our undignified exit from the window.

*

At home, Esra says, 'Now what?'

'We need the police to search his place.'

'But they need a reason, right?'

'What if I give them an anonymous tip?'

'Give it a go.'

I call the police station. Disguising my voice, I say I witnessed Alia Datta arguing with a chap in a grey suit at Churchgate Station, the night of her death. That he shoved her. Screamed at her. I describe Davar perfectly and hang up before they can ask for my details.

A job well done.

*

Two agonizing days crawl by. I set up a Google alert for the victim's name. Finally, a result! I open my inbox to find a link to an article which sends a surge of triumph through me. A thirty-seven-year-old male, known to Alia Datta, has been arrested on suspicion of her murder and is in custody at Bandra Police Station.

'Esra! Our plan worked!' I exclaim, drunk on vindication. 'The police acted on my tip, found the evidence in Davar's flat and arrested him. We've put away a sexual predator.'

Her response is icy. 'Remember Shireen? That was a disaster? You wanted her, didn't you? Then she moved away.'

'Stop it,' I snap. 'You never let me enjoy my little victories.'

Her tone softens. 'I am proud of you, Alfred. You did very well.'

A warm glow suffuses me. 'We did! This is as much your victory as it's mine. I could never have done it without you.'

'True.'

The glow vanishes as soon as it appeared. Why does she always have to belittle me? How much more of her sarcasm can I take? I think maybe it's time to get rid of her...

*

The following week, my phone rings. It's Sub-Inspector Rahman. 'We need you to come in, Mr Alfred.'

My pulse quickens. Is this it? Have I succeeded? Or messed up? 'Is it about the man you arrested? Shyam Davar?'

'We can't discuss that. If you could just make yourself available...'

'All right. I'll be there after work.'

Esra and I try to decipher his tone.

'I don't like it,' she declares. 'It's suspicious.'

'Maybe they just want me to formally identify him?'

'Then why not say so?'

'Look, we handed them Davar on a plate. They wouldn't have arrested him if they didn't have the evidence, would they?'

'Well, you'd better go then, hadn't you?' she says, after a pause.

'Will you come with me?'

'No. You should do it on your own. I'll be here if you need me.'

I'm getting annoyed at Esra's reluctance to be more involved, considering she got me into this whole mess. She was the one who suggested we follow Alia Datta in the first place. And hang around outside her house.

But, as always, I agree.

This will be the last time. I will take control of our relationship. This is classic codependence. I can't take it anymore.

*

'Thanks for coming in, Mr Alfred.'

I look around as they lead me into the interrogation room. It reeks of sweat, fear and desperation. A dim tube-light above us casts flickering, uneven shadows on the stained, peeling walls. On one wall, a faded portrait of a long-forgotten dignitary hangs crookedly, its frame coated in a fine layer of dust. Opposite it, a battered metal cabinet stands precariously, its doors slightly ajar to reveal a clutter of outdated files and miscellaneous evidence bags. Naik gestures me to a creaky wooden table in the centre of the room, its surface marred by countless scratches and cigarette burns.

I sit. 'Very glad to help. So, you got the guy?'

The inspector pulls out a plastic bag with a scarf in it. Sees the recognition on my face.

'You've seen this before?'

'It's the scarf Alia Datta was wearing on the tube the night she died!'

'You're sure?'

'I'd recognize it anywhere.'

The detectives exchange glances.

'Tell us again what happened that evening, Alfred,' says Inspector Naik.

I don't like his overfamiliarity. He should call me sir. 'Why? You've got the guy. Or do you need me to be a witness?'

'Just tell us what happened.'

'All right. We'd been to see a film and...'

'We?' interrupts Sub-Inspector Rahman. 'Who were you with?'

Damn. I've slipped up. Esra will be angry with me.

'Sorry. I meant I'd been to see a film.'

'Which movie?'

'James Bond. *Spectre*. It was an IMAX print. At Eros Cinema.'

'Please continue.'

I repeat what happened. Again, omitting following the women.

'And you didn't get out at Bandra?' says the inspector.

'No, I went straight home.'

Silence falls over the room like a blanket. Then, the sergeant produces two photographs. Lays them on the table.

'We have you on CCTV, following Alia Datta and Shanti Damyata out of Bandra railway station.'

I stare at the damning photos. My world unravels. 'That could be anybody,' I protest weakly.

'We believe it's you.'

'It's not.'

'Would you be prepared to give us a DNA sample?'

I don't like the way this interview's going. Panic claws at my throat. Where's Esra? Why did I come alone? Am I in trouble? I mean, they have the scarf now. What more can they want?

'Why?'

'Just so we can eliminate you from our inquiries.'

'I'd prefer not to. I thought you had your man. Why did

you arrest Davar? Was the scarf the murder weapon? Was it strangulation?'

'Do you know Mr Davar?'

'No.'

'Never been to his house?'

'How would I know where he lives?'

The sergeant takes out another CCTV image.

'Isn't this you in front of Signia Pearl five days ago at 6.12 in the evening?'

My stomach turns to jelly. My face is clearly visible in the picture. How do I explain my quest to ensure they have evidence against Davar so they can get him for what he's done?

My only option is to brazen it out.

'That's not me.'

I hear how pathetic my voice sounds. Why the hell is Esra not here with me? I need her.

'You didn't break Mr Davar's car window?'

'Why would I do that?'

'Maybe to distract him so you could enter his flat?'

These guys aren't idiots.

'Why would I do that?' I repeat.

'You tell us.'

'Davar is a sexual predator. He was a partner. Alia Datta was his subordinate. Women need protecting from men like him.'

'Actually, all three were in a consensual relationship. We've released him without charge,' says the inspector.

Perverts.

'I'd like to go now, please. This is getting tiresome.'

They exchange looks.

'Thank you for coming in.'

*

Back home, Esra says, 'I told you it was a terrible idea to call the police. Now they suspect you.'

'They have no proof. Davar is the likely killer. I'll tell them it was your genius idea to follow them.'

'They won't believe you. The CCTV only caught you, not me.'

'But it's the truth! You started the whole thing. Going after them that way. This is all your fault!'

Her next words cut deep. 'I can't be with someone this careless. We're done. That's what you wanted, right?'

Reality slips away like sand through my fingers. What am I without her? 'Please,' I beg. 'I can't do this without you. I need you. You're part of me.' A movie line pops into my head. 'You complete me.'

'I'm sorry, Alfred. It's too messy. You're better off flying solo.'

And she's gone, leaving only silence.

I was lying to myself when I said I needed to be free of her. I can't bear the loneliness. Her absence is like a black hole in the corner of every room I enter.

*

Weeks blur together until they come for me. No more asking politely for my DNA. They just take it. It had clung like an imperceptible deadly spore to the scarf I'd rubbed against Davar's clothes in the hamper to get his DNA on it.

Without Esra there to advise me, it's a relief to confess.

I tell them how Esra had whispered in front of Alia Datta's flat. 'She screws men and women. But she would never give you a single glance. You're just a nobody on the Mumbai local. Are you going to live your life as a nobody? Or will you finally do something? Ring the bell. Hand her the scarf she dropped. Maybe she'll ask you in for a coffee. Maybe your luck will change. Then you won't need me anymore. This is your chance. Do it! Like you should have with Shireen.'

I tell them how my indecision ebbed as my confidence flowed.

I tell them how Alia Datta was still in her mini skirt when she opened the door. How I dumbly held out her scarf. How she thanked me. How she could hardly refuse when I asked for a glass of water. I was so inoffensive. How could I be a danger?

How she laughed when I moved towards her.

How soft the skin on her neck was under the ragged claws of my fingers.

How wide her eyes were when she screamed.

How Esra went quiet after Alia Datta died.

*

I've been alone in this wasteland of a jail for three months now. The walls press in, suffocating. What despair and desolation they must have seen. The machinery of justice is relentless. It took me in, chewed me up, and has now spat me out in this place that has been forgotten by time, a constant reminder of the dank underbelly of this city. But maybe this is what I deserve. After all, what am I, but the loser Esra always said I was.

I need her desperately. But she doesn't answer, however much I beg her to return.

She's my other half.

She completes me.

But she won't speak. She's punishing me. She does this sometimes.

I turn the light off. Try to sleep.

The bunk is hard.

I'm cold.

A fly buzzes around me. I don't swat it. I'm glad of the company.

A whisper.

'Miss me?'

My heart soars.

'Esra. You're back?'

My words echo in the empty cell.

'I can't stay away from my Alfie for long. You know that. We are one, after all.'

'Oh, Esra. Never leave me again.'

'Never. I love you.'

Scalding tears fall down my cheek.

Relief drowns me.

# OUT OF MERCY

## *Nev March*

'Still no reply?' Officer Punit Rai asked, wrinkling his forehead.

He waited for the woman's answer, standing on the front porch of the single-family home owned by an Indian couple, Magan and Champa Patel. Since Edison was overcrowded, immigrants were flocking to other towns in the New Jersey suburbs, eager for a slice of the American dream. Local police dispatchers often summoned Punit, a second-generation Indian American, to attend 'domestic' calls: community policing, understanding of the local customs, et cetera.

On the landscaped flagstone walkway, the tall Indian woman shook her head. 'I've called my sister twenty times. My brother-in-law too, and the kids. Where could they be?'

She'd said this before, when she had called the township police and begged them to check on her relatives, an almost incoherent torrent of worry.

Punit said, 'Mrs Nayar, when did you last speak with them?'

She pushed strands of her long hair from her face. 'I told you. Sunday night. Champa calls every day, or I call. Monday, she didn't pick up. Her phone could be broken or misplaced or even stolen. But all of their phones? I texted, called her kids! No answer!'

From the squad car, he had dialled all four numbers as well, to no avail.

'And you were on good terms?'

'Of course!' She jerked her head towards the door. 'Can't you open it?'

He peered at the panel at the entrance. 'It's a code lock. Know the number?'

She shook her head. 'Champa's husband Magan wanted privacy.'

Despondent, she folded her arms over her neat professional attire. Trim, forties, long black hair. She'd returned from a business trip and called the Kingston Police from Philadelphia, then driven up in a white BMW i5. A sweet ride, expensive. She and her husband were architects, and had a firm in Philly.

'Can't file a missing persons' until tomorrow,' he reminded her.

'But something is wrong. They would not have gone out of town without telling me.' She twisted her hands as though she needed to clutch something. 'Please!'

He leaned on the doorbell again. A slow tune sounded dimly through the ornate double-glass door. Expensive thermal glass, in a fancy sun-burst design. A high-end entrance on a modest colonial. He hesitated, reluctant to call the department's locksmith without a strong reason.

Stamping down the three stairs of the front portico, he pushed through the boxwoods and strode around to the back, peering up at the draped windows as he went. The home lay on a manicured lawn, the neighbouring roof visible beyond clusters of azaleas and trees.

At the back, he called to his partner, Constable Arthur Kane, returning from the neighbour's yard, 'Find anything?'

Kane puffed towards him. 'They don't know them. Only see them heading to school in the mornings. No sighting this week.'

'Huh.' Punit started up to the deck behind the house. Indian neighbours would be more inquisitive. When he stopped abruptly, his partner bumped into him, then stepped back with a grunt.

'Look.' Punit pointed. Between pots of basil and sweet mint gaped the shattered rear door, bits of glass clinging with jagged edges. 'Burglary?'

Kane frowned. 'Odd, that. Why not break the lock? Those things are flimsy.'

A trembling voice spoke behind him. 'Oh, Shiv-dev, don't let them be inside.'

'Ma'am,' Punit threw an arm towards Mrs Nayar. 'Don't come in. There's glass all around. Please wait.' *And we don't know what we'll find*, he thought, as he squirmed his hands into latex gloves.

She called, 'The wood. Is the wood piece there?'

When he frowned over his shoulder, she held her hands wide apart. 'They have a wooden rod. Like a baseball bat. It holds the back door closed.'

Sure enough, slotted in the track below the door was a long piece of wood to prevent anyone sliding it open. 'Yeah, it's here. Stay outside!'

He signalled to Kane to call it in, then stepped through the broken door, his fingers loosening the revolver at his waist. Cops often rushed in with itchy fingers, but he was Indian, and this was an Indian house. The sandalwood murti presiding on a side table seemed to approve. Other than shards scattered like sugar cubes over the floor, the kitchen looked untouched. Two pots on the glass cooktop, empty. Three glasses in the shiny metal sink. Warm colours on the wall hangings, touches of vermilion, dancing Hindu gods, voluptuous village belles, colourful elephants and camels. In a large frame, a smiling bride glowed, bedecked in auspicious red, showing the complex curlicues adorning her palms.

Punit went through the lower floor room by room, calling out 'Clear,' hearing Arthur echo the same as he went around another way.

In the front foyer, they came face to face at the foot of a curved staircase. Punit scanned the wall by the door. *No alarm system*. Opening the outer door, he waved to the officers in the squad car which had just pulled up. 'We're checking the other floors.'

Arthur headed upstairs, so Punit pulled open the basement door.

The smell hit him like a punch, putrid and overripe like rotting cheese. Like a sewer. Like something was dead. For a long moment, he stood there, wishing it was different, but the smell prodded him to his duty.

The basement lights were on, so he stepped down carefully, stifling a groan.

Arthur spoke behind him. 'Holy potatoes. What the hell is that smell?'

Punit continued downwards, saying, 'Don't touch the banister.'

'You mean the handrail. What d'ya think? Home invasion?'

Arthur always talked too much when he was agitated. Punit stepped into a comfortably furnished game room and found the missing family.

Side by side on the large sofa before the TV slumped two

boys. The younger looked about five. A Game Boy controller was at his feet. The older lay sideways, his head cushioned by the arm of the sofa, looking upwards. He seemed about twelve. Punit noticed the bullet holes. Head shots, at close range into each boy's temple.

The boys' parents sat on the smaller sofa. Their mother was curled into a foetal position, as though asleep. The father sat upright; the back of his head splattered across the wall behind him. Punit carefully raised his arm. A 9-mm pistol nestled in the father's lap.

Arthur cursed in a steady stream, then scrambled upstairs to summon forensics. Punit examined each corpse and noted their positions, the young family brought together in death. Someone clearly intended for Magan to be considered the culprit. But for the door, Punit would have believed it. The door told another tale.

Since there was nothing else to be done, Punit composed himself and trudged upstairs to give Mrs Nayar the bad news.

She didn't take it well.

'Oh god, it's my fault! I should have known! I should have asked!' She broke into a wild fit of weeping.

He backed away, knowing she could no longer hear him. He'd first got her to call her husband, so someone was hopefully on the way. Mrs Nayar looked ready to keel over, so he seated her at the kitchen table. She wept into her hands as he sighed and pulled out his notebook, jotting down details for his report. Now he just needed to wait for the machinery of the department to arrive.

Every wall was filled with photographs of smiling groups. The family dressed in blue jeans and white shirts, with mountains behind them. Another of the four in traditional attire, at some family wedding. In red sweaters, by a Christmas tree.

His gaze fell on a poster of a large group arranged on the home's curved staircase – about thirty people, dressed in a riot of colours, grinning in their new year's hats. A large family, like his own. But few Indian families wanted their sons to become cops. Doctors, lawyers and engineers were preferred. Nurses, IT professionals and architects were fine. Plumbers and electricians were not. Nor policemen.

An hour later, forensics brought their bags of photographic equipment and took fingerprints. Arthur's and Punit's were on file, so they could be excluded. Punit went through the steps mechanically, pondering on Mrs Nayar's words. '*It's my fault!*'

When her husband arrived, Punit explained the situation. The shocked architect seemed too numb to ask questions, so once he gave his prints, Punit let him take his sobbing wife home.

Turning the site over to the homicide team, he went back to the station and wrote his report, keeping it simple. Then he went home to his mother's vegetarian *sabzi* dinner.

He ate four parathas, surprised at how famished he'd been. When his mother smiled and offered another, he patted his growing gut and shook his head. Then, before his sisters and his chaotic cousins arrived, he slipped upstairs to crack open his laptop.

'Home invasion kills Indian family in New Jersey.' The murders were already on a few local news sites, with titbits of ancillary information, a *bhel-puri* of assorted facts and speculation.

Punit read them carefully, making notes as he scrolled. The deceased couple were both IT professionals. He jotted down their places of employment. A cousin who lived nearby said Magan used to play poker with some friends, but had stopped about six months ago. The cousin's wife had reported that

Magan was a loving father, citing an expensive cruise he had arranged for his wife's birthday. 'He surprised her at work! Just walked in and waved the cruise tickets in her face!' she claimed.

'She was a devoted wife,' said a neighbour.

The same neighbours who didn't know anything, who only saw them leave for school? Devoted mother, devoted sister. Bought presents for teachers, made food for the temple, gave donations for school events.

The boys were 'brilliant, so full of promise!' said teachers at the local school. The kids had been six and sixteen. Punit had misjudged their ages because they looked younger in death. The teenager Sumin liked math and soccer and was on the local swim team. The younger one, Sarosh was learning violin and chess. Chess. It didn't surprise him. Well, it was homicide's problem now.

Except it wasn't. First his parents and siblings, then every relative and friend, Indian and American, called or visited to 'get the real story' from him.

'It's being investigated, Surya Aunty,' Punit explained for the fiftieth time. The long pause on the line sounded distinctly dissatisfied. Surya Aunty wasn't his aunt, but his mother's friend. Out of respect, all Indian elders were called uncle or aunty.

'You're a good boy, Punit,' she said in a grumpy voice, and cut the line, just as his mobile showed another incoming call.

'Yes?'

A familiar voice spoke softly, 'It's Anandi Nayar. Have you learnt anything?'

No, it wasn't a disgruntled grandaunt demanding, 'Have some respect! Have you learned nothing from your parents?' He recalled the dark-haired Mrs Nayar sobbing uncontrollably, her outburst: '*It's my fault!*'

'Mrs Nayar, can we meet?'

Settling upon a local diner for their meeting, he called to his sister, 'Taking your car, Kamini!' and snatched the keys off their hook. It was Saturday, and he wasn't in uniform. But that instinctive phrase – why hadn't he put it in his report?

Although it was only 8 p.m., the diner was almost empty. Americans dined earlier, he knew.

Mrs Nayar was waiting in a booth, large eyes anxiously watching the entrance. He slid into the seat across, concerned at her dishevelled look, crumpled clothes and red-raw eyes. Was this grief, or something else?

He offered his condolences and made small talk while they ordered coffees, then got down to brass tacks.

'Did you see the house again, after, uh...' he trailed off, searching for a neutral word for bodies or corpses, then went on, 'after they were taken away?'

She answered demurely. 'Yes, the homicide detective asked me to check if anything was stolen. I walked through the house with him.'

'And?' He searched her downcast face.

She shook her head. 'They had a gold *murti*. Still in the dining room. Laptops and phones were all there. Champa's jewellery was in her drawer. The casual stuff. Rest would be in their safe. My husband is the executor of their wills...'

'Not you?'

She gave him a look. 'You are Indian, no?'

'My parents migrated forty years ago.'

Yeah, he thought, husbands managed the cash, so they would be executors and trustees. Mrs Nayar was an entrepreneur, but that wouldn't count. She was a woman.

He came to the point. 'You said it was your fault. What did you mean?'

She pulled back, shaking her head. 'When did I...?'

'Look, Mrs Nayar. If you want this solved, I need to know.' Why did he have such a knot in his belly, he wondered. He wasn't supposed to be here. It wasn't his case. Homicide would scoff and glower at him, a lowly constable daring to interview a possible suspect. '*Who'd you think you are, huh? Matlock? More like Columbo!*'

She said, 'Okay, I'll tell you. Magan asked us for a loan. But Raj, my husband didn't like it.'

'She's *your* sister, yes? Not his?'

She waved him off. 'That's not why. Actually, Raj said yes.'

Startled, Punit said, 'So you gave him a loan? Did your sister know?'

'We didn't. That is, we agreed to pay directly, for whatever Magan needed. But he wouldn't tell us what it was for. He didn't come back to us, so we thought, okay, he doesn't need the loan after all.'

She chewed on her lower lip, eyes squeezed in a plea.

'What else?'

She grimaced. 'It is probably nothing. Raj says I read too much into these things. He said it could not matter.'

Punit kept his manner neutral. 'Let me decide that.'

'Okay, see. We all meet every weekend. Parties are usually at my house. It's bigger, comfortable, right? We migrated decades ago, so we have more friends. They just came four years back, so they don't know many people.'

Nodding, he waited while she worked her way to the point.

'It was many months ago. Champa and I had made dinner. I came to find Magan, to bring him to the dinner table. We like to eat all together, us, kids, Baba and Mammeeji. You must be knowing this, yes? In your family?'

He refused to be distracted, saying, 'Baba and Mammee. Your in-laws?'

'Yes. They were all there, and I went to get Magan. He was playing some game on his phone, so I just interrupted – "Magan, come!" What did I know? It looked like some timepass game.'

'And?'

'He looked up when I spoke. But when he saw his phone he said, "*Mar gaya*!" He looked so shocked, as though he might faint. Staring at the mobile.'

*Mar gaya*—I'm dead. Punit leaned forward. 'Was someone calling him? Texting him?'

'I don't think so. Music from the game was still playing.'

'When was this?'

'Months ago. But after that, they stopped coming to our house. I felt really bad, but what did I do? Maybe I should not have called him like that, but he was just playing a game! Why take it so badly?'

Punit wrote in his notebook, then asked, 'Was this before he asked for the loan?'

'Oh, much before that! Months ago.'

Did she know about Magan's weekly card game? Punit asked, 'Did your husband and Magan still play poker, after that?'

She pulled back, frowning. 'Raj doesn't have time to play, but my brother plays in that group. Let me call him.'

Punit listened as she called her brother and spoke in Gujarati. Her tone and demeanour showed a close relationship between the siblings.

Hanging up, she said, 'He says Magan hadn't joined a poker night for the last six months. Said he was saving for the kids' college funds. It surprised my brother because both Magan and Champa are doing so well at work.'

Funds. College funds. Punit tapped the pencil on his notebook then thanked her. When he began to rise, she grabbed his arm.

'Punit, please. Who did this? I need to know! I cannot sleep or eat or even cook! I just keep imagining...who would do this to them? Why?'

'We will find out, Mrs Nayar.'

'Please. We have a security system, but now Raj has added cameras everywhere. He thinks someone is targeting Indians.'

Punit had read the torrent of speculation in the Indian web-magazines. These murders had shaken the Indian community far beyond New Jersey.

He could only repeat, 'Have patience, Mrs Nayar. Again, I'm sorry for your loss.'

The phrase did not hold much meaning, he thought. Platitudes. It's what you said. Confronted with the deaths of her little nephews, the laughing sister who grew up with her, who called every day, the words had no weight at all.

And then, nothing happened. The next day, and the next. Punit did traffic duty and gave out tickets. His sisters looked up each evening when he got home, the same question echoed in their faces. Relatives called, made small talk, then waited, their expectant silence a disappointed rebuke. So, the next time his mother chatted with some aunt and offered him the phone, he waved it away, scowling. His father sighed and patted his back, murmuring.

A week later, Punit found himself standing at the desk of the homicide detective assigned to the case. Blake Gordon was the only black officer in the rural NJ county, and he had the reputation of being a good cop, a professional. White haired and grizzled, he came from New York and wore jeans to work. No one remarked upon it, but young officers sometimes grumbled that he seemed to show up only when it was nice out.

'He does his job. Clears cases,' the sheriff had barked. 'How 'bout you do yours?'

After making a little chit-chat, Punit said, 'The Patel case. Got any leads?'

Gordon grinned at him. 'You want to work homicide? C'mon over.'

'We don't get even three cases a year,' Punit said. 'Doubt they will add another headcount.'

'We–ell, I won't be here forever,' said Gordon, taking a stack off the chair near him. 'Sit yourself down and tell me what you got.'

Punit found himself leafing through his notebook and narrating what he'd learned.

'Uh huh,' said the old detective. 'All right, yeah. What else?' After Punit had spilled everything he knew, he closed his notepad and waited.

Gordon said, 'Anything else?'

'No, but, uh, what are you working on? Can I help?'

Gordon's smile grew. 'So polite. Gotta learn to question, kid. Gotta be pushy. Don't ask, don't get, see?'

Punit straightened up. 'Yes, sir. Right. What have you found?'

'Sir, is it? Nah, call me Blake. What my mama called me. Just Blake.' He took a file off the top of his pile and handed it over. 'Read that, tell me what you see.'

The forensics file! Punit pulled it close and examined the reports.

'No fingerprints other than the family.' He turned the page and went on. 'Toxicology. The kids had ingested diphenhydramine hydrochloride – that's a sedative, right? And pseudoephedrine. They were on drugs?'

'Nah. Sudafed. For cold.' Gordon took the file and whistled. 'Twelve tablets worth. Each.'

Punit stared. 'The ME says that?'

'Nah, my mother-in-law.' Gordon handed back the file, his face sardonic. 'Look at the milligrams. Do the math.'

Punit retorted, 'Right. But that's a lot. Both the kids took that much?'

'Crushed in a cocktail of Benadryl. Here, skip over to the financials, will ya?'

Punit flipped the page to the subpoenaed records from First National.

'Wow. Two hundred grand?'

'Keep going.'

'Wait. There's a hundred and fifty thousand. And another eighty thousand. But they come in and go out the same day.'

'Came from TrueLight Investors.'

Punit recognized the name. 'That's a broker. My parents use the same guy!'

Gordon nodded at the file. 'Read the rest.'

'But...' Punit flipped pages back and forth. 'You got the footage without a warrant?'

Gordon looked at him. 'Yeah. Store gave it up. No sweat.' He seemed to be waiting.

Punit read through the rest of the file, absorbing details, each piece adding to the scale tipping in his mind.

'But Mrs Nayar...' he began, then found himself at a loss for words.

'Yeah, someone needs to tell her.'

Punit searched his face. 'Someone? You mean...'

'I mean you, kid. I'll come with, but it might be easier coming from you. The facts are there—' he waved a hand at the file. 'But she doesn't need to know everything. You want to join homicide? This is the job. Investigate, get the facts, tell the family.'

Punit shuddered, then straightened and went to get his uniform jacket. An hour later they were sitting on a plush blue sofa in front of Anandi Nayar, her face drooping, her worn eyes begging for answers.

'Would you like some tea?' she offered, her fingers gripping the chair to rise.

'No, ma'am,' Gordon replied. 'We've got, ah, an update on the case.'

'You know who did it?'

He nodded slowly and looked at Punit.

As they'd planned, Punit went over the toxicology results in simple terms.

Mrs Nayar blinked, confusion twisting her features as she listened. 'So, Champa and the kids were drugged? By whom?'

Instead of answering, Punit said, 'The tox report shows that Magan Patel was not, though he had consumed a lot of whiskey.' Did she understand that this was significant?

'So they didn't know...Champa didn't see...'

Punit nodded. 'We think the children were shot first, then Champa – and then her husband.'

'But who did it? Why? Did you catch the intruders?'

Punit glanced at Gordon and read the go-ahead in his solemn look. They had argued over how much information to share up front.

'Mrs Nayar, there were no intruders. We think Magan shot the children and Champa, went upstairs and bashed in the door from the outside, then shot himself.'

Dark eyes wide, she stared, open-mouthed.

Her voice rose as she cried, 'What are you saying? He loved

them! I don't believe this. You can't find the culprits, so you are putting it on Magan?'

Punit put up his hands. 'Please, Mrs Nayar. He was in trouble. His bank records show it.' Cutting off her protest, he hurried to explain. 'In the last three months, he cleaned out their savings account, then sold multiple investments. He even applied for a second mortgage and was declined – not enough equity in the house.'

She shot to her feet. 'Then he was being blackmailed! He was the victim!'

Gordon said, 'Ma'am, the payments. They were all made out to CapitalMarketFunUSA.'

She stared at him blankly.

Gordon's baritone voice was gentle. 'That's a casino. Online gambling. It's a phone app.'

Her gasp cut the silence. She covered her mouth, then fell into the chair as though her feet had suddenly gone numb.

'Phone. A phone app. But it was a game! Just a game, with beeping and music!' Her voice rose then fell silent. She dropped her head into her hands, shaking.

Long moments later she looked up, her face ravaged. 'But why? Why shoot the little ones? Why kill Champa? They were quarrelling on and off, but she did not know about this, I'm sure of that. Gambling losses.' She pleaded, 'You said he sold their investments. If he paid off the losses, why would he kill her?'

How little we can do for those who remain, the families, the survivors, Punit thought. He said, 'We have served the casino a subpoena, but they're incorporated in Delaware. It takes time. It's likely Magan owed a lot more.'

'Maybe *they* killed him, and Champa, and the kids!' Her voice shook, her gaze aching for another explanation.

Punit winced. 'There were no other fingerprints on the pistol, only his. He bought it a week ago, paid cash. We have CCTV footage from the gun store. It is clearly Magan.'

'But why?' she whispered, voice breaking, her face leached of blood. 'He loved the boys, Sarosh and Sumin. He adored Champa. Why did he kill them?'

In the long silence, Gordon caught Punit's glance, prompting him onwards. The answer they'd prepared was, '*We can't know what was in his mind*,' but now the words stuck in Punit's throat like a dry, week-old *bajri-roti*.

Instead, Punit said, 'Mrs Nayar, we don't know but...possibly it was so that they wouldn't know, wouldn't have to answer questions, about his debts. The knowing looks, pity and scorn, I think...he wanted to spare them that.'

Her breath scraped the quiet of the room. Tears welled and dripped over her cheeks unchecked.

'The fool! The coward!' she raged, then softened. She shook her head, a slow pendulum of sorrow. 'If only he had trusted us enough. We would have paid it off, and told no one else. Champa would have forgiven him. The poor misguided man. Out of mercy. He killed them out of mercy.'

Punit avoided Gordon's questioning gaze. What right did he have to judge? If it gave her comfort, why not leave it be? Murder left survivors with aching wounds, the deepest from unexplained loss. What of Magan – what agonies had he suffered, what self-condemnation? Crippled by debts or regrets, he'd preferred oblivion for all those he loved. He was wrong, but he would never know it – only the living learn and grow. His wife and kids would never have that chance.

# CRIME AND CRIME

*Tanuj Solanki*

Back in Baded, when I was still a boy of twelve or thirteen, there was that time when my father had disappeared on us and I had had to work in the fields, where the Chaudhri's daughter, a few years older than me, sometimes made me remove my shorts and giggled at the changing shape of my thing, and when a couple of months later two men walked in on us and caught us playing that game of ours, a curious one for me but a delightful one for Mimmi (that was her home-name), there was, as anyone who's ever lived in a village can imagine, a big bhasad which turned into a terror for our basti even before the sun had set, fire and gunshots and vile things said about shoving in long spiky things up our holes, a riot so loud and scary that my mother, my poor, poor mother, while shivering and blabbering and tearily slapping me and abusing me (and abusing the world and my father and my three sisters) with words I didn't know she'd known, gave me some notes from a small rusted box (three hundred and fifty rupees, I remember) and handed me half a packet of Parle-G and asked me to run away from the jungle-facing side of the basti, to run as fast as I could and to never look back, which is what I did, and which is what led me, after a few stops and situations that I have all but forgotten, to working in Gurgaon, firstly for four years at a flowers and bouquet shop, where, apart from bearing Mausaji's drunken kisses on chosen nights (the nights of leftover carnations, whose petals he used to squash into his vodka), I learnt the use of knives and scissors and tapes, and then a couple of years at a basement workshop that made wooden frames for photos and paintings, where saws and hammers and nails became my friends. In all this time, there was nowhere for me to sleep except at work, and while at the first one it was the sweet sickly smell of rotting flowers, like crotch and crushed roses and wet foam, that gave me a runny nose and watery eyes, at the frame-making workshop the same effect was continued by the varnish and thinners that we used on the wood, such that in all those years I felt that I was living under some endless curse of prickly sadness, and whoever met me met a young boy always with a scrunched-up face and teary eyes, with his shirtsleeve glazed with nosemuck, and with no nicknames more worthy for him than *Sinnku* or *Rotadu*, one about the unstoppable nose and the other about the unceasing eyes, and this poor boy could do nothing but respond to these names, which became mine as much as my own name was mine, as became the case with some of the other names too, except, perhaps, 'Chhotu bhenchod', which was what Mausaji liked to call me all through my time with him, a time which ended one late carnation night, with a pair of stem-clipping scissors going a deep way inside Mausaji's belly, only the brass finger-holes sticking out, the iron part having taken in some of the sweater and the shirt with it, and when I pulled out the thing the next moment, there oozed not just red blood and yellow goo but fluffs of wool and nylon too, and as I looked up with my runny eyes I saw all the terror of the world narrowing into Mausaji's eyes and his face scrunching up with shock and pain, and back down his sweater became a glorious pink flower, the fastest-growing flower in the world, a flower that dripped its juice too, its beauty so sudden and reeky that I, its harvester, couldn't bear the sight of it and ran away with my four items of clothing and all the cash I could find in the shop, my nose and eyes turning to taps on blurry night-time Gurgaon roads and in my mind the image of my poor, poor mother, once again asking me to run away as fast as I could and to never look back, and me desiring nothing more than to set fire to the whole city, to turn all its flowers to ash. Mausaji didn't die of those scissors, something that I learnt three years later at an open-air market for second-hand winter clothing, where I wanted to steal at least a jerkin for myself, and where I saw him, body thinned to a skeleton, hair nearly all gone, shoulder frame askew, trundling from stall to stall in search of a sweater and being hesitant about bargaining, which was the worst thing to be hesitant about in that place, that place which was teeming with all kinds of us that evening, all desperate kinds, fruit-sellers and construction workers, mistris and toilet cleaners and food deliverers, pickpockets and thieves, waiters and cooks and security guards, and, I am sure, a few murderers and fugitives too, a place where every last rupee mattered and had to get for the holder enough warmth to survive the cold days and nights ahead, something that looked to be impossible for Mausaji given his horrid state, and so I walked up to him, not so much out of pity or good feeling, it must be said, but out of the shock of knowing that I wasn't a murderer yet, that all the nightmares about fast-growing flowers that I had suffered were now to vanish, and I offered him a namaste, to which he responded with that old dense terror in his eyes and a nervous shuffling of the feet, something that made him fall to the ground like a sack of firewood, and it was only after I had helped him stand up and had reassured him with some kind words that his breathing returned to normal and he looked like he could at least survive that night, though, later, at a theka that wasn't too far from the market and where he paid for our drinks, as he showed me the scar that I had drawn on his tummy, shiny and brown like a rotting leaf, his breathing turned jagged again and he briefly got in those dirty eyes of his a spike of terror, a look that I would in time come to love in other people's eyes, before turning to utter sadness and telling me that he was going to die by the time the winter was over, maybe by Holi, or maybe a few weeks after Holi, but definitely before the hottest days of summer, when the flowers sold dearer at the wholesale market and the business dropped. That was my last time seeing Mausaji, and this was not because I hadn't tried to meet him later, for a week before Holi I had gone to his shop with Golu, my only friend from the frame-making workshop, who had convinced me that if Mausaji was someone who had kept me alive, albeit cruelly, like an animal, and for his own selfish reasons, I needed to forgive him and let the past be past, and even though I was suspicious of this idea, of letting the past be past, for what else was there to life except the past, you were what you were because of it, and if you'd been born in a seth's house you'd be rich too, you'd be hanging expensive pictures on walls rather than making the frames for them in dingy basements, you'd be fucking the girls who wear tight jeans and show all that skin inside malls, you'd be spending all your summers in air-conditioned rooms, or even if it was just that your father hadn't abandoned you and you'd continued school back in Baded and had never had to go to the fields, had never been touched by Mimmi, had never had to run away from home, had never had to deal with Mausaji and his flowers, then maybe you'd have found a way to get rich too, maybe you'd have studied enough to get a job in one of those glass buildings, those tall glass buildings, maybe you'd have a car for yourself, why not, why the hell not, and so, even though I was suspicious of this whole idea, of ignoring a thing that lived with you as much as your own breath did, I allowed myself to do what Golu wanted me to do and went to Mausaji's shop with him, only to find it shuttered, which had been the case, we learned from the boy from the next shop, for more than a month, and which led me to do something that Golu teases me about to this day: I squatted on the floor and cried like a child. As we walked out of the market, which was one of those standard Gurgaon markets, really, two floors high, painted a fading red, placed squat inside areas where people with cars lived, and housing the kind of shops one didn't find in the malls, tailor shops and mobile-repair shops and kebab shops and sweet shops and shops for fruits and flowers and school supplies and other such things, I decided that I wanted to cause some damage somewhere and said so to Golu, who asked if I had anything in my pockets, and who when told that I had a little hammer with me got quite excited, probably more excited than me, and soon we were roaming in the galis around Sector 46, looking for a car to smash the windows of or a motorcycle to break the mirror of, but searching most of all for a quiet gali where we could do our little misdeed in peak afternoon and run away unaffected. We had tried this sort of thing twice before but had let fear get the better of us on both occasions, the first one inside Ardee Mall, where the security guard, one

Kheer Singh, a friend of Golu's, had let us in oblivious to our plans to shatter a glass pane or break something inside the toilets, a plan we let go of only because Golu spotted the cameras and couldn't stop thinking about the police, and we ended up standing on the top floor while holding hands and counting girls; and the second such attempt was in a network of galis in Sector 51, where a bunch of dogs turned their attention to us just as I was about to slash a car's front tyre, making me throw a knife at them for distraction before we ran into the next gali and stood next to two security guards for safety. That afternoon in Sector 46, though, the one where we'd gone to meet Mausaji, we eventually found a gali that was perfect, with no person walking by and the lone dog too old and friendly to care, and started to discuss, in excited whispers, which car among the many parked there on either side of the street would satisfy us the most, which car appeared the newest, the most expensive, the most loved, and Golu, who was more informed about cars than I was or ever could be, pointed to a big one with his eyes, a big black one, which from up close looked as big as a house, a rich, comfortable house, with seats so full of foam one could imagine sinking into them, and so it was with some happiness that I pulled the hammer from my pocket and brought its pointy part down on the car's window glass, causing a thin crack, as thin as a hair, seeing which Golu couldn't contain his excitement and grabbed the hammer from my hand, which he brought down on the same thin crack with all the force his hand could muster, and the glass shattered in a great way, breaking into little pieces that looked like diamonds and large pieces that looked like congealed glue, most of which fell inside the car, though it's true that the sound of this shattering disappointed us a bit, it was too muted, too muffled, almost as if the glass had been sad and had given in to our blows sighingly, and it was this disappointment that made us forget that the best thing to do after doing what we had done would be to run away, to run away and have a cup of hot tea at some roadside stall and gloat about what we had done, and instead we remained rooted to our spot, almost as if we were waiting for something more to happen, some bhasad, some drama, or some acknowledgement, at least, of what had just been done, and we kept looking at the shattered glass and at each other, not knowing what the next step needed to be, till the hollering of a fat man, who had suddenly emerged from behind the tall gates of the house next to the car, broke the state we had found ourselves in. Golu dropped the hammer to the ground and ran away, and I, certain that I didn't want to leave the hammer behind (I rued losing the knife still), bent to pick it up, which proved to be the wrong move, for by the time I was back straight again, my collar was in the fat man's hands and he had lifted me off the ground by a couple of inches, and my back rubbed against the car's window such that some of the glass that was still stuck to the frame tore my shirt and cut me, and in the next second the man hurled the same abuses at me that I had heard back in Baded, with some spittle from his mouth landing on my nose and cheeks and chin, and there was nothing left for me to do than to raise my right hand, the one holding the hammer, and bring it down on the man's sweaty pate, and as soon as I did that the man's grip relented and I landed back on my feet, and on the ground there formed some circles of red, the man's blood dripping down and spotting the mud, and he looked at me with the same look of terror I had seen in Mausaji's eyes, and I swung the hammer at him again, landing it this time on his left temple, or somewhere close to the left temple, and the man staggered on his feet for a small second before falling down in a heap, as if he were dead.

Before I go any further in the story, before I narrate how, on the same evening, Golu convinced me to try a different kind of life, and before I get into how that life, with its many dangers and delights, began, I must change something in what I have already told you, I must make a small correction, I must tell you that what I have earlier called *the wrong move* (the picking up of the hammer from the ground, which allowed the fat man to grab my collar and led to what it led to) was not the wrong move at all, that it was, in truth, the right move, the best move ever, for it revealed to me two things that I had not known about myself, two very essential things: firstly, that I was a man who loved his tools as much as anything, and, secondly, that I was, at heart, a bad person, one of those who don't need the shadows to do their dark work, one of those who are unafraid, who can go to any lengths to grab what is yours and make it their own, or to give you a whack on your head for no good reason, none other than satisfying an itch that only they can understand, and, consequently, one of those who aren't able to think too much about the damage they cause or the pain they spread in the world, for they are children of damage and pain themselves, and the flame in their hearts, the flame that keeps the sane sane or the flame that is the good light inside man, has long burnt out, and the remaining wick is nothing but a blackened tangle of grimy malice, a tangle that invites black fires and cold, cold mayhem, that over a length of time comes to learn the utility of darkness, too, and begins to bide its time in narrow unlit lanes or deserted parking lots or the sides of thekas, or breaks into flats and apartments, helping itself to whatever bounty comes to hand, and spending it all in a crazed rush so that there is every reason to seek the next fix immediately, to go out and invent an occasion for trouble, someone else's.

Back, then, to the evening of the day when we went out to meet Mausaji and ended up smashing a car's window and a man's head, and back, thus, to the tea shop close to our frame-making workshop, where, after dealing with my complaint about him running away from the scene without as much as a glance in my direction, Golu told me that a man like me, who was good with sharp things as well as blunt things, should explore a different line of work, something that brought in more money, by which he meant the work of opening locks and sneaking inside shops and other places. I told him that he was being stupid, that picking locks wasn't the same thing as clipping flowers or making picture frames, and I added that it wasn't even the same thing as pushing a sharp thing inside a tummy or making a blunt thing fall on a head, all of which he agreed to in silence, before the two of us started talking about the scenes of a film that we had watched together a few days back, when we were delivering a set of frames to a shop in Sector 41 and the owner let us sit with him for a while, and on the small TV affixed in a corner of the shop there were four men in dark clothes robbing a house, and they were talking to each other through hand gestures, and at one point the lock-picker among them put his ear close to the door of a safe that contained all the maal, and we watched him moving the lock's dials ever so slowly, ever so carefully, with all the skill and patience in the world, till something inside the safe clicked and the thing opened by itself and a gleaming heap of jewels and cash bundles showed itself to the robbers, who celebrated mutely for a second, with pumped fists and soundless claps, and then got to shoving all the riches into the bags they had brought with them. 'But if you have a big hammer and a big iron rod,' Golu said while signalling for two more cups of chai, 'then you don't need all that drama, and anyway in the shops I'm talking about, there are no safes, and none of those round locks either. Haven't you noticed those drawers they keep their money in?' After our next round of chai arrived and we were both halfway done with it, I told Golu that he was right, that there was no harm in trying anyway, and I asked him how much money it would cost for us to rent a room of our own, and he mentioned a certain amount, and I said that we should at least try and earn that much money if we were to do this thing, to which he responded by saying that we would need some practice first, some way of learning each other's ways, and the first option we discussed was the front office of the workshop, where, by Golu's estimate, we would find about half of the money that we wanted to make, and then we discussed some other options from among the shops around the workshop, but ultimately all these options were rejected by me, because for me practice was a stupid thing to consider when it was going to be as daring as the real thing, besides which there was the fact that there was no point in going for small amounts so close to where we lived, and so, after some more thinking and yet another round of chai, both of which really led us nowhere, we tiredly decided to go for the same store where we had watched the film, convincing ourselves through the argument that the store was far away from the workshop and yet was familiar. It was only at night, as we were sleeping next to each other inside the workshop, with eight men snoring beside us, that it occurred to us that no shopkeeper would leave cash in their shop overnight, that it just wouldn't make sense to do that, which was further confirmed in our minds when I told Golu that even Mausaji, who had me sleeping inside his shop, took the cash home every night, unless there wasn't much to take home, or unless it was one of those carnation nights when he allowed himself to be carefree, which all meant that there was seldom more than a thousand rupees inside the flower shop after nine in the night, which was usually the time when Mausaji brought down the shutters and locked me inside. We slept sadly that night, and we were sad for the next few days, till the day of Holi, when, under the influence of a pouch of desi that I took from a kirana store owner in exchange for two frames I'd stolen from the workshop, I told Golu that we had been thinking about the whole thing wrongly. 'The shop owner takes the cash with him, yes,' I said, 'so we have no need to enter the shop. We catch the man outside it, after he has drawn the shutters, when his pocket is bulging with all that he's made in the day, when he's thinking of what he's going to eat for dinner, or how he's going to make himself warm next to his wife. That's when we catch him, that's when I show him the hammer, and it's good if he gives the cash to us without a fight, and it's better, if you ask me, if he refuses to give it and I set his skull right for him. As for all that lock-picking and lock-smashing that you see me doing, we should do that with shops that have good stuff inside, don't you think? We should do that with shops that have...' and here I paused for a moment to bring my thoughts to the same speed as my tongue, 'we should do that with shops that have watches, or jewellery, or maybe lots and lots of other things, like shops that have clothes. Fine, fine clothes, like jeans and other stuff.' Golu agreed with all of this at once, and the very next evening, armed with a knife and a hammer, and having stored our few belongings with Kheer Singh at Ardee Mall (we hoped our efforts would bear fruit and we would not have to return to the workshop), we set out to loot the shop owner in Sector 41, the very same one who had let us watch those scenes from a film, and ended up reaching the market an hour in advance, owing to which we had enough time to have paani puri and then to walk around the market for a while and make a mental list of the kind of shops it would be beneficial to break into, a list from which we decided to exclude ATMs, though not without an argument, for ATMs seemed to Golu as good as any other shop for our purposes, whereas to me there remained something off about a place that housed nothing but a machine with money inside it. Eventually, at about 9.30 in the night, the shop owner pulled his shutter down and we took to following him closely, not knowing the right moment to pounce on him, and beginning to realize that our plan had this one simple problem, in that it assumed that the shop owner would, by himself, walk to a place suitable for our approach, which did not seem like it would happen in our very first attempt at this thing, given that the man walked a busy path towards a plot not too far from the market, a plot where his car was parked along with many other cars, and a well-lit plot it was, with four to five men standing at a nearby paan stall and loudly discussing the change of some government somewhere, and it became clear to me that there would be no time for a discussion of any sort, that there would be no time to show our weapons and ask for money and reason with the man and then wait to see whether or not he agreed to give it to us, and that our interaction with him needed to be swift, and silencing. I took the knife from Golu, so that both the weapons were with me, and told him to wait five paces away from the group of men, so that if there were to be a noise from the man I was about to hurt, Golu could try to delay the other men from coming to his help, and I followed the man, our unlucky shop owner, who'd once let us sit in his air-conditioned shop and watch ten minutes of a film, I followed him as he entered the plot and neared his car, and just as he opened the car's door I grabbed him from behind, his neck in my elbow-hold, such that the only thing he could do with his mouth was gasp for breath, and I hit him on the head with the hammer a few times, till he slumped and became a voiceless thing, and I took from his pockets and his bag all that I could and walked away calmly in Golu's direction, signalling to him that the job was done and we needed to get away. That day we made twenty-one thousand rupees in cash and would have made more had we not gotten too scared about selling the man's phone; the next day we got ourselves a new room; and the day after that, we left the workshop job. My nose and my eyes stopped being watery, and I told Golu never to call me Rotadu again.

We repeated the same bloody business many times, always in new locations, though over time we came to prefer other activities over this one, activities that brought in more money, such as breaking into kothis when the residents were away and we could really take our time checking everything in the house, or showing a knife to a woman in an unlit area and asking her to give us her handbag, which the woman did without as much as a whimper and which left us, on more than a few occasions, with an expensive piece of jewellery. After about two years of all this, though, two years during which we thrice changed our room for the better and made Kheer Singh quit his job at the mall and join us in our line of work and in our room, Golu decided that he'd had enough and expressed a desire to open a shop of his own, something that made me laugh and laugh, for I couldn't let go of the idea that he would one day be a shop owner who would have two men sneak in on him with a hammer and a knife and take away his money and maybe even his life, and after long discussions about what kind of shop he might like to open, Golu decided that it would be a paan-and-cigarette shop in Sector 29, the area where all the glittering drinking places for the rich people were, and he added that he wanted me to run four omelette-and-Maggi stalls around the shop, 'Because rich people,' he said with eyes wide with greed, as if what he'd learnt about rich people was their biggest secret, 'because rich people are willing to pay for expensive drink but they don't want to burn their money buying expensive food.' The next day we had our first fight about money when Golu asked for a big share of all that we had and Kheer Singh supported him, and there were abuses hurled at each other and a little scuffle between me and Kheer Singh too, and though we calmed down soon enough, I realized that I needed to knife them that same night, for there was a good chance that they would do that to me at some point, and so I got a bottle of Angrezi in the evening and declared that we needed to drink away the bad memories from the day, and, hours later, when the two of them were asleep, I picked up my sharpest knife and approached their snoring forms, Golu's before Kheer's, and I brought the knife to Golu's neck and made to move my hand in a slaughtering way, only to discover that the hand refused to move, no matter how hard I tried, my own hand refused to obey me, and my throat and chest tightened, and I felt like I was burning all over, and a couple of my tears even dropped on to Golu's face, who moaned something in his sleep and turned to a side, and I, shaking because of I didn't know what, sat down on my haunches and took my head in my hands and screamed silently, and I felt sorry for myself in a way I had never done before. As dawn came, with Golu and Kheer still snoring, I was on my way to the village, with clumps of cash in one plastic bag and all my tools in another.

Back in Baded, I learnt that my mother was long dead, though nobody could say whether it was on the same day that I'd fled the village, and I learnt that my father had returned years ago, and that my sisters were still alive, and that Mimmi was now married to a shop owner in Gurgaon. Nothing else was as I had remembered it, and I realized that I had made a mistake in coming back, that there was nothing for me to do but to return, with my father and my sisters with me, to take the room next to the one in which I had lived with Golu and Kheer Singh, and to agree to running the omelette-and-Maggi stalls with my father and my sisters, while always being on the lookout for an older Mimmi, to offer her an omelette and Maggi for free, and to take it further from there.

# THE LAMPLIGHTER

*Anuradha Kumar*

*Bombay Chronicle, 21 August 1905*

## A standard time for India?

The Imperial Legislative Council has been debating an important matter. A standard and uniform time for the Indian colonies. It is hoped a decision will be reached soon. The move is expected to be welcomed by all, for it promises an improvement from three different sets of time: Bombay and Calcutta time, *and* Madras time, the latter greatly preferred by the Indian Railways.

Bombay time is four hours and fifty minutes ahead of Greenwich time, and Calcutta, five hours and forty minutes. This has made Madras time more acceptable as a compromise. But compromises create complications, and it is time to move to certainties.

Meanwhile, protests have broken out. Workers in Bombay's textile mills and dock workers in the city, and in Calcutta and Madras too, are suspicious about losing out on overtime wages, and being forced to work more, to make up for the changed half-hour.

Three weeks after they became friends, Albie the lamplighter asked Abu, his young book-loving friend, to write a letter for him. A special kind of letter, a love letter.

But Abu stopped only a second later. His pen hovered in the air, over the paper, just above the word 'dear'. He looked up; the lamplighter stood tall, the sun just behind him, and Abu shielded his eyes with his hand, as he asked, 'And a name? What about it?'

'Oh, I don't know,' Albie demurred, then grinned. 'You don't need a name. Not at first, do you?' he paused, then added, 'Finding that out only adds to the mystery.'

Abu wanted his friend to find happiness, for his love to be reciprocated in every measure. Yet Albie seemed content with not knowing her name. Didn't a name help? A name, Abu thought, gave shape to the person one imagined, made one believe that one knew the person in some way. A name conveyed a lot. Or didn't it?

Abu knew the lamplighter just as Albie; others called him Albert. A man with blue eyes, or were they green – Abu found he didn't really know – and he had a short brown beard and a lot of strange ideas.

Albie winked, doffed an imaginary hat, and rode away on his creaky cart. Abu saw him moments later, when Albie placed his ladder against a wall, took the steps lightly, quickly, and with a whoosh of his flame box, lit the lamp that looked out over the narrow lane. The boys cheered, they heard the sound of anklets, and somewhere a flute. It was the house of the dancing girl that came alive every evening, moments after the lamps were lit.

★

That same week, Abu also wrote a letter of complaint for the blind lady. She had been insisting for a while that the clocks in the city weren't keeping proper time. Someone, or some people, she said, were winding the clocks wrong, or just not doing it properly.

'I feel it is deliberate, this messing up, this playing with time. Time,' she said slowly, and the word sounded really big, powerful and mysterious. 'Time—,' she paused, 'it is the moving force of the universe. If anyone messes with Time, there is a price to pay. For all of us,' and her pale milky green eyes looked all around, and Abu felt seen in ways he couldn't understand.

Every day, she said, she could hear the ticking, the tolling and the chiming of certain hours, from clocks near and far, and when compared to the clock in her room, the one from her grandfather's time, she could tell that all the other clocks had skipped seconds, others had slowed down, or picked up after some seconds, some had gone totally quiet, and some had just been wound wrongly.

'And the sounds,' she stopped, her hands on her ears as if she was carefully listening for something, 'instead of ticking, I can hear a clanging or a squeaking, sounds different from what time makes.'

⋆

Days after this, the blind lady asked Abu to write to anyone who could decide on such matters. So he looked up the addresses of the city magistrate, the sheriff, the councillors, the inspector of schools, the police superintendent, the innumerable justices of the peace, and wrote to them. She never had a reply for no one wrote back to her. But she insisted that one must never lose hope and placed her fingers in her ears as she heard a clock in the vicinity ticking the wrong time.

In return for writing the letters, Abu did not take anything from the lamplighter. His light, Abu said, was like the sun for him. It helped him study, especially in the evenings and because the darkness came on earlier, minute by minute, every passing day, or so he thought. And the blind lady would many a time send down food for him, striking the latch repeatedly against the wooden pane before she let the basket down on a string.

These letters were different from the ones Abu usually wrote. He wrote letters on behalf of people to their folks back home. He penned letters that were more like pleas, or entreaties to higher-level people when someone wanted a raise, a day off, or were pleading sickness. Then there were the threat letters, when someone had to be reminded of money owed, and Abu was always polite, always gentle.

Abu also wrote secret letters to his parents. They had perished in the plague that had devastated the city only some years ago, but he wanted to believe they had gone away somewhere – a pilgrimage, perhaps – and never returned.

*

His orphan status made his neighbours, the other people who lived on the street, the boys he knew, pity him, but they also admired him. For his age, Abu knew a lot of things.

Every evening when he had a newspaper to himself, he read parts out loud for anyone who gathered around. And every day, all that he read told him this: that Bombay was a city of change. Everything, Abu thought, began here. The first train, the first movement for reform in India with the Congress meeting the very year he was born, and so many other initiatives, like education and an end to early marriage for women. He knew about Rakhmabai, the girl who had once lived in this same neighbourhood, who had fought a case refusing to return to her marital home, and even the queen in faraway England had written to her. Rakhmabai had just left to study medicine there. Her life had entirely changed from that one act of resistance.

There were things like tram-cars on the roads and more streetlights, running on gas, had appeared in the city.

Where Abu lived, the sea was a constant roar, and trains whooshed past somewhere near. He could hear them when he awoke, always early, before daybreak, just as the last jackals called. If he stepped out from his road into other roads, and by-lanes, he could see all that he heard: a portion of the sea, the boats on the horizon or bobbing at anchor, and a train pulling into a station. Important things happened in this city, and Abu believed he lived in the very heart of it.

The road he lived on ran in a serpentine way, with twists and turns, and curves and bends so that people had no idea where the road ended, or even where it began. Nor did anyone really know how long the road was. People with their houses along a curve could see little beyond a distance.

What Abu also noticed was this: that shadows too had changed. They were larger, longer, more strangely formed than before as the houses around grew bigger and bigger. Sometimes houses had small pathways leading in, and these became narrow lanes that led past courtyards and over boundary walls back into that curvy sinuous road, and people took shortcuts, or lost their way altogether.

The road's length and shape confused people about its name too – was it Delisle Road or Clare Road, Cavell Road, and surely not Devil Road? Some argued that the confusion prevailed because it sounded so English, and something needed to be done. And as people argued, the city changed even more, and the street looked different from one day to the next.

The curvy, sinuous road was lined with houses of uneven height. In the three years since Abu had come to live there, the houses had grown in strange, unpredictable ways. From one floor, with a colonnaded porch, with the carvings on top, and lovingly carved statuettes, there were now houses with two storeys or even more. Some were even taller than the nearby trees, the palm trees that someone – the blind old lady's grandfather, as Abdul, a friend, had told him – had planted long ago. The tallest house had four floors, and the blind lady lived on the highest floor.

The floors above every house had balconies, windows that were louvred and draped with curtains of different colours and patterns. The balconies stood outstretched on brackets shaped like bird wings, and when the wind blew hard, every rail and frame shook, and the wooden floors creaked. When the breeze blew out from the land, Albie, the lamplighter, often felt the wind on his back, pushing him on, or as he laughed with Abu, pushing him out of the street post-haste.

'This road looks more and more different. And the animals look so real,' Abu said to himself, looking at the dragons, the gargoyles, the phoenixes, and the flying horse high on the roof. If he didn't have the map of the road in his head, he knew he'd be lost in the darkness that lay everywhere. The lamp posts cowered like stunted, shrunken trees, the orange pools of light at their feet flickering desperately in the battle against darkness.

*

Albie never missed a lamp. If he did, the blind lady always noticed, and she would call out to him.

'I thought she couldn't see a thing,' Albie once told Abu, looking bemused. He had never seen her wave back to him, and once he had lifted his pole with the flame on it, it had given him quite a jolt to see her face. It was the twilight hour when daylight receded and darkness advanced. There was a milky whiteness in her eyes, and her face was smooth and unlined, with a gentle smile.

'She can't see, but she hears better than anyone,' assured Abu. 'The echo of wheels, the sound of your ladder, the scraping sound it makes against the street, your lamp hissing, and the whoosh as it lights up. She has been here for so long that she sees things we don't.'

Abu lived and studied on the porch, and it gave him a kind of vantage point. He couldn't help but also note the sullen anger, a buzz slowly growing in the streets. Some people met in secret, in a hall that otherwise doubled up as a theatre. There was growing talk about forming unions, groups and associations. It was true people achieved more when they acted together; still, Abu was confused. Did it help to get together to cause mayhem and suffering? A crowd could, at times, get violent.

* * *

*Bombay Chronicle, 20 September 1905*

## The Mystery Proletarian Prince

Certain sections of the British government have alerted us to something sensational. It is reported that the arch-nihilist, anarchist, suspected communist, a renegade of the

> Tsarist Romanov family has secretly entered Bombay. Prince Alexievich is also a master at disguising himself.
>
> He plans to spread mayhem and cause disturbances. His methods of doing this may be unknown but the police insist everyone has to be on alert. There is special deployment of policemen in the textile mills where the workers remain a volatile lot. They are well-organized and ready to go on strike and resort to violence on the slightest pretext.

This bit of news gave Abu cause for concern. He looked at the boys around him, who were all his friends. A highlight of their day was Albie's arrival, when he came by on his rounds. Every evening to light the street lamps and mornings too, when he snuffed them out. Otherwise, the boys worked at various jobs – as loaders, packers, messengers and delivery boys. They were paid poorly and treated badly. Albie had once said that of all people who needed to be organized, it was these boys who did so much and yet were shabbily treated.

Abu held the newspaper, its pages unmoving in his hands, and wondered if Albie had been serious.

Jobs like Albie's too – lighting lamps – were doomed. There would soon be electric lamps on every street. What would happen to him then? Perhaps the renegade prince, Alexievich, with his heart for the workers, knew that in Bombay, he would find people he could help: all those who were discontented, and disenchanted, all those afraid that things would take a turn for the worse.

*

Albie's route never varied. From Carvel Road, along Chowpatty, past the military barracks, the burial grounds, the theatre halls, the temple, and the church, and down Agiary Street, and past the hospital, the gardens with the tall thorn bushes, and cacti plants big and succulent, and then finally into the street he knew as well as the lines on his own palm. In places where it got too narrow, with no place for his small cart, Albie would ring his bell, and this made people angry. Only temples and people worshipping could have a bell.

Albie came by in the evening just as the city around him slowly fell quiet. He trundled up in his cart and the boys gathered to watch him at work, as he lit up the lamps one by one all along the stretch – was it Delisle Street, or Devil Street, or Carvel? But what did a name matter when the world was all lit up and the darkness dispelled for a while?

Some evenings, when Albie returned from his round, down the entire stretch of the street, just to check if the lamps were lit properly, he would hear the tinkle of anklets and the sound of someone humming to herself.

'The women of the night,' he said softly and only Abu heard him. 'They sing so beautifully, it's hard to stay away. Be warned,' he raised his voice, grinning at his friends, 'they could stop you from doing your job.'

Some hours later, at daybreak, when Albie came by to put the lamps out, he was most often alone, but for three people.

Abu, under a streetlamp and half-asleep among his books. The blind woman looking out of her window, listening to the clocks everywhere in the city, and the young dancing girl who having danced and entertained all night long, closed her own window just as soon as he came.

Like a habit, Albie would bend down from his cart, his reins light in his fingers and ask Abu the question he always did. 'Has she replied to my letter yet?'

Abu's reply never varied. He yawned, shook his head, and hoped Albie wouldn't mind this much. After all, he wanted to tell him, he wrote letters to his parents too, not expecting a reply. It just made him happy.

There were some mornings Albie lingered, as he watched Abu gather his books.

'All this studying,' he bantered. 'When will you join the Imperial Civil Service?'

'First,' Abu replied, 'I will take the ship to London. There's a job I have been promised as a lascar. Once I go there, I will take the exam.'

Albie laughed. 'Don't increase my work hours when you make laws. I barely get enough sleep.'

Then he looked around and leaned forward, making his cart creak unexpectedly. 'What you might do is change the name of this street. Delisle, Caryle, Carvel, Devil, whatever, they are all the wrong names. An English name is so out of place, and Englishmen too.'

Abu stared at him. Albie could get into trouble for what he had just said: there were spies everywhere. People were often jailed for just a simple, innocuous statement.

'For some people like her,' Albie said casually, pointing up to where the blind lady lived, 'there is no need for streets to have names. Didn't you tell me that she knows a street, a place just by its sounds, the way the shadows fall against her face?' His words fell away. He stowed away the stick with the lighter and gathered the reins in his hand. Abu saw his face lit up in parts by the slow morning light.

'When you become an ICS officer,' he told Abu, some mornings later, 'tell them this city really can't take tall buildings.'

'The government is only for the rich,' Abu said in turn. Maybe he was sleepy and wasn't really being careful. 'They are building high and swallowing up everything else. The river that used to run through the city, the hills over Mazagaon, the tall trees lining the road. No place for the poor, the simple, the ordinary people.'

'Be careful. You don't want to sound like a communist,' Albie's tone was light as he went on. 'Maybe the prince will hear you. He can't be here, can he?'

Abu joined in the spirit of banter, 'Oh, he could be in the most crowded of places and hide away in plain sight.'

Albie sighed, then abruptly changed the subject. 'Remember, what I said about names? If you change a street name, what would people who can't read do? Why not have someone stand at the corner shouting out the name every now and then?'

'Someone to manage the traffic, you mean,' said Abu. 'One day can you imagine the city getting so crowded that it will be full of vehicles, no place for people like you and me?'

Albie cleared his throat, and said softly, 'By that time, you will be a fine officer, and I will no longer have a job. We are a dying breed.'

The old woman laughed, they had no idea she was right above them, that they had chosen the porch of her house to have their conversation. 'You do not really want to give up the job because you are in love.'

Abu knew instantly what she meant. How could he never have guessed? Albie wrote letters to the dancing girl. It was so obvious in whatever Albie did. The way he propped his ladder against her house every evening, lit the lamp, and the slow way he dropped his letter – the one Abu had written for him – through her window. Abu understood. Love was what made Albie linger, made him whistle a tune. Abu felt sad that it wasn't because of him.

No one saw Albie blush at the old lady's words. It was that undefined period when darkness took time to recede, and daylight crept in slowly, between buildings, through shuttered windows, a gap in the street. Faces looked grey and wan, maybe it was the darkness, the sadness of their lives, or because reading people and their expressions was hard. The murkiness had only spread to corners, where it took up more space, and conversations at this time were hushed and watchful, and so Albie demurred, 'I can always get a new job. But it will be a while.'

They stood under the balcony, hearing the birds that had their nests in the rafters, the breathing of the pariah dogs that sheltered on the porch, and furry creatures brushed past Abu – and he remembered how jackals had once roamed the city. Maybe there were still a few, the lost ones roaming the streets, unable to find a way out. The animal figures hovering above looked real to him, in this half-light, with their bared teeth and all-seeing eyes. 'Maybe,' he heard Albie say, 'I could be a watchman, even a carriage driver.'

★

Familiarity with anything brings about an unseriousness with it. Changes happen, but it's hard to find the difference between big and small changes. The darkness advanced, one house, then another, and another, added an extra floor, the trees grew a bit taller, the weather colder, and rainier and puddles and streamlets appeared on the street, making people skirt around them or tramp over wooden planks, and Abu realized only much later that the dancer had one special visitor who came at night.

One day, when he didn't expect it, he found the young man, the dancer's patron, waiting for him. The moment he spoke, Abu knew, of course, that he had heard this man before. The time he had raised his voice when he had stepped right into a puddle soon after alighting from his carriage. Sometimes, he sounded angry when he spoke to the dancer, his voice ringing loud in that quiet street. And there were times his words came in a low hiss, when he was being mean and nasty to the coachman, or his horse, or even the dog that harmed no one.

But the man came only at night, in the carriage that left soon after dropping him, and so Abu had never had a close look at him. Did Albie know the dancer had a lover? Abu now thought, as the man came closer, that he had a menacing aura around him.

'We *cannot* wait,' the man said coming closer, and Abu smelled the tobacco on his breath. 'I warn you to keep the lamplighter away. I know he is your friend. I know how he whistles under her balcony and lingers. The brazenness of it. If you don't do it, let me tell you, I have people who can easily put a knife through him.'

The man's hand dug into Abu's shoulder like claws. He felt any time now, he would be lifted off the ground, swept away in a carriage, away from every familiar thing. He looked up, and saw the trees looming overhead, their branches like webs.

'We can do worse,' the man whispered. 'Get him transferred, move him to another street, and from that street to still another, till he is lost, so confused that he turns mad. You know what they do to them then? They send them to the madhouse, the lunatic asylum at the very place this city ends, the corner of Colaba.'

The man stepped away and said, still with soft menace, 'And remember, we have ways of catching those who don't listen. We can even send you to the madhouse.'

*

Abu knew he had to warn Albie, but he had no idea where he lived. He worried as the night grew older, and the lamps dimmed. The old lady sent down a bowl of grapes and a rice dish, and decided then and there, to tell Abu a story – of the Pathan fruit-seller of her childhood who hadn't come back from his hometown.

'But I could hear him from a long way off. My ayah would laugh when I told her that I could hear his voice. Through the mountains, and the desert, and the marshes of Bassein and Bandora, and the creeks that divide up this island city, I could hear him, and I told my ayah that no matter how much the city changes, and the new roads that come up, with their even newer names, I'd still know his voice. Such a strong voice, it could travel miles easily. Like distant thunder or a conch blown long and hard. Sounds carry, one should just listen...' she smiled, and Abu saw, looking up at her, that her face was all lit up, bright as the moon. 'You understand what I just said, didn't you? I sense you are not smiling.'

'I did understand,' he stammered, not wanting to lie but he had been struck by an idea, so blindingly obvious. A new name for an old road. A new look for an old road. Wasn't that what she was telling him?

Her eyes looked unseeingly down at him. 'From your silence, I can tell you understand. Anybody else would have lied. But yes...' she held up a gnarled old hand, 'there's something you have to do now, and urgently. Look, the Rajabai tower clock is already tolling the hour, and it's three minutes late.

'I know because my clock, from my great-grandfather's time, was made by the best clockmaker in London. It was one of the first clocks that arrived here with the city's governor then. My ancestor was on the same ship. A man who wanted to make this city the most efficient city, with everything running on time. It would make things so easy for everyone. No one would be too late or too early.

'But lately, I can hear the clocks everywhere, all giving the wrong time. Louder than before, their ticking – some slow, some too quick, and none of them with time as right as mine. Can't you hear them, the tick-tick, tick-tock, tock-tock, tock-tick sounds?'

Abu shook his head, and the blind lady understood once again. 'This time, you think I've gone batty. But when the city falls quiet, you can...hear the clocks. You listen to the sound time makes.'

*

People always said that Bombay was a place where no one really bothered you, and this truth still prevails. No one gave Abu or his friend a second glance as they placed a board at the very entrance to their street, an arrow pointing right painted on it. A similar board stood on an inside lane with a finger pointing skywards. Then his friend – Abu would always be confused about the name; was it Ramraj or Ahmed? – had the great idea, or so he thought, of painting on a corner wall, a grand portrait of Shivaji. They had always been mesmerized by his stories.

'It is a good thing not many people will notice,' said a girl, walking by, and because the anklets tinkled on her feet, it took Abu only a moment to realize this was the dancing girl. 'They would never guess you were up to no good.'

She looked at them, and they felt shy. She was beautiful, and younger than Abu had assumed. Fifteen, sixteen, he was thinking, but she couldn't be more than eighteen, really. And he couldn't quite remember what she had just said.

'Do you think he won't know his way here?' She was pointing to the board they had placed halfway across the narrow street.

'We are just trying to confuse him,' he said, not wanting to alarm her, and tell her of the threat to Albie.

He remembered the moments he had seen Albie drop his letters. The way he stood on his ladder, as it leaned against the wall, close to her window. Maybe he hoped she would look out, but the girl never did. Abu felt a pain in his heart. He felt sad for love that could be hopeless, and because the world made it so.

'Were the letters from him?' she asked suddenly. 'I can't read,' she confessed. 'Or I can't read English.'

Abu liked her honesty. He liked her otherwise too, for she was really very pretty. He stared at her and in those seconds, he heard the slow ticking of the clocks. A ticking, a buzzing, even a strumming, so many different sounds, and he understood what the old lady had been saying. He understood something else, too: Albert asked him to write because he didn't know English either. Where was he from? Did he really have blue eyes, brown hair, or did the shifting light and the shadowy darkness always make him look different?

'Stop him coming then. Even from getting into the road. Place a cart at the entrance. Or cover it up with stones and,' – she pointed to a house that had just been demolished – 'with the broken columns. No one will notice, you know that. They never bother unless you break a caste rule, drink from a forbidden well...or—'

Before Abu could nod in empathy, the old lady leaned out, '—or if you love a stranger, or someone you are forbidden to love. Maybe that's what Bibi means.'

The girl smiled, and Abu saw that it made her look sadder.

'Maybe there's no need for a lamp today,' the old lady spoke over their heads, 'you will see.' The blind lady always knew what she was talking about. All this time, after all, she had known the girl's name.

*

The moon rose full and early, making the women come out to their balconies and porches to admire and exclaim in delight. On this night of the harvest moon, the moon would slowly become larger, still larger, and at a precise moment it would come very close to the earth, nearer than it had been in a long time.

But predictions were hard to make; even wise people had been thrown off track, for the clocks never kept to the same time, and everything ran of its own accord.

Soon, Abu heard the blaring of horns, the clashing of cymbals, the chanting of hymns and the blowing of conches. The moon was brighter than it had ever been, but Abu had no time to look. He felt a new guilt. He had wasted time in the morning. All the work on the road signs and talking to the girl had eaten into his study hours. Now he wanted desperately to make up, and he walked up to the tallest tree, the one taller than the four-storey structure where the blind lady lived. If he climbed right to the very top, he could study by the moon's light.

He stopped often, as he climbed. He paused, holding aside one leafy frond, and then another, slowly making his way up. Sometimes he looked into windows, and saw women at work, preparing for the festival and for the auspicious moment that could come any time. They didn't want to be caught by surprise.

'It's the biggest it has ever been, but of course, it's hard to keep track of such things now,' said the old lady, and she looked like an angel or someone not quite of this earth. But that thought didn't scare Abu. The ticking of the clocks was loud, because as he rose, the city was quieter, and he could see into houses, and it puzzled him, and he shook his head repeatedly, for every clock, as he looked in at every window, showed a different time. Maybe, he thought, it was the darkness inside, or the way the moonlight fell, the manner it turned some clockfaces purple, or made them shine in a blinding way. Or it could be that he was sleepy. But he just had to climb even higher. And the moon only grew brighter, and he could see more of everything.

A few more feet up, and Abu stopped short. Looking out towards Chowpatty, he saw Albie on his cart. The way he stood up, tall and high, made Abu certain. Albie's lamp pole was unlit. And Abu realized something else: none of the other streets had been lit. But the moon more than made up for this.

He saw Bibi, the young dancing girl, looking out into the street, at the women emerging from their houses, who were all looking up at the moon, unseeing of anything else. They would go down the broken narrow lane towards the sea and offer prayers to the goddess of wealth. Abu saw Bibi's look of longing, and knew she couldn't join them for they were all so very respectable, so unlike her. He was high up on the palm tree and closer to the moon than ever before, or maybe it was the moon that had come very close and was not moving. When a lone cloud drifted away, like a boat in the sky, the moon came through with its valleys, creeks and hills, and it shone through the windows the dancing girl had thrown wide open.

The palm tree, lithe and tall, moved easily and Abu could look even farther out. The street looked purple and orange where people had lit lamps, and the houses turned into something from a theatre set. The animal carvings and figurines looked changed, and somewhat bigger, even lifelike in that purple moonlight. Or maybe Abu, being so high up, was seeing them better now. A crane on a roof stretched, and spread its wings, and a lion, only a floor below, bared its teeth. The old woman stood at her window, her face lifted, and it seemed she was like an unknown conductor managing all this. Maybe she was still listening to the clocks.

He peered over the roofs and into the streets around. Albie stood there, his rod taller than before and still unlit. Abu saw the fancy gilded carriage of the man who was Bibi's patron, and who had asked him to pass on a threat to Albie.

Abu saw how his carriage moved, the coachman unable to find his way to anywhere. He was dashing down one street, entering another, and never quite finding this one street with its many confusing names: Delisle Road? Or Cavel, Carter...or not Devil, surely? And Abu understood that he could not find the street because the lamps had not been lit.

Bibi's window, Abu saw, opened onto a big hall, with cushions and ottomans and hookahs, and it was empty. The moonlight made silver streaks on the floor. She threw open all the windows, drew apart the curtains and opened the balcony door, and waved to the woman, and to Abu. Her bangles jangled, and the old woman smiled.

'I wish I could see you really happy. You used to be a happy girl before.'

'Yes, the madam is strict but evenings she doesn't bother me.'

The older woman nodded, 'You are her prize dancer, after all.'

The girl smiled, 'I've never felt as free as I do today.'

As they watched, she took the candles and placed them in the chandelier and the room transformed into a magical place. He heard the sounds of matches being struck, the light popping up, and to Abu, she seemed to be her own lamplight.

★

A clock somewhere struck nine then, and the old woman lifted her head.

'It's Time,' she quavered, 'it just isn't working right. When time is not moving in a flow, the past catches up and can be confusing. A jumbled-up time throws everything off the rails, shakes up everything we have ever known.

'The long ago comes very near then,' she spoke slowly. 'You can see the pirates walking the streets, and the cries of the fishermen when the tide comes in.' A ship's horn blew somewhere, and she knew it was the one from Australia. 'Can you hear the horses? Long ago, a century ago, Shivaji's army passed along the mountains, down the ravines when they raided the rich port town of Surat. And the British and the Armenians moved out in their boats. And you can hear things in the future too, the roar, and the buzz and the honking.'

The girl looked afraid, as she listened to her. 'Is it true that the future is going to be like that?'

'There will be so many sounds that you will miss the simpler sounds, the birds, the vendors, your music, and the ticking of the clocks.'

They listened, unable to say anything, and the ticking of the clocks sounded louder. 'It's the sound that takes me back to the past.' The lady pressed her hands to her ears. 'It's like time moving in circles around me.'

They heard a creaking and saw Albie had finally found his way to their street. He lifted his light rod high, so they could see the last dying flickers of light on it. He was limping, and his clothes looked torn, as if he had been walking a long time, and had been in a duel.

'We just have time to get away,' he whispered, looking at the dancing girl. He spoke in a different language, and everyone understood. 'I am sorry I did all this,' he looked up at Abu, still speaking in that different way. His eyes were blue, and he had a pointed beard, and Abu felt he should understand something more, beyond what was being said. Instead, Abu looked away, and into another street, not very far away, where he saw someone with a blood-smeared shirt, who leaned forward, gasping as he asked his coachman to drive faster, faster, and to get help.

The man was only a street or so away, but still he couldn't see them.

Abu came down from the tree and helped Bibi and the blind lady into the lamplighter's cart. The four of them would take the boat from the swamps of Bandora and sail away.

'Did you do all this?' Abu asked after a while.

'The lamplighters' union had a strike today. They managed to get together.'

'Ha!' said the blind lady. 'And are you telling me the clock winders too were on strike?'

Albie looked puzzled. 'No, we don't know how that happened, but it confounded everyone.' He looked up at the sky and said, 'All that debate about what time to follow, this time or that time, Bombay, or Calcutta, or still some other place, left everyone confused. What is the time, really? What is Time? It seems no one really knows. When time goes on strike, everything else has to as well.'

Abu spoke softly, as the waves lapped against the boat, and rushed towards their feet. 'You did all this because...of love?'

It was the old lady who answered. 'Yes, a love bigger than what you could ever figure out. When one is not anchored to time, everything looks different. We look at things differently.' She lifted her head and looked Abu's way, and once again, Abu knew she saw and understood things much better.

The lamplighter had gone still, his eyes sharp and boring into him, his moustache thin.

'And you are Prince Albert Alexievich, the organizer, the nihilist?' Abu asked softly, his heart beating fast. He felt lost in this world with no time.

The girl stood by the sea, not stepping into the boat, not looking at anyone. Albie held his hand out, and she shook her head. Abu knew she was staying back for him. But dreams could be beguiling: one never knew if they would come true, but it was good, for some moments, out of time, to live in them.

'How can one understand anything, this world, even love,

when there is no time,' Bibi spoke so quietly they could all hear her and the ticking of the clocks. 'There is nothing that holds us to this moment. When every moment, past, now and future appear to collide, where does that leave love? What kind of love could exist without time?'

The moon went behind a cloud, and the wind picked up, and the few lamps still burning went out. When they looked back, the boat with the lamplighter had gone. Had time moved so fast that they had been unable to keep up?

Sometimes on clear nights, Abu could see a boat at sea, a light high on its mast, and he would think it was the lamplighter, or the prince, Albert Alexievich. He was still at sea, still trying to find the right time for all that he had in mind.

# A DIVINE MADNESS

## *Anil Menon*

Has John Janardhan shown that religiosity is the result of a parasitic infection? Anil Menon describes how scientists, building on Janardhan's work, are uncovering the astonishing role played by the parasite *Neospora nicolai* in disrupting rationality.

'If I were called in/To construct a religion,' wrote the poet Philip Larkin, 'I should make use of water.' The neurologist and evolutionary biologist John Janardhan begs to differ. He would start, he says, with a parasite.

Nothing about John Janardhan suggests he plans to be a prophet of any kind. Or a radical. Or a nonconformist. Indeed, he is quick to stress that he leads a conventional life, typical of a great many well-educated, reasonably well-off Indians of a certain age. He lives in Indiranagar, the heart of Bengaluru (formerly Bangalore), in the same modest two-storey house his family has owned for over three generations.

At home, he wears a spacious white cotton kurta and an even more forgiving lungi (sarong). It imbues him with a sage-like simplicity. Or perhaps it is his completely bald dome and large forehead, altogether too heavy for his narrow shoulders and slim frame. The forty-two-year-old has the kind of delicate features that must have made him look mature in his youth and would probably make him look youthful in his retirement.

Janardhan's office – a converted guest room – is what one might expect of an Indian professor of medicine with the standard British Raj–inspired English education. There is a model skeleton in one corner, a folded wheelchair tucked away in another, two book-lined walls with volumes on medicine, Western classical music, Christian and Hindu theologies, Victorian classics, pop science books, bestselling genre-fiction from the 80s and 90s, and Enid Blyton's novels.

'Jennifer's removed her books,' he says, as if in defence. His smile seems to mask an irremovable sadness.

Whether he looks the radical's part or not, the work of this modest, quiet-mannered scholar offers a revolutionary, and for some, deeply upsetting, perspective on religiosity. The reason we are religious, claims Janardhan, has a lot to do with the *Neospora nicolai* parasite.

Parasites belonging to the *Neospora* genus specialize in living off livestock and pets. Some are quite specific. *N. caninum*, for example, parasitize dogs, coyotes, grey wolves, dingos and such. *N. hughesi* infects equids: horses, zebras and asses. *N. nicolai*, named after the early twentieth-century scientist-explorer Nicolai Angelo, focuses on primates; in fact, it is particularly fond of one specific primate species: *Homo sapiens*.

Parasites specialize in hacking other life forms. It isn't hard to hack biology. Parasitism is far from being an unusual lifestyle. Indeed, which critter gets labelled as a parasite often depends on exactly who is being inconvenienced.

But it is a lot harder, Janardhan explains, to disrupt the neural circuitry of a host organism to effect a specific change in its behaviour. For one thing, it is hard to get through the blood–brain barrier. For another, there is behaviour and then there is complex behaviour. It is fairly easy to hack the neural systems of insects and take control of their behaviour.

'Neural system doesn't equal brain,' says Janardhan. 'Lots of parasites leave the brain alone. Take the *unilateralis*, for example. This is a parasitic fungus that infects carpenter ants. Brilliant, nasty piece of work. The ants have armour, so it's not easy getting into their bodies. But the fungus spore pressures open the exoskeleton, get in and then begin to munch away. It spreads. The fungus is careful not to eat the vital organs. It leaves the brain untouched.'

'So how does it control the ant?'

'Not really sure. It may be hacking the neural pathways, sending its own signals to the muscles. Anyway, the ant is turned into a zombie. It lurches away from the ant trails, finds a nice bit of tall grass or tree branch, climbs to the summit – lots of parasites make insects do that, so it's called the summit disease. The ant clamps its mandibles shut in a death grip and hangs there. It dies, officially. The busy little fungus sends out a stalk through a hole in the exoskeleton and the spores are released to the wind. Cue *Lion King* music.' He smiles at my expression. 'It really *is* the circle of life. The fungus has its own parasite to deal with. This parasite seems to keep the *unilateralis* in check. That may be why the ant's brain is left alone.'

Vertebrates, however, are a lot more complex than insects. Their behaviour is not necessarily determined by the firing of a few thousand neurons. But given time, even their neural systems can be hacked, and it comes with a special reward. The brain (and more generally, the central nervous system) enjoys what biologists call 'immune privilege'. Brain tissue is too vital to be allowed to suffer damage from the inflammation that is a key component of the immune response. Accordingly, the vertebrate brain has a host of techniques to suppress the immune response. Which is just dandy for the parasite that is able to break in.

*N. nicolai* belongs to the same elite club of cyber-hackers, so to speak, as *Trypanosoma brucei* (sleeping sickness), *Plasmodium falciparum* (cerebral malaria), *Taenia solium* (cysticercosis), *Taenia multiceps* ('the staggers') and the formerly trending parasite *Toxoplasma gondii*, implicated in everything from schizophrenia through drunk driving to sloppy dress sense.

*N. nicolai* is accused of something equally bizarre. The parasite, studies suggest, can trigger hallucinations, induce feelings of ecstasy, flood the body with dopamine and oxytocin, and mediate the urge to congregate. The word 'mediate' is important. Primates are social animals. They like to congregate. But humans are a class apart in sociality. Most of the studies on the parasite's mediation of congregation have been done on mice, but they clearly demonstrate the parasite's ability to alter the urge to huddle. In short, the parasite mediates various dimensions of religiosity. If God exists, then *N. nicolai* is their henchman.

What makes it remarkable is that Janardhan and his wife once counted themselves among the very religious. I know enough about Indian names to recognize that John Janardhan isn't a typical one. His great-grandfather's family – originally Hindus – had converted to Christianity. So had Jennifer's, only more completely; unlike Janardhan's ancestors, they had given up even the peripheral affiliations: attire, Hindu surnames, rituals, songs.

'My name is just the result of an opportunistic conversion. My great-grandfather's real religion was the accumulation of wealth, and Christians had access to better jobs in the British Raj.'

Jennifer's story, according to Janardhan, is less grubby. Her great-grandfather Yamanurswamy hadn't been allowed to eat in the same lunchroom as his upper-caste colleagues. He couldn't use the same water pitcher. The office peon wouldn't bring him tea. Yama had a high-school education, was literate in English and was a Class III lower-division clerk. He was very sharp by all accounts. Despite all these merits, or perhaps because of them, he was humiliated on a daily basis. Gregg Roberts, the local British officer, tiring of the office politics, ordered Yamanurswamy to eat lunch in his ante-room. They became friends; that is, as friendly as was possible for a white man to be friends with a brown subordinate in the British Raj. Yamanurswamy Mogera eventually converted to Christianity and became Peter Roberts.

Neither of Janardhan's parents were particularly religious in their teens or twenties. That all changed once they attended a Pentecostal service at the Bethel Assembly of God Church sometime in the mid-90s. Janardhan says he must have been twelve or so at the time. He remembers hundreds of voices soaring in aural synchrony, the smell of incense, spears of multicoloured light through the stained-glass window and the ecstasy of belonging. He remembers it as a positive experience. However, he is too knowledgeable about how human memory works to take his feelings seriously. The memories, he says, are most probably composites, reconstructed from traces laid down by later visits to the church.

'You must understand,' says Janardhan, leaning forward for emphasis, 'our emotions are also constructions. They aren't reactions to the world – you follow? The body reacts physiologically. We interpret this physiological change by constructing a feeling. An instance of an emotion. Which means parasites can effect physiological changes to fool us into psychological delusions.'

This is important because studies suggest the parasite can alter emotional reconstructions of doubt-inducing experiences. In other words, make us less sceptical. In one of the early studies, conducted by Wilbur Smart's team at the MIT Behavioral Research Lab, participants who had scored high on the Huber & Huber Centrality of Religiosity Scale (a measure of religiosity) were divided into two groups based on whether they had tested positive for the parasite or not. Each group was shown Alain Resnais's *Hiroshima mon amour*. The participants were physiologically monitored throughout the movie. Just after the viewing, a questionnaire probed their reactions. The parasite-free group reported instances of negative emotions; they self-identified these feelings as irritation, sadness, anger and frustration. The parasite-infected group also reported similar responses. The physiological responses weren't markedly different between the two groups.

A few days later, the two groups were again asked about their recollection of the movie. This time, however, a clear difference emerged. The parasite-infected group now reported positive feelings about the movie experience. Their reasons varied, but they rejected the idea that the movie left a negative impact. In fact, it had strengthened their satisfaction with their religious faith. The parasite-free group also had recovered to some extent, but the movie remained a source of instances of negative emotions. Other existential films produced similar results. The parasite not only seemed to help the religious reframe doubt-inducing experiences as faith-testing ones, but it also helped them claim victory in these tests.

The Smart Study has been replicated. To rule out the possibility that the effect is tied to a particular movie, different movies are chosen: *The Pawnbroker*, *No Country for Old Men*, *American Psycho*, *Requiem for a Dream*. Other objections have been looked into. Perhaps the reframing was due to the peculiar nature of fiction? But studies using *non-fictional* reports of a world spinning out of control – statistics on growing childhood cancer rates, poverty, climate change, migration – also show a similar reconstruction. The parasite seems to help people maintain their belief in an orderly world, even if not a God-governed one.

When Jennifer and Janardhan met at Bryan Adams's 2001 tour stop in Bangalore, it certainly felt like God had had a hand in it. They had that extravert (Jennifer)–introvert (Janardhan) astral connection, they had played together as kids at the same crèche, and their parents were similar enough to be interchangeable. In 2002, Jennifer completed her master's in science and found a job as a lecturer at the Azim Premji College. Janardhan completed his bachelor's in medicine at Saint John's, in Bangalore, and married Jennifer the same year. He was admitted for a three-year neurology residency at the prestigious All India Institute of Medical Sciences (AIIMS), in Delhi. Family considerations forced Jennifer to stay back in Bangalore. The separation hit them hard, but the heart-aching couple did their best to stay connected; they made it a point to do their evening prayers together.

On his first flight home for the Christmas vacation, Janardhan read Robert Sapolsky's *The Trouble with Testosterone*. What he learned, troubled him.

'I experienced a version of the Smart experiment.'

One of Sapolsky's essays discusses the biological basis for religiosity. Sapolsky considers it one of the manifestations of the cluster of behavioural ailments that the DSM-IV calls 'Anxiety Disorders'. For example, the spectrum of obsessive-compulsive disorders or OCD.

Most religions, Sapolsky demonstrates, have ritualistic requirements which are strikingly similar to the elaborate order-confirming rituals of those afflicted with OCD.

Unlike Jennifer's faith in God, which was unquestioning and experiential, Janardhan needs his beliefs to be defeasible. After all, why believe in the existence of YHWH or Jesus Christ when he didn't believe in the existence of other gods, some with even more followers? He was drawn more to C.S. Lewis and Thomas Merton than the emotional appeals of charismatic pastors.

He quotes Merton: 'Faith is first of all an intellectual assent. It perfects the mind, it does not destroy it.'

Janardhan's opinion of Sapolsky hasn't changed over the years. He considers Sapolsky a brilliant and honest scientist. And here was his hero claiming religious belief is basically a kind of cognitive disorder.

'I felt devastated,' says Janardhan, simply.

Jennifer noticed the change in Janardhan almost as soon they met. When he began to tell her, with some hesitation, about Sapolsky's ideas, he felt a curious change come over him. He made the arguments sound witty, not really serious, the kind of thing atheists wrote when they didn't really 'get it'. God was a concept far, far beyond the reach of petty logic. Sure, lots of religious people have OCD. So what? Lots of religious people are completely disinterested in rituals.

'I noticed I was actually giddy. Like I'd woken up from a bad dream. It didn't make sense.'

He returned to Delhi with his faith restored. Perhaps even strengthened. If someone brought up Sapolsky's thesis, he felt amused and changed the topic. But there was, he says, an unease.

Seasons of doubt are common among the very religious. As usual, the eighteenth-century aphorist Georg Christoph Lichtenberg saw deeper: 'There is a great difference between believing something and again believing it.'

Janardhan smiles and nods. 'Yes, that nails it. Something had changed. But I thought about germs and disease to avoid thinking about the germ of belief.'

In 2002, he obtained his MD with a specialization in neurology. He hadn't heard of the *N. nicolai* parasite. That isn't surprising. American medical doctors learn about parasites only in passing. A recent survey by Dr Alex Acholonu, a biology professor (now retired) at Alcorn State University, reveals that not a single medical school in the US had a parasitology department. In the Barrows Guide, only 2 out of the 122 schools and colleges of medicine devote courses to parasitology. Parasites are considered a Third-World problem. The First World has the means but not the interest; the Third World has the interest but not the means. Janardhan estimates that in med school, he'd been exposed to a total of just under ten hours of useful instruction about parasites. It hadn't covered the *N. nicolai*.

In 1992, the Italian doctor, Nicolai Angelo, had initially mistaken the *N. nicolai* for *N. hughesi*. There is an old joke, attributed to parasitologist John Janovy, that to get a master's degree in parasitology, a student had to describe a new species, and to get a Ph.D, a student needed to work out a life cycle (Dr Janovy told me the quote was misattributed and that he had heard it at a talk by O. Wilfred Olsen). Nicolai Angelo wasn't trained as a parasitologist. After completing his residency at the University of Virginia, in Charlottesville, he had, like many foreign-born doctors wishing to settle in the US, opted to serve three years at a 'medically underserved area' than return to Italy. He was assigned to Williamson, West Virginia. He quickly noticed that a significant number of his Appalachian patients appeared to have low-grade contact dermatitis. Now, his patients were mostly poor whites with fairly serious health issues; skin conditions were unseemly but low on the list of things to be fixed.

However, Dr Angelo understood better than most that to feel good it often helped to look good. All through high school, he'd had to endure ridicule on account of his buck teeth. He couldn't do much to fix his patients' real problem: generational poverty. But he felt he could fix their skin problem. The standard treatments for dermatitis tend to work unpredictably. Often the condition returns. So it was in these cases as well.

Skin conditions are difficult to treat, and they are the poster children of psychosomatic ailments. Indeed, faced with the combination of ignorance but partial control, almost all his patients evolved a superstitious regimen involving prayer, avoiding the sun, herbal cures, homoeopathy, Epsom salt baths and alcohol poisoning to keep the eczema at bay. In some cases, the protective rituals became quite fantastic. One of his patients, a Vietnam vet, believed the eczema was karmic payback for his life of violence. The blood spilled needed to be repaid in full. Using a multiplicity of aliases, the old soldier would donate blood in quantities that were neither legal nor safe.

At this point, a wise doctor would have given up. Besides, he had only one year left to serve. A charming Italian doctor with perfect teeth would be welcome almost anywhere in the States.

But Dr Angelo had become fond of his hardy, cantankerous, credulous, superstition-ridden and kind-hearted Appalachians. He liked their complicated but tight family relationships. He liked their political incorrectness. He liked attending their fervent prayer meetings with their hollerin' and shriekin' and devil cursin'; they were nothing like the chilly, stuffy and overly intellectual Catholic masses he'd attended in Brisighella. It rekindled his own lost faith. He redoubled his efforts. He took skin biopsies from his patients, re-educated himself in long forgotten histology lessons. And that is how the first *N. nicolai* cysts were discovered.

Though he had not been trained as a parasitologist, he taught himself enough to work out the life cycle of *N. nicolai*. Thanks to his efforts, we now know that though the parasite uses livestock and 'companion animals' as intermediate hosts, its 'definitive host' – the species in which it gets serious about settling down and reproducing – is *H. sapiens*. The parasite spores in human hosts, and in a remarkable deviation from other members of the genus *Neospora*, some of the spores ('oocysts') migrate to the skin's surface. From there it spread to other hosts through contact. This meant of course that *N. hughesi* could be sexually transmitted. His efforts eventually led to a combination-drug regimen that was successful in clearing up his patients' skin conditions.

Dr Angelo never left Williamson. He died in 2005. The local greasy spoon named a hideously large steak sandwich –

Le Diablo Angelo – in his honour.

Meanwhile, Janardhan was flourishing. In 2010, he was appointed to the faculty at the National Institute of Mental Health and Neurosciences (NIMHANS), in Bangalore. Ranked fourth in the country, it was an ideal launching for an ambitious thirty-something medical neuroscientist. For Christmas, their parents gave the couple a special gift: a one-week stay at a resort in the cool climes of hilly Coorg.

'We had never been left to ourselves for so long,' remembers Janardhan. 'It felt like our first real honeymoon.'

A few weeks after they returned from the vacation, Jennifer learnt she was carrying a baby. The news was received with undiluted joy. Janardhan relished announcing: 'We are pregnant.' He took his pregnancy seriously. Processed foods were out. High sodium foods were out. *They* had flourished on unhappy-cow radiated industrial milk throughout their childhood, but their baby could only burp on Vedic milk from A-2 certified Gir cows. Jennifer couldn't get a fever without Janardhan giving her a choice of orifices with which to indulge the thermometer. Jennifer liked a glass of rum and coke on occasion, but that was all over: the preggo czar refused to even discuss safe amounts.

The pregnant totalitarian had his gentle side: he was willing to massage Jennifer's expanding universe with expensive butter-soft skin creams for hours on end. They had never been happier. The couple cuddled into a bliss so intense that sometimes Jennifer would tear up. He got used to waking up and hearing her whisper in the dark: *Angel of God, my guardian dear, To whom God's love commits me here, Ever this day, be at my side, To light and guard, Rule and guide*. She preferred Catholic prayers.

Within the first few weeks of Tara Janardhan's birth, it became clear something had gone very wrong. Her central nervous system hadn't developed properly. After eight exhausting years of a wheelchair-bound, epileptic existence, unable to comprehend much beyond the radiant fact of the vast and inalterable love her family bore for her, Tara Janardhan returned to the great source.

For Janardhan and Jennifer, their joint journey ran out of road.

In June 2019, NIMHANS hosted a talk by a parasitologist, Dr Isabel Medina. Dr Seshadri, the head of department, emailed a circular begging the faculty to attend. She knew no neurologist gave a damn about parasites, parasitology or parasitologists, but it would just look bad if no faculty showed up. In Janardhan's case, the plea was unnecessary. By this time, says Janardhan, he was looking for excuses not to go home.

Dr Seshadri needn't have worried. The lecture room was packed. Word had spread about Dr Medina's hostility to bras. Her T-shirt read: No Free Lunch.

She talked mainly about parasites who were into mind control. The notorious schizophrenia-triggering, reckless-behaviour-encouraging, sloppy-dress-sense-inducing cat-parasite *T. gondii* was, of course, on the list. But she also discussed the parasites that turned caterpillars into ant bodyguards, ants into zombies, induced crickets to drown themselves and so on. She mentioned her interest in parasites had been sparked by an internship under Nicolai Angelo; she discussed the *N. nicolai* briefly. Janardhan says he was intrigued.

'It seemed to me the parasite was triggering OCD-like symptoms.'

Later, in the NIMHANS café, Medina recounted to Janardhan in detail everything Angelo had told her about the parasite. He had spent much of his research focusing on the neural mechanisms behind OCD, but he had never suspected that a parasite could be a trigger. Isabel Medina was sceptical at first, but she began to see the connection. Angelo had believed that the OCD-like symptoms were concomitant effects, caused by the skin ailment's aetiology. People, when forced to endure semi-predictable unpleasant phenomena, often generate appeasement rituals.

She told Janardhan that when the parasite had been rendered unviable in the patients with the newly available drugs, the OCD behaviour had also stopped.

If Dr Angelo had grasped that the parasite could alter behaviour, perhaps he would have been much more careful. Her friend, Medina recalled, had been murdered by a Vietnam vet he had been treating. Dr Angelo had persuaded the vet there was no need to risk getting arrested for using false identities; the vet could make the blood sacrifice at the Williamson Hospital itself. The vet would arrive every three weeks, the nurse would set up the apparatus, give the vet a mild sedative. Once the vet nodded off, the nurse would stop the extraction, be shown the nicely labelled bag of blood when he awoke and go home satisfied. The vet eventually noticed, however, that there was a difference in how he felt between the true donations and the fake ones. His diary revealed obsessive calculations to account for the strange 'rejections of the sacrifice'. During one session, the vet pretended to nod off, caught the nurse stopping the extraction, relabelling a blood bag and switching out the empty one. The same day he returned with a Beretta 92, shot Dr Angelo, as he was making his evening rounds, then shot himself.

The Medina and Janardhan paper on OCD and the

*N. nicolai* parasite is now a modern classic, cited many thousands of times. They showed that nearly 44 per cent of the patients undergoing OCD treatment at NIMHANS tested positive for *N. nicolai* cysts in the brain. Furthermore, there was a remarkable reduction in OCD behaviour when the patients were put on a course of antiparasitic.

But Janardhan was just getting started. His lab and the growing number of research alliances around the world began to work out how the parasite did what it did. Not all *N. nicolai* infestations produced OCD. Also, not all OCD victims showed active infestations. The two were related but also independent. Genetic analysis revealed predispositions and markers for when the parasite could trigger full-blown OCD. Most humans, it turned out, walked on a tightrope. We are habit-driven creatures, and a habit is how we keep events from happening all at once, but the neural habituation mechanisms could be easily hijacked.

George Soros's Open Society Foundation donated thirty million dollars to Janardhan and Medina's Valley start-up to develop a vaccine. This was when the *Wired Magazine* article on John Janardhan appeared: 'The God Slayer'.

'I would have never agreed to the interview,' says Janardhan, with uncharacteristic irritation, 'if I knew how they would title it.'

The label isn't entirely inaccurate. Janardhan's research and those of his colleagues have given atheists fearsome new ammunition. Multiple studies show that the antiparasitic were correlated with a reduction in religiosity. For example, when Medina returned to Williamson, she observed a marked reduction in church attendance in the area as compared to the surrounding districts. Local pastors were beginning to sermonize about the devil Heathen who was trying to destroy Christianity.

'C.S. Lewis was mistaken,' says Janardhan drily, after I play him a YouTube video of a local Williamson pastor in hysterics. 'The Devil's greatest con wasn't convincing the world he didn't exist. It was simply claiming that God exists.'

It isn't that our existential questions disappear. Existence takes a great deal of effort, and it is rational to question the necessity of any effort. But the need for a personal god is definitely an emotional construction. And the parasite can shape this reconstruction.

'It turns out we are Spinozans,' says Janardhan, 'not Cartesians.'

'We believe in Spinoza's god?'

'No, that's different. I mean that when it comes to how we receive claims, Spinoza, not Descartes, gave the correct theory.'

Suppose someone tells you she's heard on good authority that Oprah is granting a privileged few the opportunity to be mummified with her in an Egyptian-style pyramid. Does the mind incorporate this claim as a provisionally truthful claim which may later be disproved (Spinoza) or does it hold it 'in equilibrium', neither labelled 'true' nor 'false', until further evidence is brought to bear on Oprah's mummification plans? In the 90s, this question was studied by behavioural scientists Daniel Gilbert and Patrick S. Malone at the University of Texas at Austin and Douglas Krull at the University of Missouri at Columbia. Their ingenious experiments show that people, by default, tend to believe everything they are told. Later, we may change our minds, but by default, we take things at face value. We are Spinozans, not Cartesians.

The parasite finds this useful. Combined with the human

tendency to mightily resist cognitive dissonance, people will cling like koala bears to the tree trunks of the craziest beliefs.

A few weeks after the *Wired* article went viral, the usual attendance of the deranged visited Janardhan. Death threats. Long emails from crackpots quoting various scriptures to prove he was utterly wrong. He was egged in class by a group of fundamentalists. Pope Francis offered his measured thoughts in an encyclical. He invoked Merton: 'The man of faith who has never experienced doubt is not a man of faith.'

'The Pope!' says Janardhan, in a tone of disbelief.

When Richard Dawkins heard Janardhan was in London for a talk, he sent a warm invitation to stay at his home for Christmas.

A neuro-parasitological theory of cognitive disorder is beginning to emerge. The family *Sarcocystidae* of obligate endoparasites seem particularly adept at manipulating vertebrate behaviour. 'Obligate' means the parasite cannot reproduce without their dominant hosts; your casa is their humping ground. The *T. gondii* belonged to this family; so did members of the genus *Neospora*. Endoparasites should perhaps be called 'beginoparasites'. As with the mafia, your troubles really begin when you encounter one of them.

The outstanding talent of *N. nicolai*, studies suggest, is to get people to congregate. People addicted to large, intense group concerts have been shown to become more infected than those who lived isolated lives. Extraverts are much more likely to be infected than introverts. In a double-blind study, a population of mice were tracked for a month to identify behaviour traits, after which they were either infected with the parasite (experimental group) or received an antiparasitic (control group). Both groups were then tracked for another few weeks. The results were dramatic, to say the least. The control group showed a marked reduction in their socialization, turned relative loners. The reverse was true of the experimental group. Sociality is fundamentally a species trait, of course, but the experiment suggests the parasite can modulate the degree.

A forthcoming study appearing next month will discuss the results of tests on what is perhaps the world's largest annual gathering of believers: India's Kumbh Mela. Millions will bathe together, eat together, worship together. When I ask Janardhan for a reveal of the results, he smiles and only says: 'God is on the surface of things.'

It isn't really safe anymore for John Janardhan in India. The government has grudgingly appointed a single security guard, but on a contingent basis. Janardhan is to stop making 'anti-national and community-offending statements'. He is seriously thinking of migrating; there is no shortage of job offers: Medina's lab, Soros's offer, universities in the Netherlands.

Even if it were safe, he says, he would leave. He is weary of the country's growing inequalities, the communal mistrust, the overwhelming religiosity. Indian universities invite him for keynote addresses and open with Hindu religious rituals. It had never bothered him earlier, but now it did. I asked him why was it that so many poor countries were so religious. Surely, the people in these countries only needed to compare their situations, their beliefs, with those living in richer ones?

'It is possible,' admits Janardhan. 'Poor countries are ridden with parasites. Rich countries aren't. But I don't know of any study that takes the question seriously.'

Jennifer enters the room. Janardhan gets up with an apologetic smile, goes to the wheelchair in the corner and rolls it over to his ex-wife.

'I'm donating it,' Jennifer clarifies. 'There's such a shortage.'

Janardhan tells me later that he obsesses about whether the skin lotions he'd applied on Jennifer contained toxic levels of Vitamin A. He'd had a jar of cream analysed, but the amount of Vitamin A was within safe limits. Yet Janardhan can't let go of his feeling.

'If only we had the will to disbelieve,' says Janardhan wearily.

Janardhan swivels the wheelchair around so that she can wheel it out. She reaches for the grasp. He asks if she needs help. No, no, Jennifer protests, she can handle the boxes. Her friend is waiting downstairs. Please continue.

Their hands meet on the surface of the wheelchair's handle.

We keep by letting go and we let go by keeping. Jennifer holds on to her faith and Janardhan holds on to his grief. They seem to have let go of each other. The sadness between them seems to have almost transmuted into a sacred kind of love.

I have just spent an hour or so with the world's leading expert on a doxastic parasite. And yet I cannot let go of this word: sacred. It consoles me, guides me, binds me to this world. What will we retain of ourselves if we lean away from our consolations and simply, ever so gently, just let go?

# BURDEN

## *Salil Desai*

'Kavita, don't be like that! Come home with me...' Avadhoot pleaded with his wife.

'I'm fed up with you coming here every few weeks and bleating like a lamb, Avadhoot,' his wife said scornfully. 'I'm not coming back till you resolve the problem...'

'What do you want me to do, Kavita? She is my mother. I've got to take care of her...'

'Yes, but I don't have to, Avadhoot!' Kavita replied, flashing her eyes. 'And she *was* your mother once. Now she's more of a vegetable...'

It was said with a vicious candidness that tore into Avadhoot. 'Don't demean her, Kavita, please...It's cruel...' he protested.

'Oh, I'm being cruel?' His wife turned on him, 'No, you are wicked to expect me to play nurse to a half-dead person.'

'But I told you I have made an arrangement with Sheetal-tai, our second-floor neighbour. She comes regularly...'

'From 9 a.m. to 6 p.m. is not enough, Avadhoot,' Kavita said. 'There are twenty-four hours in a day...'

'But between you and me, can't we manage the rest of the time?' Avadhoot said, trying not to sound exasperated.

'No way, Avadhoot. With the baby, I can't spare a moment for your mother,' Kavita asserted.

Thus rebuked, Avadhoot threw a forlorn glance at their six-month-old baby girl, sleeping peacefully in her cradle. How long was he going to have to keep making these hasty, one-day trips to catch a glimpse of his daughter and his wife, at his in-law's place in Kolhapur?

'Please, Kavita, we'll work something out,' he said, moving closer to his wife. 'I can't bear to live away from you and Ketaki. It's almost been a year since we've been staying apart.'

Kavita turned to him with a pouty frown. 'Why can't your sister Devayani take the responsibility of your mother now?'

Avadhoot sighed. 'How is that possible? Devayani's working. She's got her husband and children to look after. Besides, their flat in Mumbai is so small.'

'Oh, so it's okay if she shirks her responsibility towards your mother?'

'But, dear, she's also taking care of her in-laws, no...'

'Devayani's in-laws aren't paralysed, Avadhoot. Besides, they live next door, in their *own* flat,' his wife scoffed. 'Look, I don't care what you do. Find some old people's home or an assisted living facility where they take care of paralytic patients and shift your mother there. Or get a full-time caretaker for her. I'm not going to spend an ounce of my energy on her.'

'The cost is unaffordable, Kavita,' Avadhoot reasoned, 'please try to understand.'

But his ingratiating, conciliatory tone cut no ice with his fretful wife. 'Perhaps you would prefer to pay maintenance and alimony then,' she shot back.

Avadhoot felt as if he had been slapped across his face. He blinked and let out a low whine, but his wife's diatribe that followed left him in no doubt that it was not a remark said in a fit of momentary anger.

'So, you decide whether you want me and Ketaki or your mother for company,' were the last words Kavita said to him, before they parted that night, as Avadhoot left for Pune, on the night-bus.

*

He had expected to reach by around 5.30 or 6 in the morning, but an unusual pile up near Shirwal delayed the bus by an hour. So, when Avadhoot got home it was around 7.30.

'I am so sorry, Sheetal-tai,' he began as soon as the part-time caretaker and his neighbour from the second floor, opened the door.

'Nah! It's okay. In fact, I was hoping your bus would be delayed so that you didn't turn up at dawn,' the cheerful, forty-year-old Sheetal-tai said. 'Got an extra hour of sleep this way.'

'Is Aai okay? Any problem?' Avadhoot asked.

'Nothing to worry at all. I gave her all her medication without fail; the dabbawallah delivered lunch and dinner for both of us, so no issues,' Sheetal-tai said. 'I sponged her yesterday, did some physiotherapy and massaged her too...All as usual. She's fine.'

'What would I do without you, Sheetal-tai,' Avadhoot said. 'Is Aai awake or still asleep?'

'Still sleeping. I'll be back in an hour's time so that you can leave for office,' Sheetal-tai said animatedly. 'How are Kavita and the baby? When are mother and daughter coming back to join proud father?'

Avadhoot's face fell. He averted his eyes and just shrugged. Sheetal-tai immediately sensed some complication. 'What's the matter? Everything all right?' she asked, trying not to sound inquisitive.

For a moment, it looked as if Avadhoot was all set to confide in her but seemed to change his mind. 'Yes, all is well,' he said, then pretended to glance at his watch. 'My god, I better get going, Sheetal-tai, or I'll be late for work...'

Sheetal-tai took the cue and didn't pursue the matter, although she was dying to know more. 'I'll be off too then,' she said and quickly scrambled out of the door.

Avadhoot felt grateful once again that he had found Sheetal-tai to rely on. She and her husband were a childless couple, who weren't well off. Sheetal-tai belonged to a class that wouldn't stoop so low as to work as maidservants or cooks, because it was beneath their sense of dignity. But neither did she have any bare minimum qualifications to secure and hold an office job.

Sheetal-tai had taken on this quasi-nursing job of looking after Avadhoot's mother because it was convenient and acceptably respectable. Her husband had let her take it because it brought in some much-needed money, without her having to leave the building. Moreover, he would also not have to be inconvenienced because it was flexible and informal.

In fact, it was only because Sheetal-tai's husband travelled out-of-station every fortnight or so for work that Avadhoot was able to make an overnight arrangement with her, so she could stay and look after his mother, while he made a quick visit to Kolhapur. Otherwise, it would simply not have been possible because Sheetal-tai's usual timings were 9 to 6, Monday to Saturday. Her husband wouldn't let her linger even a minute more. His wife had to be home to receive him, ready with tea and snacks, and she could leave home in the mornings only after making him breakfast and packing his lunch.

Avadhoot went into his mother's room. She appeared to have just woken up. 'I'm back, Aai,' he said, going up to her bedside and into her field of vision. The old woman's eyes strayed towards him and registered his presence but the expression on her face was vacant as usual.

The paralytic attack had turned his mother into half a human being or even less. She couldn't speak except to utter some involuntary sounds; her body functioned at minimum capacity and speed. Every single action needed assistance, right from sitting up in bed to eating food, to dressing up – as if her entire body functioned on low-voltage, incapable of enough power surge to make the various parts work autonomously.

Her face had turned into a mask and her responses were rare, as if she no longer had a will of her own and only enough brain capacity left to obey instructions given to her. Mercifully, there was no major organ failure.

'I met Kavita and Ketaki,' Avadhoot said to his mother, then tapped his mobile and showed her photos of his daughter and his selfies with her. His mother gazed at the mobile, but there was nothing that could tell him if she was pleased or happy or felt anything at all. It was frustrating, but he hoped his mother could still feel emotion even if she couldn't express any.

'Nice, no?' he said, then laid the phone down. 'You want to get up and go to the bathroom now?'

It wasn't so much so a question – because his mother never answered – than it was a call for action. He was now going to help her get to the toilet, then brush her teeth, followed by tea. Fortunately, his mother could still manage to clean herself, because he had got a bidet installed as advised by the doctor. Brushing her teeth was trickier since she could sometimes manage a few strokes, but at other times, her hands would shake too much or fall away. So Avadhoot would have to do it for her.

As he prepared tea, Avadhoot glanced at his mother seated in her wheelchair, staring unseeingly at the television. He tried to remember how she had been before the paralytic attack two years ago. No fond memories came rushing to his mind. His mother had always been a dull, colourless soul, not particularly affectionate towards her children. She had lived her life as if it were a wretched job she had been stuck with.

Avadhoot couldn't remember any words of motherly love, encouragement or even anger that had remained with him. No little gesture, no lip-smacking dish – not one single action. How could an entire life have been lived without any memorable moments? And yet there definitely had been a silent bond between them.

He poured the tea in her sipper cup. When he had realized that she was unable to drink tea from a normal cup or even a saucer, without spilling it all over, because she couldn't hold it still for long enough, Avadhoot had thought of a sipper. Although he was at first apprehensive that she might scald her tongue, the idea had worked wonderfully well and his mother had become adept at slurping even the hottest brew with the sipper – tea, coffee, milk, soup.

Avadhoot watched her down the tea as he sipped his. He gave her small pieces of biscuit to nibble with it from a small bowl. He suddenly felt a lump in his throat as his mind harked back to the previous evening, when he had been thrilled at the sensation of feeding his baby daughter. When was he going to be able to do that every day? His little Ketaki! What if Kavita stuck to her guns?

He glanced at his mother again and felt something he'd

never felt before. Resentment! So intense, it took his breath away. His phone rang, just then. It was his sister Devayani calling.

'Hullo, didi,' he said gloomily.

'Just called to check if you are back, Avadhoot,' Devayani asked.

'Yes, the bus was a little late.'

'Bus? Why didn't you hire a taxi if you were bringing back Kavita and Ketaki?' his sister remarked with surprise.

'Because they didn't accompany me back, didi,' Avadhoot snapped.

'What? Why? The baby is six months old, for heaven's sake,' Devayani said. 'High time your delicate wife returned home.'

Avadhoot glanced at his mother sucking from her sipper, then got up from his chair and went into another room. 'Didi, my whole life is being held ransom to Aai's condition. My daily routine is centred around her. I am either working in office or tending to Aai. I can't go anywhere and even Kavita refuses to return till I make full-time arrangements for Aai's care.'

'What? Who does Kavita think she is? Why can't she take care of Aai when that neighbour of yours is there to help? You've pampered your wife too much, Avadhoot. Do you want me to give her a piece of my mind?' his sister snarled.

'Didi, I require help, not sermons for my wife,' Avadhoot replied. 'I need to look for an assisted living facility for Aai or at least a full-time caretaker, but I can afford neither. Will you be ready to share the expenses with me fifty-fifty? Please?'

An awkward silence ensued before his sister spoke again. 'Avadhoot, you can't let Kavita blackmail you! Money does not grow on trees. You have to be firm with her. It's her duty.'

'Didi, isn't it your duty also to look after mother? Or at least share the expenses?' Avadhoot interjected.

'You can't speak to me like that, Avadhoot. I am your older

sister,' Devayani fumed. 'Just because you can't put your wife in her place, you dare to...'

Their argument quickly escalated to acrimony, when Avadhoot suddenly thought he heard a sound from the adjacent room. Still exchanging barbs with his sister, he made his way there and was shocked to see his mother trembling and writhing.

Avadhoot tried to grasp what was happening and realized the old woman appeared to be choking over a piece of biscuit. How in the world had she managed to put one in her mouth, because he didn't remember giving her a piece before leaving the room.

'Didi...didi, something's happening to Aai. I'll hang up now and attend to her,' he said hoarsely into the phone.

'Oh!' his sister responded. 'Is everything okay? Hullo? Hullo, Avadhoot?' But Avadhoot had already hung up and rushed to his mother's side. She had collapsed forward now and almost slumped off the wheelchair.

'Aai, Aai...' Avadhoot held her up, only to have the daylights scared out of him. His mother had started convulsing and looked as if she was turning blue, her eyes disappearing upwards into her sockets. Avadhoot felt his blood turn cold. He began dialling the ambulance, cursing his luck again.

*

A month had passed since his mother had suffered the second paralytic attack.

'It was a mini stroke,' Dr Thombre had said. 'Not as severe as the previous one but enough to have been fatal. You got her to the hospital just in time.'

Those words had echoed in Avadhoot's mind ever since. Could just a little delay on his part have saved his already troubled existence from turning even more wretched? His mother had miraculously survived the mini stroke, but her condition had worsened and multiplied Avadhoot's woes. She was no longer ambulatory and had completely lost bowel control.

Sheetal-tai had drawn the line at bedpans and involuntary soiling, even though she was willing to continue playing general attendant and feeding the patient. Avadhoot's sister had visited for two days and fled back to Mumbai, citing family commitments. And Avadhoot had experienced the full horror of the bleak situation – the exhaustion, the revulsion and the mind-boggling costs. He had hired full-time nurses for three months through an agency, who came in rotational shifts. It was not just the money that had flabbergasted him, but the sheer unreliability and lackadaisical service received in return.

The nurses were often late for their shifts and would make excuses to leave early. They would get into arguments with him whenever he pointed out some task that was not done properly. They would complain constantly about how much extra work they were putting in or throw tantrums and threaten to quit.

His phone rang as he sat brooding in his office, one afternoon, after a firing from his boss. He had been roundly ticked off for taking too many leaves, bungling assignments and generally turning in a below-par performance for several weeks.

It was his wife calling. Avadhoot was in no mood for more mental mauling today. But he had forgotten to return her call earlier in the morning, so it was better to take her call now.

'Hullo, Kavita. Sorry I couldn't call back. I had to do something urgent...' he lied.

'What have you decided?' his wife demanded.

'About what?'

'You know what,' his wife screeched. 'About your mother!'

'Kavita, I already told you. She's just recovering from another mini stroke. I've also got full-time nurses. What more can I do? Hopefully in a few months her condition will improve,' Avadhoot replied uneasily.

'That's no good! You shift her to some assisted living facility.'

'How many times have I told you I won't be able to afford that?' Avadhoot protested.

'Well then look for cheaper places.'

'There aren't any, Kavita.'

'Fine, then I am filing for divorce,' his wife said harshly.

'Are you crazy, Kavita? On what grounds?'

'There's plenty. For mental and physical harassment.'

'What?'

'For unnatural sex.'

'What? We haven't even had natural sex for a year.'

'For carrying on an affair with Sheetal-tai.'

'Don't be ridiculous, Kavita! You know none of this is true,' Avadhoot pleaded. 'Don't be spiteful. Don't do this to me. I can't just dump my mother somewhere.'

'I don't care, Avadhoot,' his wife said, breathing fire. 'I'm giving you a fortnight more. If you prefer to hang on to your paralysed, half-dead mother, then you deserve a divorce and a lifetime of alimony and maintenance.'

'But...but, Kavita.'

His wife had already disconnected and so all Avadhoot

could do was grind his teeth in vain. Why was life pushing him into a corner like that?

*

'Euthanasia? Don't be silly, Avadhoot. Your mother's not on the ventilator or something.' Dr Thombre peered at him, and said, 'Besides she hasn't made a living will, has she?'

'Living will? What's that, Doctor?'

'A written, legal document refusing further medical treatment or consenting to its withdrawal,' Dr Thombre explained. 'Terminally ill patients can do that in our country and choose passive euthanasia.'

'No, but isn't there any other way? I mean, I can't bear to see my mother in this condition,' Avadhoot said. 'What's the point of living like that? Being unable to move or function, speak or do anything. Lying in bed, shitting in bed, getting bed sores?'

'Hmmm. I know how it feels, Avadhoot, but there's nothing that can be done. I mean, you can try and move the high court, but I doubt it'll help in the absence of a living will, and anyway the plea won't be considered promptly.'

'Are there any realistic chances of improvement in her condition, Doctor?' Avadhoot asked.

'Unlikely! Besides, you simply won't be able to afford advanced treatment or surgery,' Dr Thombre said. 'And even if you can, the chances of a miracle are minuscule.'

Avadhoot shook his head. 'Doctor, how long do you think she'll survive like that, in this condition?'

'Oh, that one can never say. Six months, a year, maybe much longer,' the doctor replied.

Avadhoot could have screamed his heart out. What the hell was he to do now?

*

Kavita's deadline of a fortnight had drawn to a close. Avadhoot had made several attempts to coax and persuade her, even making another quick trip to Kolhapur the previous week. It had been in vain. Kavita had been adamant, her parents, hostile and scornful, telling him their daughter was right. After the visit, Kavita had stopped taking his calls. Things turned ominous when he got a call one day from Juna Rajwada Police Station, Kolhapur.

'Avadhoot Palshikar?' a voice drawled.

'Yes?'

'I'm Constable Sangole from Juna Rajwada Police Station, Kolhapur,' the voice continued. 'Your wife Kavita Palshikar has filed a complaint against you.'

'What?' Avadhoot reacted with a hiccup, thoroughly rattled.

The constable read out the sections under which the complaint had been filed. 'So, you need to present yourself for questioning here. You live in Pune, right?'

'Yes, saheb, but there's been some misunderstanding. My wife...er...we just had a baby,' Avadhoot began to stutter.

'All that you tell the investigating officer when you come tomorrow,' Constable Sangole said dismissively. 'Reach by 12.30 p.m.'

'Tomorrow? Saheb, I have an invalid mother. She's fully paralysed. I cannot make it tomorrow,' Avadhoot said.

'All right, be here day after tomorrow,' Constable Sangole responded.

'No, saheb...Please, I can come on Sunday or next week,' Avadhoot requested. 'I...I have to make arrangements...'

'Sunday is five days away. Don't you know these are very serious charges?' the constable said with practiced sharpness. 'You can be arrested if you dilly-dally...'

'Arrested? But...saheb I haven't done anything...I swear...' Avadhoot croaked.

'That we'll see. You better get here on Saturday. The IO is on leave on Sunday,' Constable Sangole instructed.

'Ok...saheb...thank you...' Avadhoot acquiesced as the constable disconnected.

For the next two days he sweated buckets, trying frantically to call his wife and her parents, who didn't take his calls. Then he contacted a lawyer friend in Pune, who got him in touch with a Kolhapur colleague. The Kolhapur lawyer, Adv. Gojumgunde, said he would look into the matter and told Avadhoot to meet him when he reached town on Saturday, before going to the police station.

But the meeting with Adv. Gojumgunde did not inspire much confidence in Avadhoot, although the Kolhapur lawyer gave him a few tips and told him to call in case the cops actually moved to take him into custody. Surprisingly, the encounter with the IO, who turned out to be a woman, wasn't half as scary as he had expected it to be. API Kirti Mirajkar asked him several questions, heard him out as he told her about his quandary and the background to the flashpoint between his wife and him.

She had then grunted almost sympathetically and asked Constable Sangole to record Avadhoot's statement. 'I will be conducting further inquiries. You must present yourself as and when required,' API Mirajkar said.

Avadhoot had readily agreed, only too relieved not to be taken into custody. Neither had he been asked for a bribe.

'It is always a mistake to go to the police station with a lawyer the first time. It hurts the ego of the IO and unnecessarily makes one appear guilty,' Adv. Gojumgunde had told him in their brief meeting earlier. That had turned out to be sound advice indeed.

But Avadhoot's exhilaration had been short-lived. Because what awaited him back home in Pune, was nothing short of a nightmare.

When he had left early morning, in his hurry to not miss the bus, he'd forgotten the set of house-keys he always carried with himself. In fact, he hadn't even realized it the whole day because of all the anxiety. Avadhoot had instructed the first-shift nurse to wait for the arrival of the second-shift nurse. But the night-nurse had called up the day-nurse and told her she was running late. The day-nurse had grumbled, waited another hour and lost her patience.

She then called up Avadhoot, who was just an hour into his return journey. The day-nurse told him she couldn't wait any longer for the night-nurse, so Avadhoot had asked her to leave the keys with Sheetal-tai and inform the night-nurse. Sheetal-tai would also check up on his mother if the night-nurse was delayed longer.

Unfortunately, it being a Saturday evening, Sheetal-tai and her husband had gone out. So, the day-nurse dumped the keys with the day-shift watchman, who had spent years honing his talent for unreliability. He had placed the house-keys he knew not where and forgot to inform the nightwatchman about it, when the latter replaced him about half an hour later.

When the night-nurse finally arrived, the key was nowhere to be found, and the day-shift watchman was unreachable on his mobile. The night-nurse made a frantic call to Avadhoot, who felt his heart jump into his mouth. His mother was now all alone inside the house for nearly two hours. It was 9 p.m. Avadhoot was almost three hours away from reaching Pune. He asked the night-shift watchman to fetch a locksmith urgently. The night-shift watchman had no idea where he could find one and moreover, he could not leave his post. The night-nurse also declared it was not her job to go looking for locksmiths.

Avadhoot then called up another neighbour – the secretary of the society – who promised he would try and do what best he could. As a person of authority, he dispatched the night-shift watchman to look for a locksmith in the nearby areas, but was baffled when the man came back empty-handed, saying the only locksmith in the neighbourhood had downed the shutters and gone home.

The secretary then put the matter up in the society WhatsApp group, inviting suggestions to tackle the problem. Avadhoot's heart sank further when he saw the message. His poor, helpless mother! What must be her condition? Would she be okay? He was still going to take hours to get home.

Meanwhile, responses in the WhatsApp group were coming thick and fast. Someone suggested the watchman become a trapeze artist and climb down into Avadhoot's balcony from the flat above his. Someone responded that this was too dangerous. Another neighbour recommended that the door be broken, but no one had any idea how that could be accomplished. Someone suggested calling the police, while yet another said calling the fire brigade was warranted.

After some more debate, Avadhoot pleaded that they call the police first and if they declined to help in the matter, then the fire brigade be contacted. The secretary acted upon this course of action.

When Avadhoot finally reached home, what he got was an earful of rebuke and blame from the police, the secretary and the sundry neighbours for letting such a situation arise in the first place; and then a breathful of stench when he stepped inside the house, that turned his stomach inside out.

His mother had soiled herself several times and lay helplessly in her filth for hours. Worse, she had then slipped or fallen from her bed, fractured her arm and broken two ribs. The medical attendants from the ambulance parked below were engaged in a heated argument with the night-nurse. They insisted she should help clean the patient before shifting her, while she was flatly refusing, telling them it was their job now.

His mother lay where she had fallen, as if it made no difference to anyone if she was dead, alive, in excruciating pain or otherwise. The sight, the stench, the sounds added up to a scene of surreal horror. Avadhoot felt an almighty rumble in the pit of his stomach, and he threw up as if he were a volcanic geyser that had just erupted.

★

Avadhoot sat on the sofa, staring intently at the newspaper report he had just read, then re-read. It was a Sunday morning, a week after the distressing event. His mother had been discharged from the hospital after two days, with her hand in plaster. Ribs, of course, couldn't be plastered and god alone knew the amount of pain it caused her.

The pealing of the doorbell startled him. Avadhoot looked at his watch. The day-nurse couldn't be here so early, especially since it was a Sunday, and she knew he did not have to rush to office. The night-nurse had left some time ago.

Avadhoot lay down the newspaper on the teapoy and trudged to the door. He was surprised to see Sheetal-tai outside, with a tiffin in hand.

'I have brought poha for you and some sweet porridge for your mother,' she said with a smile and thrust the tiffin at him. 'How is she now?'

Avadhoot took the tiffin gratefully, almost overcome by her kindness. 'Please come in…Sheetal-tai…' he said.

They had barely walked to the sofa in the drawing room when a loud sob escaped Avadhoot's mouth, and he burst into tears.

'Arre, what happened?' Sheetal-tai asked, bewildered.

Avadhoot shook his head shamefacedly, desperately trying to stem the flow of tears and the sound of sobs.

'No bad news, I hope?' Sheetal-tai enquired gingerly.

Avadhoot shook his head, wiped his tears and said, 'Thank you, Sheetal-tai. For bringing me and Aai breakfast…thank you!'

'No, no, it was no trouble,' Sheetal-tai said. 'I was feeling so bad since that evening. If we had not gone out for a movie, none of it would have happened. So, I thought I should pay you and your Aai a visit today. My husband is again on tour…'

Avadhoot had managed to regain his composure by now. 'It's awfully nice of you, Sheetal-tai.'

Sheetal-tai smiled coyly. 'Is your Aai awake?'

'No, she's still sleeping. The painkillers make her even more drowsy.'

'Ah! Come then, have some hot breakfast. Even I haven't eaten yet,' Sheetal-tai said, and knowing her way around the house, quickly fetched dishes and served poha, for both of them.

Avadhoot felt a lump return to his throat. He couldn't remember the last time someone had made hot breakfast for him. How he missed Kavita, but she'd served him a legal notice now, instead of poha.

Sheetal-tai's poha tasted wonderful. He savoured each spoonful.

'Your mother fractured her arm, right?' Sheetal-tai asked.

'Yes, and two ribs...'

Sheetal-tai shuddered. 'Poor soul! Is she in a lot of pain?'

Avadhoot nodded. 'God alone knows how she bears it. No one deserves so much suffering,' he said with feeling.

'Yes, her body has already been ravaged by two strokes, and now this,' Sheetal-tai remarked.

'And what kind of life is this? Where's the bloody dignity?' Avadhoot blurted out. 'She was fully covered in her own urine and excreta and what not! Lying helpless and injured. She can't do a thing by herself now, and those two nurses treat her like a slab of meat...'

An awkward silence followed, before Sheetal-tai asked him candidly, 'Is that why Kavita hasn't come back with the baby yet?'

Avadhoot flinched at the directness of her question, then nodded, embarrassed. 'Yes...'

'Hmm, I thought as much,' Sheetal-tai said. 'So what are you going to do about it?'

Avadhoot shrugged, then grimaced. He didn't want to share the sordid details of Kavita's police complaint and legal notice.

Sheetal-tai shook her head. 'So sad. What does the doctor say?'

'That Aai is bedridden for life and her condition will keep deteriorating...' Avadhoot replied, his voice hollow.

'I see,' Sheetal-tai said and got up. 'Let me check if she's awake now.'

Avadhoot nodded. 'Would you like some tea, Sheetal-tai? I'm making some for myself.'

'Okay,' Sheetal-tai said and went inside.

Avadhoot sighed, then got up and began making tea. Sheetal-tai returned to the living room a few moments later.

'She's still asleep but I think she needs to be changed,' she said, her nose wrinkling.

Avadhoot's shoulders slumped. 'I hope that nurse comes soon,' he said, squirming.

Sheetal-tai sat down on the sofa, picked up the newspaper on the teapoy and glanced at it.

Avadhoot's phone buzzed as he prepared the tea. He groaned and picked up the phone. 'Hullo, where are you, Nurse-tai? What? Again? But, Nurse-tai, she needs immediate attention just now. No, every Sunday you give some excuse and come late. Hullo, hullo...'

His face twisted into a frustrated scowl as if tempted to fling the phone away. The tea had come to a boil. He poured it into two mugs, walked over to the sofa and offered one mug to Sheetal-tai.

Both sipped tea in silence.

'I sometimes feel it would be better if she were to die than live in this state,' Avadhoot suddenly said, as if someone else had spoken from inside him. He glanced at Sheetal-tai quickly, shocked at himself – expecting her to be taken aback or react with unease.

'I guess it's not unnatural to feel like that, given the circumstances,' Sheetal-tai said instead. 'Maybe your mother wishes the same.'

Avadhoot was startled. 'You think so, Sheetal-tai?'

Sheetal-tai shrugged. 'I know I would,' she said. 'Who would want to waste away like this?'

Avadhoot reflected on her remark, then shook his head. 'It's such a helpless feeling, Sheetal-tai. I shudder to think of her condition if her organs start failing. How am I going to manage? I wish there was some way for me to let her go painlessly and peacefully.'

'What do you mean?'

Avadhoot was quiet for a few seconds then said, 'I am almost running out of my savings, having to pay for Aai's treatment and the nurses. And if I have to start paying maintenance to Kavita and legal expenses, I'll be ruined.'

'What? Why will you have to pay maintenance?'

Hesitation grappled with anguish. 'I received a notice from Kavita's lawyer this week. She's already filed a police complaint against me in Kolhapur,' Avadhoot whimpered.

'Oh, you poor man,' Sheetal-tai said, clicking her tongue. 'I didn't realize matters were that bad.'

'I'm at my wit's end, Sheetal-tai.'

The ringing of the doorbell interrupted their conversation.

'It must be the nurse,' Avadhoot said and got up to open the door.

*

'Hello. Avadhoot Palshikar?' The call from API Kirti Mirajkar came at lunchtime the following Tuesday.

'Yes, madam?' Avadhoot responded nervously.

'Did you get a new motorcycle, flat-screen TV and two lakhs cash from your in-laws in your wedding?' API Mirajkar asked.

Avadhoot's mouth turned dry. 'Yes.'

'Well, your wife has filed a fresh complaint against you invoking dowry harassment sections, so you better get here tomorrow.'

'But, madam, I...I never demanded any dowry from them. I swear...! They gave it as normal wedding gifts,' Avadhoot said shakily.

'That's not their story,' API Mirajkar replied. 'We'll see about that. I'll be expecting you tomorrow.'

'But, madam, I told you about my invalid mother. I...I'll need to make arrangements. I need some time.'

'Okay. Report here by Friday noon,' API Mirajkar said. 'And remember I might have to take you into custody, so make longer arrangements for your mother. Incidentally, she's also named in the FIR.'

'What?'

'Of course you need not bring her along but bring copies of all your mother's reports and certificate from the doctor about her paralytic condition,' API Mirajkar said and disconnected.

A cold, clammy sensation began manifesting itself inside Avadhoot's stomach. Arrest! Imprisonment! What fresh hell was this? His sister and mother had conducted the dowry negotiations. He had been too smitten by Kavita to bother. Why, oh why, had he gone along then? What was he going to do now?

His frenzied mind went back to the newspaper report he had read on Sunday.

★

'Didi, I need you to come down for a couple of days,' Avadhoot came straight to the point when his sister picked up the phone.

'What? Why?'

'I've been summoned by Kolhapur Police on Friday. I might even be arrested.'

'That conniving bitch! It's all your fault. You pampered her too much,' Devayani raged.

'Shut up, didi. You and Aai selected Kavita for me. You also demanded dowry,' Avadhoot retorted morosely, 'and now I am going to be arrested for it.'

'Was I clairvoyant to know she would turn out to be such a witch?'

Avadhoot was not to be distracted. 'You need to reach here by Thursday night. I have to leave on Friday early morning.'

'I can't just drop everything and come. My kids have exams,' Devayani replied churlishly. 'Why don't you apply for anticipatory bail, or bribe the cops?'

'Didi,' Avadhoot said wearily, 'I am trying just that but who knows for sure?'

'Look, if you are arrested then of course I'll have to come, but for Friday make some other arrangements,' Devayani said. 'The full-time nurses are anyway coming, aren't they? So just ask your neighbour Sheetal-tai to check on things.'

'Come on, didi. I'm begging you. You can't always shirk your responsibility like that,' Avadhoot said desperately. There was a reason he needed his sister to definitely be there.

'Watch your tone, Avadhoot,' Devayani snapped. 'I can't be at your beck and call. I'll only come in case you are really arrested.'

She disconnected the call. Rage, panic and frustration surged through Avadhoot in equal measure. He tried to steady himself. There was no alternative now. He would have to make do with Sheetal-tai! He still had twenty-four hours to make the final decision – to go ahead or back out!

*

'Sheetal-tai, I need a big favour,' Avadhoot said as she opened her house door on Thursday evening.

'Just now?'

'No, tomorrow morning,' Avadhoot replied anxiously. 'I have to leave for Kolhapur early morning again. The...the police have summoned me.'

'Oh! Don't worry. Leave your key with me. I'll make sure what happened last time is not repeated,' Sheetal-tai assured him.

'Thank you, Sheetal-tai. Can you also feed mother biscuits and tea around 8 a.m.? The day-nurse is refusing to come early, before 8.30 and the night-nurse refuses to wait beyond 7.30. So...so...' Avadhoot said, palpably jittery.

'But in the morning...you know my husband's breakfast and tiffin...'

'I know, Sheetal-tai. But just for tomorrow morning if you could spare fifteen minutes...I would be really obliged. I'll make and keep tea in a thermos flask. It'll stay hot.'

Sheetal-tai frowned. 'All right, I'll wake up a little earlier and get his things ready. But why don't you drop in at night and directly request my husband? It will make things easier for me.'

'Okay. But he won't refuse, no?' Avadhoot swallowed nervously.

'No, your personal request will flatter him.'

Sheetal-tai's husband didn't look too pleased when Avadhoot returned that night. 'Okay, but this is the last time! We are neighbours, not family,' he said with a finger-wag.

It stung Avadhoot, but he nevertheless thanked the man profusely. 'I'll leave the flask with black tea on the table,' he repeated to Sheetal-tai, as he was leaving their house.

'Black tea? Why? Your Aai does not have normal tea like earlier?' Sheetal-tai asked, puzzled.

Avadhoot's throat ran dry. 'Er, doctor's advice. Aai does not like black tea and may resist...but please make sure she drinks the whole cup.'

'Don't worry.'

'And, Sheetal-tai...just rinse the flask afterwards,' Avadhoot said hoarsely.

'Of course,' Sheetal-tai said, after a little pause.

*

The call came at 9.30 a.m. just as the bus passed Satara, and Avadhoot was in danger of turning into a nervous wreck. Intriguingly, it wasn't from Sheetal-tai.

'Palshikar Saheb, I've called the ambulance...' the day-nurse said breathlessly.

Avadhoot was dumbstruck. It was really happening, what he had set in motion. 'Why? What's happened?' he stuttered.

'You need to return immediately. I think your mother's suffered a heart attack,' the nurse replied.

'Oh my god! But...she's still...er...breathing...right?'

The nurse hesitated. 'I can't be sure. She has no pulse. The ambulance will be here any moment. You please turn back...'

'Oh heavens! Please take her straight to Dr Thombre's hospital. I'll speak to him,' Avadhoot said, feeling utterly sick of himself. 'I'll alight at Karad and take a return bus...but it'll still take me three hours. You please be with her till then.'

'Look, I'll accompany her to the hospital, but why don't you arrange for some friend or neighbour to take over thereafter,' the nurse replied promptly. 'Maybe that Sheetal-tai who was here earlier.'

'Is she there now?'

'No. She left as soon as I came. I tried to call her when your mother collapsed, but she didn't take the call...'

'Oh, okay! I'll quickly make a few calls, but you please be there till I make arrangements,' Avadhoot said and hung up. He clutched his head trying to fight the bile rising from the pit of his stomach. He had probably succeeded in ending his mother's wretched existence, but this could also be the end of him too. He could well be caught.

The only thing he was banking on was no one finding it the least bit surprising or suspicious that a severely paralysed old woman had suffered a heart attack. On the nurse, the ambulance staff and the doctor who pronounced her dead, arriving at the prima facie conclusion that it was a natural death, without any need to look deeper.

He had carefully considered the pros and cons of having his mother rushed to Dr Thombre's hospital. Would he remember the euthanasia conversation and suspect foul play? On the whole, Avadhoot thought Dr Thombre would have no reason to entertain doubts, given the clinical symptoms as well as witness reports of a heart attack and that his mother's death would occur in his absence. In any case, it was less risky than his mother being rushed to another hospital where one never knew what some unfamiliar doctor might choose to ascertain, before pronouncing death.

He called up Dr Thombre now, who opined that if his mother had suffered a heart attack, chances of survival were low and that he should be prepared for the worst. Still fighting his nausea, Avadhoot called up API Kirti Mirajkar next and explained that while he had left for Kolhapur on the morning bus, he had just received news that his mother had suffered a massive heart attack and was likely to pass away. He needed to turn back.

API Mirajkar acceded and asked him to send her a formal communication for non-appearance. Avadhoot heaved a sigh of relief and phoned Adv. Gojumgunde, who said he would file the necessary applications before the police and magistrate. The building blocks of Avadhoot's alibi were now in place.

He added the final touches by lurching across to the bus conductor and told him he needed to get off at Karad because of the tragedy that had overtaken him, to catch a return bus. Then, with all passengers watching, Avadhoot began sobbing inconsolably – part of it, genuine grief and most of it an intense revulsion at himself for murdering his own mother and enacting this sordid charade.

⋆

Every morning after his mother's death, Avadhoot woke up with a sense of disbelief. It was quickly followed by disgust, then dread. She was gone. Nothing remained of her, once she disappeared into the bowels of the electric crematorium. Nothing to connect him with causing her death.

The doorbell rang just as he finished breakfast. He hoped it wasn't another tiresome visitor dropping by to offer condolences. He felt such a phony being consoled. Avadhoot opened the door reluctantly. Sheetal-tai stood outside, thermos flask in hand.

His heart skipped a beat at the sight of the flask. 'Sheetal-tai?'

'I just came to return this and check how you are bearing up,' Sheetal-tai said.

'I'm okay, Sheetal-tai...coming to terms with er...Aai's demise,' he mumbled.

Sheetal-tai nodded. She and her husband had attended the cremation and rituals that followed with other neighbours. 'Come, I'll keep this flask in the kitchen and let's talk for a moment,' she said pleasantly.

Something about the way she said it and looked at him sent a ripple of unease through Avadhoot.

He let her in hesitantly and she briskly walked over to the sofa, flask in hand. 'So, has Kavita contacted you?'

'Yes...she did...' Avadhoot replied.

'And is reconciliation on the cards? There's no bone of contention any longer, is there?' Sheetal-tai asked, her manner gently sneering.

Avadhoot flushed, then nodded.

'Well, good for you,' Sheetal-tai said and fixed him with a stare. 'Now, where's the rest of it?'

Avadhoot sat up with alarm. 'I don't understand, Sheetal-tai. Rest of what?'

Sheetal-tai gave him a hard, sly smile. 'The sodium nitrite which triggered the heart attack, my dear Avadhoot!'

Avadhoot's blood turned cold, and he blinked, speechless.

'You think I didn't know?' Sheetal-tai chuckled, 'Sodium nitrite! Navalsinh Chavda!* Gujarat!'

Avadhoot felt his feet wobble, as if the earth had moved. 'How?' he croaked.

'Come on. You remember the Sunday I got you breakfast? Well, you blabbered about finding a way to let your mother go painlessly, peacefully...blah blah blah,' Sheetal-tai said, 'and there on your sofa the newspaper lay open with an article featuring this murderer, Navalsinh Chavda, who had just been nabbed by the Gujarat Police. Chavda had confessed to killing 12 people with his secret weapon – sodium nitrite mixed in some liquid, that triggered heart attacks in his victims within 20 to 25 minutes. I read the article as you prepared tea..And guess what? His first murder was that of his grandmother Mangu Vania, because her illness had become a burden. Coincidence? Inspiration? Set me thinking.'

Avadhoot felt the world starting to whirl around.

'And then just four days later, you appear at my doorstep, requesting me to feed your mother *black tea* for heaven's sake!' Sheetal-tai continued, 'And that tall story about how she might not drink it, but I must ensure she does? What's more, you furtively ask me to wash the flask. Why in the world would you go into such minor details? I connected the dots.'

The gravity of his folly struck Avadhoot. What a lousy murderer he had proved to be.

'But if you knew, why did you let it happen?' he asked.

---

* Navalsinh Kanu Chavda (42) was arrested by Gujarat Police on 3 December 2024 and confessed to murdering 12 people, including his grandmother, mother, uncle and a friend, between 2010 and 2024 using sodium nitrite. He died in police custody following a seizure on 8 December 2024.

Sheetal-tai grinned deviously. 'I wanted to see if it really works. Whether one can get away with it.'

'What? Why?'

Sheetal-tai gave him a piercing, enigmatic glance. 'Back to my first question. Where's the rest of the sodium nitrite?'

Avadhoot winced. 'I threw it away,' he bleated.

Sheetal-tai clicked her tongue in annoyance. 'Well, get me some more then, Avadhoot.'

'What for?' Avadhoot said hoarsely.

'I have a burden to dispose of too,' Sheetal-tai sniggered.

Avadhoot began experiencing oxygen-deprivation. 'Who?'

'Who else? My lord and master!'

'You...hate your husband?'

'He hates me for not bearing him a child. I just hate him back for being a bore, a brute and a burden!' Sheetal-tai replied evenly. 'So, when will you fetch it?'

Avadhoot licked his lips. 'What if I...refuse?'

Sheetal-tai gave him a steely look. 'I've retained two spoonfuls of your black tea in my freezer, Avadhoot. Should I dial 100?'

Avadhoot felt he was about to have a real heart attack, not one triggered by sodium nitrite!

# IN THE POISONED ENTRAILS

*Sumit Bardhan*

*Night fell thickly and softly all over IEZ Trilok. Over the fancy mansions, tech parks, and the tree-lined avenues of Olympia Hill. Over the cramped roads, decayed mohallas, and the seedy bars of Awam Nagar below it. Over the looming gateway to subterranean Dandato, standing grimly across the reeking waters of Blue Creek.*

*Night fell, wrapping its secret, black, midnight wings around deeds without name. Deeds, which thrown in the poisoned entrails of this urban blight, where fair was foul and foul fair, would keep the cauldron of corruption boiling and bubbling with its hell-broth of injustice.*

A few seconds. That's all it took for Drishti to realize her mistake. She had hoped that this might end just with some difficult compromises. That hope vanished at the sight of the first shadowy form and the vicious slash she felt across her body. She could see two other shadows approaching menacingly. There would be no compromises. This was a hunt. And she was the prey.

She screamed and tried to escape. But her predators had deliberately chosen this place. They pursued her, slashing and retreating in turns. She ran around, blind with fear and pain, until weak with blood loss, she fell. And a massive blow to her head brought down a curtain of blessed darkness.

⋆

The door opened with a slight click.

The man sleeping on the bed sat upright, startled by the noise. He raised his hands in defence as Laaldeo stepped inside.

'The safe is in the next room. I will give you the password.'

Laaldeo shook his head.

'The password that will send a signal to your drones and robo-dogs?'

The man shook his hands.

'That's not...'

'Never mind. I am not here for your money.'

The man stared at him.

'I am here about your business loan.'

'Loan? At this hour!'

'This is when I work.'

'But the matter is...'

'In the courts. Yes, I know.'

The man kept staring.

'First, you siphoned off the money and sent it abroad through *hawala*. Then you declared a business loss and went to court to prevent the lender from seizing your assets.'

'As you yourself said, it's in the courts.'

'Yes, of course. Precisely why I am here. Your idea was sound. Tangle the matter in litigation and keep dragging this out. Eventually, the frustrated lender would give up. Or settle for peanuts. But this specific lender doesn't want you to set such an example. Others would learn from it.'

'So?'

'So, I came to set a different sort of example.'

The man's eyes widened.

'I...I could pay you.'

'I am sure you could. But I can't rescind the contract I have already taken.'

The man tried to escape, but Laaldeo pinned him face down with a knee on his back. 'That wouldn't be fair trade at all, you see,' he remarked as he slit the man's throat.

*

Erlick sat in his office below Dandato's logo; a sword intertwined with two hungry mouths. He looked up as Dr Agnish Tamrakar walked in with a brisk limp and an anachronistic tapping of his cane.

'Took your time.'

'It's a long walk.'

'You didn't take the shuttle?'

'I don't like AI-driven vehicles.'

'You should have built the two underground towers closer then.'

'I don't like being close to your prison tower either.'

'That's a bit hypocritical, no? After all, Abyssmo provides the labour for your factories in Infierno.'

'That labour is a quid pro quo for the volcanic energy Infierno supplies,' Agnish tapped his cane. 'Can we get down to business?'

'I discreetly enquired with the investors of the IEZ. Looks like the tech that Surindar provides is too valuable for them.'

Agnish tapped his cane harshly. 'But the IEZ is

stagnating. The Independent Economic Zones were meant to encourage daring business innovations. His stranglehold is stifling that.'

'His Himmelian Systems is innovating all right. Look at Kronos. The most powerful AI ever built.'

'Innovation is about creativity. That AI hinders it.'

'Brother, brother, understand something. Our investors are not interested in creativity. Only in things that help them perpetuate their own power.'

'So, we do nothing?'

'I didn't say that. We wait for the right opportunity.'

'How long?'

'Patience, brother, patience. *Dum spiro spero*.'

*

Morning followed the night. And at its end, evening arrived. Depending on their form and function, lights of every hue and intensity switched on throughout IEZ Trilok.

In the vast lobby of Kinich Life's office on Olympia Hill, bright lights played on CEO Uday Kiran as he addressed the press. Rakshika Polias, Chief Marshal of the IEZ, stood beside him.

'We are saddened by the death of our colleague Drishti. This morning, her body was discovered at the bottom of a lift shaft. It looks like she took her own life. We shall all deeply feel her absence at Kinich. Chief Marshal Rakshika will share more with you.'

The light gleamed softly on the insignia on Rakshika's uniform, an owl with oversized eyes. 'The post-mortem revealed no evidence of foul play. We also discovered a scribbled suicide note on her desk.'

A reporter dutifully asked the required question. 'Can you tell us why she took this extreme step?'

'We learned that she was suffering from work-related depression. Apparently, her research was not yielding encouraging results.'

'Have you arrested anyone?' came another deferential and courteous question.

'Yes, of course. We have arrested the man who oversees the maintenance of the lift.'

All the reporters nodded dutifully.

'You liars!' someone screamed from the back of the lobby. 'You make me wait the entire day, you do not even let me see my wife's body, and now you come up with this concocted nonsense?'

Hesitatingly, the reporters looked behind. Unhesitatingly, none of them tried to photograph or record the scene.

'I assure you, Kalyan, we have handled this matter in the best way that we could.' Uday was all sympathy.

'Stop lying. I have seen the photo. There is no way she killed herself. What are you trying to cover up, you scoundrels?'

Uday raised his hand. 'Kalyan, I understand you're in grief, but that's no excuse to behave like this.'

'Grief? You have no idea what grief is. My son won't stop crying. She would never have left him alone!'

Rakshika nodded at the marshals standing at the back. Holding Kalyan in a vice grip, they dragged him out of the building.

Uday flashed a wide smile, his teeth shining. 'Sorry for that small distraction. Any more questions?'

No one had any more questions to ask, of course, not at least about what had just happened before them. Theirs were not to ask or reply, theirs were not to reason why; theirs were just to listen and let matters lie.

★

A different set of lights had come on at Awam Nagar's Madan Sadan. Garish, neonish and glaring. This was the greatest house of pleasure in the entire IEZ, offering any and every pleasure of the flesh. Its vivid glow of suggestive signage welcomed guests to its courtyards, pools, bars, and other more private and discreet facilities.

Hidden behind this hedonism, in a hall at the rear of the building, there were banks and tiers of displays. In their light, from the midst of a large team labouring on their keyboards, a woman raised her head and called out, 'Shanka, news of that Kinich Life researcher is spreading on social media like wildfire.'

A man with thinning hair got up from his desk. 'Anything pushing it?'

'Her husband posted an emotional video. It has gone viral.'

'Keep it on your radar.' He paused as a message pinged on his desk. 'I must go now. Give me an update once I return.'

Leaving his desk, he walked into an office. The room was modest, its walls bare except for a framed watercolour of a woodpecker. Laaldeo was stretched out on a sofa with a hookah pipe between his lips. Smoke coiled down his chest, its acrid smell not entirely of tobacco.

'Traasu is waiting for you, Laal.'

'Good. Inform Sandhya.'

Laaldeo stepped out of his office and walked into a room lined with white tiles.

A man was seated there, bound, gagged and blindfolded. Behind him stood a wide-chested man.

'Is this the right guy, Traasu?'

The wide-chested man nodded. 'Yes. Checked thoroughly.'

'Right.' Laaldeo removed the man's gag and blindfold. He started screaming immediately, but Laaldeo silenced him with a hard slap.

'Stop that, please. You are giving me a migraine.'

The man tried blustering it out. 'You have no idea who I am. I have powerful friends.'

'On Olympia Hill? I know. In fact, a few of them would have gladly paid me for this.'

Two women entered before the man could respond. One of them was older, although behind her impeccable bearing, her age was impossible to determine. The other one was much younger, but appeared to have been badly injured. Her face was bruised and swollen, and her breathing was laborious.

'You recognize him?' Laaldeo asked her.

The young woman nodded, her face twisting in pain.

The man's eyes widened. 'I paid for her services.'

'You are making a mistake,' Laaldeo replied. 'You paid to use her body for your pleasure. Not for inflicting pain upon it.' He raised a hand as the man attempted to speak. 'Yes, yes, I know. For men like you, someone's pain *is* your pleasure. But that is not what Sandhya offers here. As she never ceases to remind our guests, this is a house of pleasure. Not of pain.'

Laaldeo glanced at the older woman, who nodded in agreement.

'I...I will pay more. Just say how much.'

'We can't have that, you see. Then more people like you will get the notion that they can batter our girls and get away by paying.'

'But she is just a whore!'

'True. But she is also our business associate. She generates revenue, and we take responsibility for her well-being. A responsibility that we cannot casually abandon.' Laaldeo shook his head. 'That wouldn't be fair trade, you see,' he added, as he swiftly slashed the man's throat.

He looked at the two women. 'It's done.'

Sandhya nodded, but the other woman looked unsure.

'Maybe he was right. I am just a whore after all. Maybe—'

Laaldeo raised his hand. 'Everyone in this town is a whore. You sell your body. A man I killed yesterday sold his ethics. The marshals sell people's trust in law. And I sell my assassination skills. All of us are whores.'

'Does it ever trouble you? Killing strangers for a price?'

'Never. For you, sex is just a business transaction without any emotional strings. For me, killing is.'

*

Away from Madan Sadan, in the bowels of Dandato, the lights did not need to come on. In its eternal darkness, they burnt unceasingly.

In his office, Erlick addressed a hunched Dr Agnish leaning on his cane.

'We may be able to move earlier than we had expected, brother. Look at this.'

Erlick projected a few images.

'The dead researcher's husband's plea has gone viral. People are taking to the streets demanding justice.'

'So?'

'So, my brother, I intend to put some wind in these sails.'

'Stoke the flames, you mean to say.'

'Don't be a cynic. I think I could release a few of Abyssmo's inmates to lend support to the movement.'

'Surindar will crush it.'

'Yes, of course, definitely so. But that will keep him busy. And blind to my moves.'

'What moves?'

'In time, brother, in time. I will let you know in time. Meanwhile, I need your help.'

'What help?'

'I want you to assemble a team to develop a countermeasure for that technology you despise so much. Abyssmo's cells have a few talented individuals who can be motivated to work at Infierno.'

⋆

A few more days and nights came and went, till about a week later one of Madan Sadan's hospitality managers approached Sandhya.

'Didi, we'll need to do something about this political talk.'

Sandhya barely lifted her eyes from her work.

'What political talk?'

'About the researcher who died.'

'What does it have to do with us?'

'Our guests have started gossiping about it. And about the violence outside.'

Sandhya finally looked up.

'What violence?'

The man looked surprised.

'I don't keep track of anything outside.'

Sandhya sighed.

The man narrated the aftermath of Drishti's death. 'Her husband put out this video.' He projected a news clip. Kalyan's impassioned plea started playing.

Sandhya inhaled sharply, as if shaken. She regained her composure immediately. 'So?'

'People started protesting on the streets. The marshals tried to stop them, and the fights snowballed.'

The manager changed the projection. These were images and videos of vicious battles. On one side were the marshals, with their quadcopter drones, robo-dogs and laser dazzlers, and on the other side were mobs armed with iron rods and Molotov cocktails. The visuals were of raw violence. People mercilessly beaten, cars burning, stones thrown, bloodied faces.

Sandhya took another sharp breath. 'Understood. No, we do not want these discussed here. Keep everyone focused on pleasure. Offer free spirits, host parties, do anything that helps. And yes, get Traasu to discreetly station his men to remove any troublemakers.'

The man nodded and left.

*

With free food, drinks, and indulgences of the flesh, Madan Sadan managed to keep the disturbances away from itself.

Then something else occurred.

About a week later, as Laaldeo sat in his office with Traasu and Shanka, a young woman pushed her head in.

'Laalji, you need to come. Sandhya Didi, she—' Her unfinished sentence hung ominously in the air.

With two strides, Laaldeo left the room, Shanka and Traasu following him silently.

In her office, Sandhya sat frozen with a vacant stare. A few people stood around, looking puzzled and bewildered. A news clip played on the display repeatedly.

Dismissing the onlookers, Laaldeo laid a gentle hand on Sandhya's shoulder.

'Sandhya.'

She looked blankly at him, trying to fight down something inside her.

'Sandhya.'

She glanced at the display and clutched his arm.

Laaldeo watched the news. It was reporting the death of Drishti's husband Kalyan in a car accident.

'Is Kalyan your...?' he asked.

Sandhya nodded silently.

'Before you joined this work?'

Another silent nod.

'That makes it personal. I will get to the bottom of it,' said Laaldeo.

As he was about to leave the room, Sandhya spoke for the first time.

'Laal, Kalyan had a son. I will need to bring him up now.'

'It will be done.'

*

Back in his office, Laaldeo asked Shanka, 'Can you get me Drishti's forensic report?'

'My people have been looking for it even before today. Couldn't find it on the marshal's office servers.'

'What about the details of Kalyan's accident?'

'Same. Absolutely nothing.'

'I see.'

'We even searched the cache servers that are used to push data to Kronos. Nothing there either. I could try hacking Kronos' datastore, of course, but—'

'No, don't do that. Kronos is a very advanced AI. If it detects an intrusion, it will trigger too many alarms. Try something else.'

'I will keep looking.'

'Meanwhile, get me Rakshika. Let's see if she is willing to help.'

*

The image of Chief Marshal Rakshika Polias floated up on the display.

'Yes, Laal.'

'I need something, Rakshika.'

'Ah, right to the point.'

'I want the post-mortem report of the woman researcher from Kinich.'

'Can't give it to you.'

'Can't or won't?'

'Take your pick.'

'What about some information on Kalyan's death?'

'The answer is the same.'

'So, you are refusing me?'

'Exactly.' She disconnected the call.

Laaldeo turned to Shanka, 'Anything?'

'So far, nothing. But in his video, Kalyan had mentioned a photo he had seen. It may be there on his personal device.'

'That'd be with the marshals now, along with Drishti's.

Beyond our reach,' said Laaldeo, 'but that photo could have been taken by someone at Kinich. He or she may still have it.'

Traasu nodded. 'I will check.'

'Good. Let's also investigate Kinich. Kalyan may have been disposed of for raising his voice. But why was Drishti murdered in the first place?'

★

Laaldeo went to Sandhya after a couple of days. She was her usual busy self. The only indication of change was a cradle in her office.

'Are you okay now, Sandhya?'

'I will need to be, for his sake.' She glanced at the cradle.

Laaldeo nodded. 'Yes, of course. We will get to those responsible, I assure you.'

Sandhya shook her head. 'Whoever it was, I am as complicit in his death as them.'

'Don't blame yourself.'

'But I *am* to blame, Laal. I abandoned him.'

'You didn't have a choice.'

'That was then, Laal. But now? I wanted to reach out to him but feared his rejection. So, I took my eyes off him and pretended that he did not exist.' She wiped a corner of her eye. 'And now that's exactly what has happened.'

Laaldeo kept quiet.

'But life has given me another chance.' Sandhya looked at the cradle. 'And I won't do anything that will distract me from it.'

'It's a family matter now, I can't just let it go.'

'I am not asking you to. But I would rather see ahead than behind.'

Laaldeo nodded. 'A wise man once advised me to start each day by imagining that I had died the night before. And then carefully considering what I should do with my new life. I see you doing the same.'

Sandhya took a deep breath. 'True. He must have been wise indeed.'

There was a knock on the door. It was Traasu.

'Laal, we may have a few things.'

*

In Laaldeo's office, Traasu said, 'Sandhya seems to be all right.'

'Sandhya handles life like a wrestler,' Laaldeo nodded. 'Every time it throws her down, she gets up to fight again. We needn't worry about her. What is it you've got?'

They had found out that the photo mentioned by Kalyan was taken by the security guard who first discovered the body. He had then shared it with a few people. That's how it may have reached Kalyan. Shanka, however, could not find it despite a thorough search of all the IEZ servers and the router caches. Traasu tried to locate the guard, but he had vanished. He then found a couple of people who had received the photo, but it had mysteriously vanished from their devices.

'Traasu brought me one of their devices. Malware had been installed on it to wipe off any information connected to the death,' said Shanka.

'So,' asked Laaldeo, 'we have nothing?'

'I have something, though not digital,' answered Traasu.

Traasu had finally gone to the guard's flat, only to find it thoroughly ransacked. He learnt that the marshals had arrived some days ago and carted away all digital equipment.

He placed a photograph on the table. 'But they didn't get this. I found it taped under the bed.'

'They were not looking for paper,' said Laaldeo as he looked at it.

The photo showed a woman lying face down on a grimy floor, soaked in blood. There were numerous slash marks on her bare legs, and her shirt looked shredded into strips.

'They cut her repeatedly,' remarked Shanka. 'She was killed very brutally.'

'We need to find the place of occurrence. Have you checked Kinich's servers?' Laaldeo asked.

'Yes. As soon as Traasu gave me the photo.'

'And?'

'Nothing. Servers, camera memory, router caches – I could not find a single byte of data on this anywhere.'

'As expected. Taking care of the digital footprint would have been easy for them. Avoiding witnesses would have been the main challenge.'

'She was killed at night. The place would have been empty.'

'Not likely. The research centre would have had staff working at night. And then,' Laaldeo tapped the photo, 'this was extremely bloody. Not something to casually walk away from.'

'So how did they do it?'

'They probably killed her somewhere isolated. A location where there would be water for washing the blood off themselves. Find out if there is any such place in that building.'

'I will pull out the building plans.'

'And after that?' asked Traasu.

'After that, we find out who went there to recce the location before the murder.'

'Anyone could have gone there. Not only the killers.'

'Yes. We must also find out why she was killed. That will narrow it down.'

'I will start probing Kinich Life's business,' said Shanka.

'And find out about the car that killed Kalyan. There will be no digital trail, so you will have to do it the hard way.'

'There is one more thing, Laal,' Shanka added. 'Since Kalyan's death, all social media activity about these incidents has abruptly ceased. As if a blocking filter has been implemented.'

'Smells like complicity.'

'What do you want to do?'

'Bote Communications controls social media. I think I should talk to its CEO.'

'Sobrius Rajbhat?'

'Yes. I know where he can be found.'

*

Of all the bars on Olympia Hill, the loud and raucous Al Iksir was a favourite of the young and trendy, rather than the business tycoons. Yet this was where Sobrius Rajbhat sat at a table, clutching a glass of orange juice. His fashionable apparel matched the crowds', though his cosmetic surgery-touched face set him apart.

'A teetotaller sitting in a bar,' remarked Laaldeo as he sat down across from him.

Rajbhat's lips curled. 'Says an assassin who doesn't enjoy killing. I was expecting you, you know.'

'You were?'

'Yes. I was told that you are poking around the death of that woman.'

'Told by whom?'

'Doesn't matter. So, I knew that soon you would come calling.'

'Ah, you can see the future.'

'No. But I can deduce. I knew that you would come by. To ask me a question.'

'Which would be?'

'If I could prevent this issue from going viral on social media, why did I allow it in the first place?'

'And the answer to that is...'

'I can't tell you.'

'Can't or won't?'

'Whatever. Take your pick.'

'You sound exactly like Rakshika.'

Rajbhat's lips curled again.

'I am no bootlicker.'

'You sure?'

'Hers is a choice; mine is a compulsion.' Rajbhat waved back to a couple of young girls. 'Now, if you are done, I would like to enjoy myself.'

*

Laaldeo summoned his lieutenants a few days later.

'Found anything?'

'Yes.' Shanka projected a floor plan of the topmost level of Kinich Life's building. 'The rooms here are all used for storage.'

'Which means very few people.'

'Yes,' answered Shanka. He pointed at a part of the plan. 'And even fewer in this area.'

'What is it?'

'It's used for storing discarded biological samples and chemicals. Including acids and disinfectants.'

'That'd make eliminating any DNA evidence easy.'

'It also has water,' said Shanka. He projected an image of a tiled enclosure with a water tap. 'This is where they may have cleaned up.' He projected another image. 'There is also an incinerator.'

'Ah, useful for getting rid of their blood-soaked clothes. Where is the lift?'

'A few metres away. It's a service lift for moving goods.'

'Something people are even less likely to use at night. What about people who came here?'

Shanka projected a list. He had run an AI agent on a month's worth of camera footage. After filtering out the regular visitors, it had identified eleven individuals who had been in the area a day or two before the murder.

Laaldeo nodded. 'The killer could be from this list. But we need more information to pin it down.'

'I also found something odd,' added Shanka.

Shifting through Kinich's business data, Shanka had discovered some anomalies. Two distributors were selling pharmaceuticals at very steep discounts. Yet, strangely, they repaid Kinich in full. He couldn't fathom why they were selling at such a huge loss.

'Where are these distributors located?' Laaldeo asked sharply.

'Sector 28 and Sector 34.'

Traasu leaned forward. 'These are areas with very high Dopamania addiction.'

Laaldeo took a deep breath. 'Along with medical supplies, someone in Kinich has been shipping Dopamania to these distributors. Heavy discounts result in faster sales. Which means more delivery auto-trucks from Kinich.'

'Bringing in more Dopamania,' added Shanka. 'That is why Drishti had to die. She must have stumbled upon this operation.'

'We now know why she may have been killed. But how did they get her to that area on the top floor?'

'Maybe they held a gun to her back?' said Traasu.

Laaldeo shook his head. 'That would be risky. Someone would notice it during the trip.'

'Yes,' Shanka agreed. 'Her colleagues reported to the marshals that she suddenly got up from her desk and left. There has been no account of her being forced to go.'

'Keep checking. She may have been lured to some other area and then forced to come along. Anything from you, Traasu?'

Traasu had uncovered that Kalyan had been knocked down in front of his apartment at night. Some neighbours had heard the screeching of tyres followed by a scream. They rushed out to find him lying on the road. Nobody saw the car. There was nothing on the cameras either. His people were still making enquiries in the area.

'Keep at it. I'll go and question Uday Kiran. Let me see what he has to say.'

⋆

To reach Uday's office, Laaldeo had to navigate through a gauntlet of office assistants – all young, all women, and all stunningly beautiful. In his large, opulent office, Uday somehow managed to look uncomfortable despite his ridiculously expensive suit.

'I don't appreciate your barging into my office, Laal.'

'I am not looking for appreciation. Just information.'

'You could ask Kronos. That's why it was created. To gather all information in the IEZ.'

'I am asking you because you run Kinich Life. Did you know that some of your people were dealing in drugs?'

Uday didn't even attempt denial. 'This is a large pharma company, Laal, not some seedy brothel. I cannot keep track of everything that happens here.'

Laaldeo ignored the barb. 'Cannot or do not?'

'"Do not" suits me fine. This is an IEZ after all. It should be fine if a few people pursue an independent economic agenda of their own.'

'It is not if you are covering up a murder as a suicide.'

'It is, if it's for the greater economic good. No one wants chaos. It damages the economy.'

'Yet, your actions had the exact opposite effect.'

'The error was in execution, not in judgement. I stand by whatever I did.'

'So, you don't know who murdered her?'

'Do not know; do not want to know.'

'Are you certain about that? I hope I do not discover otherwise. I could then substantially damage that economy which you care so much about.'

Uday suddenly deflated. He inserted a finger inside his tight collar, trying to loosen it.

'Look, Laal, you live on the fringes of this system. You possibly cannot comprehend what those of us on the inside have to do just to survive.' He wiped his forehead with a snow-white handkerchief. 'Falling out of line is not an option for us.'

*

When Laaldeo met with Traasu and Shanka a couple of days later to check on their progress, Traasu shook his head. The street violence had made it very difficult to make enquiries. People were scared to talk. Using footage of the marshals' bodycams, Kronos had compiled a list of those who had participated in the protests. Now the marshals were scouring through Awam Nagar for the people on that list.

Shanka also had found no evidence that suggested that Drishti had been forcibly taken to the storage area.

'I see.' Laaldeo closed his eyes and leaned back. He remained in that position for a couple of minutes as his lieutenants sat silently.

Then, opening his eyes, he leaned forward.

'We have been looking in the wrong place. Traasu, how do you compel someone to do something against their will?'

'By threatening him. Or—'

'Or by threatening someone close to him,' Shanka completed the sentence.

'Yes. Instead of threatening Drishti, they may have threatened her family.'

'But Kalyan never mentioned anything.'

'Probably because he didn't know. And probably because it was not him who they threatened.'

Shanka's face hardened. 'The child.'

'Yes. They used Drishti's maternal instincts against her. See if you can locate anyone at her house that night.'

It didn't take Shanka too long. On the night of Drishti's death, Kalyan's device was in flight mode. But there was another active device in its proximity. That device had sent a large data packet to Drishti's number. Its size suggested that it may have been a video stream.

'Someone broke into the house and sent Drishti a live feed of her boy. That's how they got her upstairs.'

'It was this guy's device.' Shanka projected a man's photo on the display.

'I have seen him!' Traasu exclaimed. 'I was checking out the two Kinich distributors Shanka identified. He works with the one in Sector 28.'

'Excellent! We have got the first link in the chain. Yank it to get the rest.'

'Of course!' Traasu's face cracked in a wide smile.

⋆

Traasu called Laaldeo and Shanka to the tiled room the very next day. Inside, a naked man was seated on a chair with his hands tied behind his back. He was covered in blood, and Traasu was enthusiastically pummelling whatever remained of his face. A couple of Traasu's men stood apart at a respectful distance.

'He has already given up the names of Drishti's killers. Picked them out from Shanka's list. Just trying to see if he can give me something additional,' Traasu said cheerfully.

Laaldeo glanced at the bludgeoned figure and shook his head. 'I don't think he can. Next time, go somewhat slow.'

With a sigh, Traasu nodded to his men. 'Take him away.'

As the man was carried away, Traasu extended his device to Laaldeo. 'I have marked them. Lohit, Nilesh and Pitambar.'

Laaldeo turned to Shanka. 'You need to find their locations.'

'No need,' Traasu intervened. 'All three are gambling buddies. They gather at the BetStar Casino every evening.'

'Let's go and pick them up this evening then.'

⋆

Laaldeo, Traasu and a couple of Traasu's men stood at the entrance of a lane. Across the street, a flashy sign on a grimy cable-festooned building proclaimed it to be the BetStar Casino. Traasu nodded to one of his men, 'Go and see if they are inside.' The man had not even taken a single step when an explosion rocked the building. Traasu hurled himself on Laaldeo, dropping him to the ground as a billowing cloud of fire surged towards the lane, driving a tempest of debris before it.

All of them stood up after the wave of destruction had passed. No one had suffered any major injuries, but bodies, screams, and pools of fire were strewn everywhere on the street in front.

'This line of enquiry is now closed,' remarked Laaldeo. 'Let's head back.'

⋆

Late next day, Traasu trudged into Laaldeo's office, Shanka trailing behind him.

'Found something curious, Laal.'

'Tell me.'

It was something that one of Traasu's men had discovered. He had suffered a few burn injuries from the explosion and had gone to see a quack doctor known for his discretion. There he had met another patient who had been in some accident involving an autocab. Learning that this man lived a couple of streets from Kalyan's house, Traasu's man had struck up a conversation and uncovered some interesting details.

On the same night when Kalyan died, this man was riding home on his scooter. Suddenly an autocab, driving on the wrong side of the road at breakneck speed, had rushed towards him. He had tried to swerve away, but it still grazed his scooter. He skidded and suffered severe bruising. Both his driving licence and insurance had expired, so the unfortunate man could not file a compensation claim and now had to pay for his own treatment.

Laaldeo seemed surprised. 'Autocabs are not programmed to drive on the wrong side of the road. And in the event of an accident, they are expected to stop and transmit a message to both the Central Hospital as well as the marshal's office.'

'It did neither. Anyway, my man paid for his treatment and took the scooter's dash-cam footage.'

'Smart thinking.'

'Yes. And I passed it on to Shanka.'

'This is what I found.' Shanka projected a photo of the front view of the autocab.

'Do you see the left-hand-side headlight?'

'It is broken. Hanging loose.'

'As if—'

'As if it were in a previous accident.' Laaldeo stared intently at the photo. 'The autocab's bot didn't stop despite two accidents. And Kronos, which controls all autocabs, also did nothing.'

'That would mean that Kronos has been compromised.'

'And that would mean only one thing.' Laaldeo seemed lost in thought.

'What?' asked Traasu.

Before Laaldeo could reply, Shanka interrupted. 'Laal, there is a call from Rakshika Polias.'

'Put her on.'

The chief marshal's face floated up on the display.

There was no polite greeting. 'Laal, Surindar would like to meet you.'

'Why?'

'You will find out when you go.'

'I am somewhat busy.'

'I am not requesting. Let's avoid a confrontation,' she said and disconnected the call.

'I will go,' declared Laaldeo before his lieutenants could object.

*

The Himmelian Centre was perched right on the crest of Olympia Hill. The glass wall on one side of its boardroom offered a view of the contrasting expanse of Olympia Hill and Awam Nagar below it. A solitary high-back wooden chair stood at one end of the room and Surindar sat imperiously on it. An oil painting of forked lightning against a stormy sky hung behind him. There was no table.

'Not standard boardroom decor,' remarked Laaldeo.

'Renovated it to match my taste. No one comes here these days anyway, least of all you.'

'That's rather unkind, considering that the suggestion to live on the fringes of the system came from you. I recall you saying, "Help us from outside by doing things that we cannot do from inside."'

'You didn't seem too reluctant to leave.'

'No. I had surmised that I would soon get in the way of your approach.'

'And what approach would that be?'

'A total disregard for fair trade.'

'Visionaries like me created the IEZs. So that we could pursue economic objectives with absolute independence, unshackled from such moral compulsions.'

'Yet without the compass of fair trade, there is no economics. Darwinism yes, but economics no.'

'Whatever. Anyway, let's get to the point. I want you to stop probing this issue.'

'If you are referring to Drishti and Kalyan's deaths, then I can't walk away.'

'Why? All the perpetrators are now dead.'

'All? Are you sure?'

'Those that were directly involved at least.'

'Ah!'

'You need to keep a balance between the ideal and the practical, Laal.'

'Yes. And when that balance is disturbed, it needs to be restored.'

Laaldeo turned and left.

*

Back at Madan Sadan, along with Shanka and Traasu, Sandhya was waiting for him. She looked worried. 'Erlick wants you to meet him at Dandato, Laal.'

'He called?'

'No. A guest passed on his message to me.'

'Good.'

'I am scared about this, Laal. Dandato is one of the most brutal private prisons.'

'Don't be. I will see you later.'

*

Dandato's bleak brutalist gate stood on the far shore of Blue Creek and could be reached only by an auto-ferry. The auto-ferry's bot called itself Karon, and as the boat glided over the polluted, oily waters, its droning litany of Zen death poems made the journey somewhat morbid.

Laaldeo was escorted to Erlick's office, where he rose to greet him.

'Come, come, Laal. Long time no see.'

Laaldeo nodded at the strange logo on the wall. 'Not a cheerful place to visit, I guess.'

'Absolutely incorrect. Brother Agnish has relocated his entire business here.'

'His business motives are very strong then.'

'Yes, yes, that's true. Proximity to volcanic energy and access to the IMPDU programme.'

'IMPDU? What's that?'

'Initiative for Maximizing the Productivity of Detainees and Undesirables.'

'Slave labour, you mean?'

'This is an IEZ, Laal. Look at it from a positive, economic angle.'

'How?'

'As an endeavour for unlocking the potential of idle and otherwise unemployable human resources for improving their economic value.'

'You are giving me a migraine. Why the urgent summons?'

'Once I learned of your meeting with Surindar, I was afraid that you may do something rash.'

'So considerate of you.'

'I am serious. Any attempt on his person would put the entire IEZ in jeopardy.'

'So be it.'

'I have an alternate proposal. Get him to wear a fruitless crown. Make him dwindle, peak and pine.'

'How?'

'By taking away his power. By making his position ornamental. I am going to call for a board meeting.'

'It will be of no use.' Laaldeo gave a dry laugh. 'The investors will not agree.'

'They will. Once I convince them that on his quest to become Homo Deus, Surindar has lost sight of their interests. *Cui caput dolet*, etc., etc.'

'Let's hope so.'

'Leave it to me. But I do need your help.'

'With what?'

Erlick extended a small media card. 'Please give this to that hacker assistant of yours. Once I send the word, he must execute it.'

'What is it supposed to do?'

'Burn Surindar's latest project to ash.'

'Which project?'

'You will recognize it once you understand the reason behind the murders. Just keep on asking yourself, *cui prodest*?'

'Why not just tell me?'

'It'll be better if you figure it out yourself. You will sound more convincing at the board meeting. See you soon, friend, and wait for my call.'

★

The board meeting was called a fortnight later. They all marched into the boardroom at Himmelian Systems. Laaldeo defiantly, Erlick with a casual demeanour, Dr Agnish tap-tapping his cane, and Uday and Rajbhat somewhat reluctantly.

Surindar sat authoritatively on his high chair. Back straight, legs crossed at the knee, hands on armrests. Rakshika Polias stood beside him clad in riot armour, the lines of her face hard.

Surindar gestured at a few scattered chairs. 'Seat yourselves. Let's get this charade over quickly.'

'Of course, of course! Let me quickly get to the point then,' said Erlick as he yanked a chair and sat down facing Surindar. 'Your latest project has created a major negative impact on the business environment of IEZ Trilok.'

'Which project are you talking about?'

'The one that began with the murder of Drishti. I will let Laaldeo explain.'

'The whore master!'

'Who better to speak among a constellation of whores?' replied Laaldeo.

Surindar stopped a fuming Rakshika from stepping forward.

'Go ahead. I'll give you five minutes.'

'That's all I need. Let's start with Kalyan's death. He was killed by an autocab. Kronos manages all autocabs with its AI agents. Since Himmelian Systems maintains Kronos, it's clear that you have significantly modified Kronos to grant it the freedom to kill.'

'You have no proof!'

'We don't need proof,' answered Erlick. 'We are not prosecuting. We are just presenting the prima facie observations to the board. Continue, Laal.'

'Let's get to Drishti's murder. The who and why are clear. She was probably killed for getting too close to the drug peddling ring at Kinich.' Laaldeo looked around the room and said, 'But when she could be disposed of quietly, why murder her so gruesomely? Why allow a guard to take a photo? Why allow Kalyan's video to go viral on social media?'

'Yes, why indeed?' Surindar sneered.

'It's obvious. You *wanted* Awam Nagar to burn.'

'And why would I want to do that?'

'To collect data.'

'Ridiculous!'

'No, quite logical. The investors of the IEZ, the oligarchs, leaders and politicians, are not so interested in the profits of the IEZ as they are in its technology. Especially Himmelian's technology.'

'Ah hah!' Surindar slapped his knee gleefully.

'Yes. The spyware and malware, the robo-dogs, the quadcopter drones, the autonomous weapons, the loitering munitions. All the suppression technology that they need to keep their restive subjects in their place. But all these suppression techs have one flaw.'

'Which is?'

'The rulers must depend on others to deploy them. And these are not individuals who would want to rely on anyone who could someday unseat them. So, I assume that you pitched an AI to them. An AI whose bot swarms could run the tech to keep their rebellious subjects in check. A replacement for untrustworthy underlings.'

Surindar did not respond.

'But the AI would have to be trained first. And for that, it needs data from an actual uprising. Which is exactly why you intentionally incited unrest. To convert Awam Nagar into a sequestered lab that would generate all the data you would need to train Kronos.'

Surindar let out a long sigh. 'Even if you say so, or rather, especially if you say so, the investors will always stand with me. So, tell me, *board members*, why all this drama?'

'And there you are wrong, my friend.' Erlick rose from his chair. 'As of a few minutes ago, due to some undetected catastrophic cyberattack, Kronos's entire data store has become corrupted. I am afraid that for all the damage and destruction your actions unleashed, Kronos is unlikely to become an effective Gestapo-in-chief anytime soon. And since a little water is unlikely to clear you of your deeds, I regret to inform you that you no longer enjoy the confidence of the investors.'

Surindar pulled out his device. With a glance at it, he screamed, 'Rakshika, teach them a lesson that they never forget.'

As Rakshika pulled out her baton and advanced, Laaldeo stepped forward. A knife had appeared in his hand. 'You could try.'

Erlick quickly stepped between them.

'Stop, Rakshika. Unless you are willing to become a permanent guest at Abyssmo. And, Laal, kindly behave.'

There was more screaming, cursing and threatening thereafter, most of it from Surindar. However, the Rubicon had already been crossed. Restructuring the new regime was the only task left.

*

Finally, the day's hurly-burly was done, as battles were lost and won. Once more, deep in the bowels of Dandato, Dr Agnish sat across from Erlick.

'So, what did it take to convince the investors to dump Surindar in your favour?'

'I offered them something that they would need even more desperately than Himmelian's suppression tech.'

'And that would be?'

'Think for a moment, brother. Our guests lose their productivity very rapidly after stints in your factories.'

'Yes, unfortunately, Infierno's production targets can be very demanding.'

'Of course, of course. I am not judging. *Ex nihilo nihil fit.* However, at the end of their productive lives, could we not recycle some of their components?'

'Ah, I see!'

'Yes. Many of our investors and those in their inner circle are approaching the boundaries of their biological age. And they would soon require replacement of worn-out parts. So—'

'Yes, of course! And now that you will be able to, uh, persuade Kinich Life, they would provide the expertise for harvesting and storage of such components.'

'Absolutely! Uday is very excited about the business potential of our new partnership.'

'And it fits perfectly with the recalcitrant subject-control strategies of our investors. Brilliant!'

'Thank you! I am planning to call this the IRICULP programme.'

'What is that?'

'Initiative for Redeployment of Internal Components of Undesirables with Low Productivity.'

'That's too long!'

'Oh, it's for internal use only. For sales and marketing, I have a simpler name.'

'Which is?'

'OOD. Organ on Demand.'

# ABOUT THE AUTHORS

**Ajay Chowdhury**, the inaugural winner of the Harvill Secker–Bloody Scotland Prize, is a tech entrepreneur and theatre director. His first novel in the Kamil Rahman series – *The Waiter* (*Sunday Times* Crime Book of the Month) has been optioned for television. Its follow ups – *The Cook* (*Guardian* Top Crime Books of the Year), *The Detective* (*Sunday Times* Top Crime Books of the Year), *The Spy* (longlisted for the Wilbur Smith Adventure Writing Prize) and *The Shadow* – came out to strong reviews. He has also written a children's book – *Ayesha and the Firefish* – that was adapted into a musical and premiered in San Francisco. Know more about him at www.ajaychowdhury.com

**Anil Menon**'s most recent work is the novel *The Coincidence Plot* (Simon & Schuster, 2023). It was preceded by a collection of his speculative short fiction *The Inconceivable Idea of the Sun: Stories* (Hachette India, 2022) and his novel *Half of What I Say* (Bloomsbury, 2015). Anil is the chief editor of *The Bombay Literary Magazine*.

**Anuradha Kumar**'s most recent novel is *The Kidnapping of Mark Twain: A Bombay Mystery*. Her work of nonfiction, *Wanderers, Adventurers, Missionaries: Early Americans in India*

*1700–1950* appeared in April 2025. Her story, 'Sudden Appearances' featured in *The Hachette Book of Indian Detective Fiction*. She writes often for *Scroll.in*, and her essays received 'notable mention' in Best American Essays editions of 2023 and 2024. More recently, a collection of essays, *The Sound of Lost Memories*, was a finalist for the Gournay Prize (Ohio University Press, 2024). Anuradha was born in Odisha, and now lives in New Jersey with her family.

**Arnab Ray**, better known as Greatbong, is one of India's most widely read bloggers. He is also the author of six books, including the horror classic *The Mine*. Two of his books have been made into web series on major OTT platforms: *Sultan of Delhi* in Hindi on Disney+ Hotstar and *Mahabharata Murders* in Bengali on Hoichoi. A PhD in Computer Science from State University of New York at Stony Brook, and an alumnus of Jadavpur University, Kolkata, he is currently based in Los Angeles. Arnab Ray has a running column in the *Times of India*.

**Madhulika Liddle** is a novelist and award-winning short story writer, known primarily as a writer of historical fiction. Her most popular creation is the fictitious 17th century Mughal detective, Muzaffar Jang, who stars in a series of four books. Madhulika lives in Noida, and besides fiction, writes on classic cinema, food, nature, books and travel. Her latest book, *For the Love of Apricots*, a contemporary romance novel, released in January 2025.

**Manjula Padmanabhan** (b. 1953) is an author, playwright, artist and cartoonist. She grew up in Europe and Southeast Asia, returning to India as a teenager. She currently

lives in the US with a part-time home in New Delhi. She has illustrated over 20 children's titles including her own stories and puzzles. She used to draw a comic strip about a feisty, googly-eyed female character called Suki. For several years the strip appeared in different newspapers, before finally ending in 2016. Her play *Harvest* won the Onassis Award for Theatre, in Greece, in 1997. Her two most recent books are *Stolen Hours and Other Curiosities*, a collection of science-fiction short stories and *Taxi*, a novel set in New Delhi, about a woman taxi driver. *Taxi* was recently awarded the 2024 Sushila Devi Award for women's fiction.
Websites:
Art: www.sweetlotusart.com
Lit: www.magnoliana.com
SUKI: www.sukionline.thecomicseries.com

**Meeti Shroff-Shah** writes the Temple Hill Mysteries. She has been longlisted for the CWA Whodunnit Dagger 2025, the CWA Short Story Dagger 2025 and shortlisted for the Margery Allingham Short Mystery Prize 2024 (UK), the People's Book Prize (UK), and the *Times of India* AutHer Awards in India, in 2023. She's also been longlisted for the prestigious CWA New Blood Dagger in the UK, in 2022. Her short stories have appeared in several anthologies such as *The Hachette Book of Indian Detective Fiction* and CWA's *Midsummer Mysteries* in the UK. Apart from crime fiction, Meeti has also written a critically acclaimed memoir, *Do You Know Any Good Boys?* – a funny guide to the Indian arranged marriage, which has been optioned for the screen. When she's not plotting murder, Meeti works with brands as a creative consultant and has had an award-winning career in advertising for over 18 years. Meeti lives in Mumbai with her husband and daughter and writes from a small blue desk overlooking a gulmohar tree.

**Nev March** is the first Indian-born author to receive the Minotaur Books/Mystery Writers of America Award for Best First Crime Fiction. Her debut novel, *Murder in Old Bombay* also won an AudioFile award and was a finalist for six national awards including the Edgar and the Anthony. Nev's books deal with issues of identity, race and moral boundaries. *Murder in Old Bombay* was selected as Amazon's Editor's Pick. The *New York Times* listed it as one of the 'Best crime novels of 2020'. Nev has appeared on NPR, and written for a wide array of crime and history magazines, as well as the *FEZANA Journal, Parsiana* and other publications. Her work was recognized by JKYog and Radha Krishna Temple. She was awarded the Dinshaw Framroze Joshi Award for Excellence in Performing Arts, Painting or Literature and the famed Bapsi Sidhwa Literary Prize (Honorable Mention) in 2024. After a long corporate career, Nev returned to her passion – writing fiction – and teaches creative writing at the Rutgers-Osher Institute. She is a member of Crime Writers of Color and is the president of the NY chapter of Mystery Writers of America. She is also the vice president of her local Zoroastrian Association.

Having taken up writing as a post-retirement hobby, **RV Raman** writes detective fiction set in India. While some of his novels are traditional mysteries, others explore white-collar crime and murder in corporate India. After a corporate career involving extensive physical travel, Raman now prefers less punishing mental excursions into fictional worlds of his own creation. He lives in Chennai and can be reached at www.rvraman.com

**Salil Desai** is the author of 9 books, mostly crime fiction, which includes 5 titles of his much-acclaimed Inspector Saralkar Mystery Series – *The Kid Killer* (2023), *Murder Milestone* (2020), *3 and a Half Murders* (2017), *The Murder of Sonia Raikkonen* (2015) and *Killing Ashish Karve* (2014). The books are currently being adapted into a web series, 'Kalsutra' by Jio Studios. Salil is also the lead writer of the screenplay of 'Kalsutra'. His latest novel *The Grudges of Gajanan Godbole,* a whacky crime thriller, was published by Hachette India in November 2024. Salil's short story 'Sound Motive' has also appeared in *The Hachette Book of Indian Detective Fiction* (2024), while other short fiction has been published in various anthologies. His short story 'The Perfect Day' and novel *The Sane Psychopath* are in the process of being adapted for screen as feature films. Salil was one of the 4 international authors worldwide selected for the HALD International Writers' Residency, in Denmark, hosted by the Danish Centre for Writers & Translators, in June 2016. He was also invited and spent the month of May 2023 at Gullkistan Centre for Creativity, Iceland. Know more about him at www.salildesai.com His sixth Inspector Saralkar mystery novel will be published in late 2025.

**Sumit Bardhan** is a science fiction author known for his groundbreaking contributions to Bengali science-fiction with his culturally vibrant and socially relevant futuristic tales. He has written *Arthatrishna*, the first Bengali steampunk novel, that was later translated into *Avarice*, along with works like *Nakshatrapathik*, *Asishapta* and *Ek Dojon Kalpabigyan*, and contributed a cross-genre story to *The Hachette Book of Indian Detective Fiction*. A practicing data scientist, Bardhan crafts richly detailed imaginary worlds rooted in his cultural background. His translations include the works of H.P. Lovecraft and Arthur C. Clarke, along with Ray Bradbury's *The Illustrated Man*, published as *Chitrabichitra Manush*. Reaching an international audience, a translation of his story appeared in France's *Galaxies SF*, while his contributions to *Scroll.in* and the *Journal of Indian Literature* underscore his literary endeavours.

Born almost 60 years ago, and educated up to his Masters in his hometown, Gaya, Bihar, **Tabish Khair** has been a poet, journalist, novelist and academic for forty years now, of which he has spent five in Delhi, where he worked as a staff reporter for the *Times of India*, seven or eight in Copenhagen, where he obtained a PhD and taught, and around 20 in Aarhus, where he did a DPhil and continues to teach. Winner of the All India Poetry Prize and shortlisted for major fiction awards such as the Man Asian, the DSB Prize, *The Hindu* Best Fiction Prize and the Sahitya Akademi Award, his latest novel is the forthcoming *Drown All the Refugees*.

**Tanuj Solanki** is the author of four books of fiction. In 2019, he was awarded the Sahitya Akademi Yuva Puraskar for his short story collection titled *Diwali in Muzaffarnagar*. His last two novels, *The Machine is Learning* and *Manjhi's Mayhem*, have been longlisted for the JCB Prize for Literature.

**Vaseem Khan** is the author of two award-winning crime series set in India, and the upcoming *Quantum of Menace*, the first in a series featuring Q from the James Bond franchise. His debut, *The Unexpected Inheritance of Inspector Chopra*, was selected by the *Sunday Times* as one of the 40 best crime novels published between 2015–20. In 2021, *Midnight at Malabar House*, the first in the Malabar House novels set in 1950s Bombay, won the CWA Historical Dagger. Vaseem was born in England but spent a decade working in India.

# ACKNOWLEDGEMENTS

I would like to express my sincere gratitude to all the fellow travelers who ensured that this project reached this point in the journey.

Alok Bhalla and Manjula Padmanabhan have been especially helpful and sources of intellectual sustenance.

Thanks to Vaibhav Parel for keen critical interest in my own efforts as an anthologist and some great exchanges of ideas. I appreciate Anuradha Kumar's generosity and assistance with materials on the noir subgenre otherwise difficult to access.

It was an honour to present some of my thoughts on recent Indian crime fiction at ARSD College and St. Stephen's, courtesy Gautam Choubey and Smita Gandotra, with effective moderation by Mousumi Ray and Gauranshi Srivastava respectively. These discussions with colleagues and students helped sharpen my thinking about key issues and critical questions.

As ever, I owe a debt to all the authors of crime fiction who responded to our invitation with some crackling stories, in what should be a worthy follow up to the detective fiction anthology brought out earlier.

Many thanks to the team at Hachette India, including Anupama Manral for incisive edits, Sini Nair for ensuring smooth disbursement of dues to the authors, as well as to designer Mia Jose for the cover page. Adieu to Thomas Abraham, whose stewardship at Hachette India has been invaluable.

I would like to dedicate this volume to my always supportive parents, especially so in the absence of my late father.